Beware
the Little
White
Rabbit

Beware the Little White Rabbit

EDITED BY
SHANNON DELANY AND JUDITH GRAVES

Beware the Little White Rabbit © 2015 by Shannon Delany and Judith Graves

"Alice, Through the Wormhole" © 2015 by Charlotte Bennardo
"They Call Me Alice" © 2015 by C. Lee McKenzie
"Alice, Last of the Beating Hearts" © 2015 by David Turnbull
"The Watchmaker's Ball" © 2015 by Christine Norris
"Rabbit Fever" © 2015 by Jackie Horsfall
"Mustang Alice" © 2015 by Medeia Sharif
"White Is a Human Construct" © 2015 by Laura Lascarso
"Alice and Her Shadow" © 2015 by Tom Luke
"Alice in Wilderland" © 2015 by Jessica Bayliss
"The Aviary" © 2015 by Crystal Schubert
"Broken Tethers" © 2015 by Holly Odell
"Undercover Alice" © 2015 by Jennifer Moore
"Follow the Steam Rabbit" © 2015 by Liam Hogan

Cover Art & Typography by Quixcy Designs
Cover Art: Gaetano Pezzillo
Cover Model: Miranda Hedman
Interior Art by Shannon Delany
Interior Layout by NovelNinjutsu.com

Leap Books, LLC, P.O. Box 63, Otego, NY, 13825
www.leapbks.net Contact Information: leapbks@gmail.com

First Leap Edition 2015
ISBN: 9781616030421

Published in the United States of America

CONTENTS

Introduction

At Leap Books, we know a little about taking leaps of faith and falling down rabbit holes to see where they lead us. That's pretty much how we ended up taking on this small, but mighty, publishing house.

We can't thank Laurie J. Edwards, Leap's founder, enough for leaving us with this gem of an idea: Why not publish an Alice-in-Wonderland inspired anthology in 2015 to celebrate the 150th anniversary of the original publication of Alice's Adventures in Wonderland? Written by Charles Lutwidge Dodgson, under his pseudonym Lewis Carroll, a few short years before its publication in 1865, the book quickly became a commercial success, challenging its author to keep penning stories with such popular appeal.

Over the years, Alice and Wonderland has become deeply connected to the experiences and psyches of readers, moviegoers, and art and music lovers alike—the world and inhabitants of Wonderland have seeped into the common lexicon. This year, the celebrations are worldwide and span the entire year. There will be tea parties, film releases, more related books, cosplay balls, croquet matches, and much, much more.

And what a glorious adventure it's been for us at Leap! Our call for submissions was met with great enthusiasm, and we've retained the very best stories for your curious minds to devour. From heart-wrenching tales of the plague, stories of joyriders, explorers, romantics, and adventurers, to Alices just struggling to survive—this collection has something for everyone.

Alice is an icon of curiosity, zest for life, and a willingness to do more and be more, so we strove to do her justice. Cover artist Gaetano Pezzillo created a striking ode to Alice, which, combined with the typography of designer Ashley Poston, gives *Beware the Little White Rabbit* eye-appeal aplenty. The talents of Shannon Delany were also put to use creating dazzling silhouette pieces for the interior title page of each Alice tale contained within this anthology.

We couldn't have gotten through the submissions without the keen eyes of our Editorial Intern, Heather Elia, and Copy Editor, Kelly Hashway. Judith Graves's keen vision and nonstop enthusiasm kept everyone on track and inspired, and she was quick to jump in and do whatever needed doing. In every way, this truly has been a team effort, and we're thrilled the hour is finally at hand.

Don't be late ... It's time to follow the white rabbit ...

Alice

Through the Wormhole

Charlotte Bennardo

Nothing in the galaxy satisfies like tea.

FOR THOSE WHO DREAM OF ADVENTURES
BEYOND OUR EARTH; FOR MY DAD.

It was seedy, even for a bar; dim enough to hide the dirt, smoky enough to blur faces, and loud enough not to overhear the illicit trading. Drinks were overpriced and watered down, but for making deals that were best kept secret, this place was golden.

The scariest aspect was the clientele. Murderers, slave traffickers, drug dealers, and mercenaries – all in a mix of the worse scum. Keeping one hand on her blaster was a justifiable precaution. It also let anyone who looked her way know she wouldn't go without a fight.

An Oryctolagian, a species resembling a white rabbit once popular on the now-dead Earth but here as big as a human, hopped past, his gravity boots clunking heavily on the stone floor. She had no use for the creatures. Sneaks, thieves, and liars, they fit in with these bottom-feeders. The only good Oryctolagian was a stuffed one – on the dinner table.

Alice rolled the grimy glass between her hands. No way would she drink it. Everyone knew that consuming anything in this place carried a certain risk. One never knew what might happen. Bartenders could be bought off to slip something in that would knock you out, alter your appearance – or kill you. But to not buy anything would insult both the bartender and the mysterious owner who'd appear by hologram to remind you that you hadn't purchased a beverage or worse, a dish, from this fine establishment. It was safer – and cheaper – to order the swill. As always, before she left, she'd "accidentally" spill it onto the table sticky with

previously slopped libations and leave a generous tip to cover the housekeeping expense.

She looked at her chronometer again.

Her dealer was late.

Usually he was prompt, even getting there earlier than she on occasion. They both seemed to prefer being the first to arrive and snag the best seat: not far from the exit and with their back to the wall. She'd already been waiting ten minutes and was beginning to sweat under the breather and hood she wore. One did not advertise the fact one was a female Earthling, blonde, blue-eyed, and alone. That was shouting for trouble.

A blue skinned, white-haired Lexan walked over and sat at the table. His dark cerulean eyes, with no pupils, gave her a cursory once-over.

"Sorry, not looking for company," said Alice. Her voice, electronically disguised, sounded piercing enough that several patrons looked over in annoyance.

"I'm not offering you company. Pak sent me."

Yeah, so not falling for that.

"I've always dealt with Pak personally."

He sat down, tucking his six and a half foot frame, small by Lexan standards, into the chair, and pushed a small packet toward her.

Surprised, Alice palmed it, swiping it into her lap. With a surreptitious glance to check that she hadn't been observed and that no one was paying them any attention, she opened it. She stuck her pinky into the mix, then sniffed the fingertip.

Pure. Aromatic.

The best Remarkann tea in the galaxy. Just what she'd ordered. For some species, like Cuyhangas, a cross between something reptilian and humanoid, it was highly addictive. Others, like most Icythoids, or fish hybrids, found it euphoric right before death. Humans, exempt from ill effects, relished the taste reminiscent of smooth chocolate, spicy wine, and a hit of cannabis combined. It awarded calmness and pure bliss.

"And you are?" she asked.

He didn't answer right away, but she knew those large ears of his heard her question.

"Myca. Payment, please." He put a sealed canister on the table.

"Where's Pak?" This messenger must be his middleman. While Pak always concealed his identity, there was no mistaking this blue errand boy for a human. At least Lexans, while not poster boys for law and order, were one of the less dangerous alien species. Humans were outnumbered and under armed, spread out in thinly populated areas over several galaxies. Alice spent most of her time traveling about in her ship, not trusting her safety in a building. Her ship had better security, and a big gun. Plus, she could jet into space in seconds.

"Detained on business. I don't know when he'll be available again, so make this last."

She pocketed the canister with one hand and pushed over the platinum coin with the other, real easy. Pak didn't accept credits. Their deal concluded, she rose and quickly left, checking on the sly to see if Myca or anyone else followed. The way clear, outside the fiery orange skies and charred

black bedrock – the only things this planet boasted besides being in neutral space – filled the landscape. She slipped through the milling crowd of varied species.

Until the white rabbit slammed into her, hard, knocking her back.

"Watch it! Stupid rabbit," she growled.

"Sorry! I'm late!" he mumbled, checking his chronometer. He scampered off.

Suddenly suspicious, she checked her inside pocket and noticed her canister of rare tea was missing.

"Son of a…" She gave chase, but he was faster, those strong hind legs taking two leaps for every one of her strides. She managed to keep in him sight, but he gradually pulled ahead. He hopped into a battered cruiser. Knowing she couldn't catch him on foot, she reached into a side pocket, pulled out a tracker, and threw it at the cruiser's hull just as it began to lift off. The tracker stuck and a tiny light started flashing, letting her know it was working. By the time she'd jumped into her ship and taken off to follow, the rabbit was a good distance ahead, but she could catch that damn, thieving – and soon to be dead – rabbit.

Until he slipped through the wormhole.

She cursed him roundly as she ripped off the cumbersome breather and hood. That white abomination didn't want to pay the high price for the good stuff and thought he could simply take hers? Now it was really going to cost him – an arm and a foot when she caught up with him.

She could easily turn around, write the experience off as a lesson learned – always secure everything on her person,

rather than risk pirates or hostile aliens in this strange stretch of space. But she couldn't let it go. Not just for the precious tea, but for the fact that she refused to be bested by a damn rabbit.

She closed in. He had to have realized it, because he began weaving erratically in that antiquated pile of junk. She snorted. Like that feeble attempt could slow or stop her. She laughed at the absurdity.

The thought crossed her mind to simply blast the ship into space debris. The canister should survive the explosion intact if she targeted the side of the ship, not the engines. But since she didn't know this individual, killing him was taking a chance that he was unarmed, and she refused to consider killing a life-form who wasn't armed. Plus, if the rabbit was connected to any of the cartels or guilds, or someone as powerful, it could result in a bounty on her head, dead or alive.

No, best to play it safe and chase him down to take back what was hers. Of course, that didn't mean he wouldn't get his fuzzy ass kicked. At least there was that for fun. Fur was gonna fly.

She slipped through the wormhole, the guidance system momentarily losing track of the rabbit's ship as space folded and cut the distance between galaxies. Once she shot out through the other side, the beeping resumed on her console as the tracker and system linked again.

Alice laughed. "Got you now. Think I'm getting a new fur coat for my birthday this year," she mumbled. No one took advantage of Alice. It was hard enough being a roaming

Earthling, harder still being alone with no one to watch her back. Many times she'd had to send the message "don't F with me." Most times it worked; others, it had been close. She had the scars to prove it.

Being that her ship was faster, she caught up to the white rabbit when suddenly his ship slipped into hyperdrive and disappeared among the distant stars.

"Oh, want to play catch, do you?" Following the trail of disturbed space, she set a course. Because her ship was specially outfitted with the latest tech, she was right behind his older craft as he descended toward the planet below. If he could survive there, it was an Earth-like planet. She wouldn't need a breathing apparatus, environmental suit, or gravity shoes. Nothing would slow her down. She loaded her pockets with a tranq gun, water, and a meal pack. There was no telling how long she'd have to track that walking coat.

With her com link she ordered the ship to go into sleep mode and lock down. If she needed, she could start it on the run with a verbal command and blast off within seconds.

She hoped it wouldn't come to that, but getting her tea back from that thieving rabbit was worth it.

Although the atmosphere was breathable, everything around her had a reddish hue. Possibly an abundance of oxidizing iron, but if that were true, it should be on the brownish side, like dried human blood. The vibrant red tones of plants, grass, and even tree leaves looked akin to fresh blood. She shivered. She'd seen enough blood in her short seventeen years, all different colors; some she'd drawn, or lost, herself.

The white rabbit's ship landed just ahead. He jumped out the hatch and scurried away, heading for the forest. Even though he ran faster, she tracked his heat trail with the targeting sensor on her blaster. He seemed to be the only large living thing she picked up. If he tried to disappear, she could always stun him enough to slow him down. That white fluffy tail made a perfect target.

Feeling a little guilty for thinking about shooting him there when he couldn't defend himself, she ran faster. There were basic ground rules one followed: she did not shoot unarmed life-forms in the back – unless her life depended on it.

Through trees and low growth, and over rocks and streams of red water, she chased him. She thought that she'd stayed out of his sight, but he ran like the very devil of Heilyun, a creature that lived on a planet of molten lava, volcanic eruptions, and noxious gases. She paced herself, running steadily but swiftly enough to keep him in sight. Up ahead, she saw a hedge, and he ducked through a small doorway. It was a strange place for both hedge and door, so deep in the forest. The wall of red foliage was too high to see over and too long to see around. And although the doorway wasn't large, the rabbit easily squeezed through.

Right behind him Alice came. And ran straight into a robotic sentry. His lance, with a glistening cruel edge, halted just a hair's breadth from her throat – too close for her to even gulp without fear of nicking her skin. Breathing slow and easy, her eyes slid away from the blade to its face. Like

everything else, he was suited in red, even his metal shell was scarlet toned.

"Halt!" Luckily for her he had a universal translator. This was not a time for a misunderstanding. "You may not proceed further."

"That rabbit, the white one who just ran in here, stole something from me. I need to get it back. Then I'll leave. I'm not looking for trouble."

The sentry lowered the lance away from her throat, but not completely out of striking distance. "You must obey the laws or suffer the penalties."

Alice sighed. "Fine. Whatever. What do I need to do?"

"Royal decree says that all who enter the kingdom must be presentable." He stepped aside, the lance still within handy striking distance, and two pages, also in red, rolled forward on silent wheels and gears. They aimed a spray gun at her.

"Wait – "

They pulled the trigger, and Alice was no longer in her blue flight suit – it was red. As was her skin, her shoes, and – leaning so her braid fell forward – her hair.

There wasn't a spot on her that wasn't red. She wondered if the whites of her eyes were red too, and more importantly, if it was permanent. If she were running from the authorities, that might come in handy, but she wasn't and this was going to be a problem. Contacts like Pak knew what she looked like. She was going to spend a lot of time explaining she really was Alice and not some resident of the planet Taurus.

"Now you are presentable and may enter the kingdom," said the sentry, ushering her forward.

"Fab." She scowled. She wasn't thrilled about the skin, but the hair color was cool. With a quick glance at her hands, she looked enough like a Tauran that she could get through the Parsellian Gate without question and get back to her home galaxy a heck of a lot sooner. The gatekeepers weren't fond of Earthlings. That was some benefit anyway.

Now to catch the rabbit.

She took off at a run, marveling the sentry hadn't taken her blaster or tranq gun or anything from her pockets. Bonus for her. Not so much for that rabbit.

He must have been here before because he was no longer white but a fiery red and she hadn't been far behind him. Getting sprayed hadn't taken him much time. He was a quick little fella. She dug down deep to pour on the speed. He sprinted around a corner. Huffing, she rounded the corner and stopped short. There was a long table set with at least forty places.

Someone was expecting a lot of guests.

Almost every seat was occupied by red rabbits, looking nearly identical, although some wore hats, or sported armor, all sitting around the table wildly waving teacups. At the head of the table sat a queen. Her metallic scarlet exoskeleton, like her crown and gown, sparkled with brilliant ruby crystals. A matching visor blocked her face, so Alice couldn't see if she was machine, organism, or hybrid.

"For interrupting my tea party, off with your head!" the red queen screamed, pointing a scepter at Alice.

"I'm sorry," Alice stuttered, holding up her hands. She didn't want her highness or the sentries who rushed to the queen's side to mistake her intentions. "I didn't mean to intrude, but that rabbit" – and she looked around, unsure which one was the actual thief, so she waved her hand in the general air in front of her face to include them all – "stole my canister of tea and I want it back."

The queen's head swiveled around as she seemed to take in each guest. "Which one of them? I'll have his head on my platter!"

"Well, that's the problem," Alice mumbled.

Behind her, a laugh rose up. She spun around, and perched in the tree sat a cat-like creature. It possessed large eyes, a malicious grin, and stripes like a common Earth tabby cat she'd seen pictures of. The reason she questioned it was a cat was because of the webbed paws and small feather cluster on its head.

A hybrid cloning experiment gone comically wrong.

She'd seen a lot of that on many worlds.

"Don't know which one, do you?" it purred.

Alice glared. "Give me time, cat, or whatever you are. I'll figure it out."

"Call me Cheshire." Its grin became even more malicious, showing sharp shiny teeth. "And that I'd like to see."

Alice turned away from the creature. She scrutinized each rabbit at the table. Some she could automatically rule out, like the one with a cyborg arm. And the one with a darker streak down its back. A few more could be eliminated

for various reasons, but even with them removed from the suspect list, that left about twenty others that were identical. Trying to figure out which one of them was her miscreant rodent was going to take some sleuthing.

"While we're waiting for her to make up her mind and Cheshire to make a fool of her," one of them said, "let's have tea."

They all clapped and cheered, and banged the long table with their paws until the queen stomped her foot. They quieted instantly.

"Serve the tea!" she ordered.

And there stood Pak's canister on the table.

"Wait!" Alice cried. "That's my tea! I want it back!"

The queen stood. "You said first that you wanted the rabbit. The tea was second, and therefore, you didn't want it as much." She pointed to the canister. "It's on the table, so now it belongs to all. And we want tea. Take any rabbit you choose. There are too many here, and they are a noisy lot." The rabbits' noses twitched nervously, each looking fearfully at their neighbors.

Alice moved closer. "I changed my mind. I paid for the tea, so you can keep the rabbit. I'll just take the canister and be on my way."

"Too late!" the queen cried. "You can't change your mind now. That would be rude!"

Alice's hand froze in midair.

"Is it worth losing your hat holder?" Cheshire winked at her.

When Alice inhaled to argue, the queen waved her scepter wildly in the air, causing the sentry on her right to duck. "Not another word, unless you wish to lose your head, too!"

The sentinels raised their lances with menacing intent. There was nothing Alice could do. Her heart fell as she watched a sentinel open the canister and spoon it into a very large, shiny vermillion teapot. The sentinel was using too much, wasn't letting it steep properly, and worse, was carelessly spilling the precious leaves on the tablecloth. After she'd saved so long for it.

Alice gritted her teeth.

"Stop! You're doing it all wrong!" Much as she hated the thought of having to share her treasure, the pain of watching it desecrated was more than she could stand. She shoved her way over to the sentinel's side. "Let me do it, you mechanized dishwasher!" She took tea and spoon away from him and started over. First, she set more water to boil on the little burner on the table. It was strange to use red water, but maybe it wouldn't affect the taste. When it boiled, she spooned the correct amount of purplish red tea leaves into the pot and put on the lid to let it steep.

"Hurry it up!" the queen demanded.

I could just shoot them all, take my tea, and run…

It sounded like a good idea, but she wasn't sure if the queen's bodyguards had other weapons besides their lances. She couldn't see under their tunics. And being robotic or cybernetic, any number of weapons could be built into them, ready to fire in a nanosecond.

"Good tea takes time," she countered, feeling a bit cross.

"Maybe more time than you have," Cheshire snickered.

"I'm just as good with a knife as I am with a blaster," she responded crisply over her shoulder at the creature. It continued to grin but didn't offer any more comments.

There was still a good half of her tea left in the canister. She'd hang around long enough to find her thief. Maybe if she created a distraction, she could swipe the container.

"We want tea! We want tea!" chanted one rabbit, banging on the table with spoon in hand. The rest soon followed, creating a loud din.

They are all mad. Maybe they have space psychosis.

Whatever the reason for their boorish behavior, thankfully the tea was ready. Soon, this place would be only an annoying memory.

"Quiet, or all your heads will hang in the wind!" the queen shouted.

Alice was tiring of hearing that threat.

"Tea's ready. I'll pour." She gave a nasty look to the sentinel who'd moved forward to grab the teapot and snatched it first. "I said I'll do it!" The sentinel wheeled back.

Etiquette demanded the queen be served first. Since she had a cup and saucer placed in front of her, she had to be part organic life-form, but who knew what breathed underneath that manufactured exoskeleton? Alice filled the teacup but left enough room for milk or lemon or whatever else these creatures put in their tea.

"Don't forget me!" shouted Cheshire.

Alice ignored him. Even if he was part living creature, he was sitting in a tree and didn't have a cup. She certainly wasn't going to bring him one.

Next, she started down the long line of guests. As she filled the cups, she scrutinized each guest. One was too fat to be her rabbit. One was too skinny. Another was too short. Down the table she continued. When she'd finished, there were only five viable suspects.

"Have you narrowed it down to ten or less?" Cheshire chided. He still hadn't moved from his spot on the overhanging branch. Could he move at all?

Turning back to the party, she debated once again about stunning them all, grabbing the tea, and getting out.

'Til she saw the look on the sentinels' faces. They watched her intently, their eyes and movements following her. Maybe she'd better hold off for now.

"I know what you're thinking," Cheshire sang.

Alice raised an eyebrow. "Not all of it." Right now she was thinking if she tranqed that thing, she could sell it to a zoo somewhere and make enough money to replace the wasted tea if this plan failed. Pak had connections.

Cheshire laughed and promptly changed from striped to zigzag lines.

If he could do that, he'd be worth two canisters of tea.

The rabbits got raucous. They sloshed their tea, wore the crumbs of scones on their chests, and stomped their feet as they sang loudly – and off key. It was a nightmare.

"Make your choice!" ordered the queen.

Alice had to figure out a way to find her rabbit. How? She sat in a chair, observing them. All eighty eyes stared back. There was no expression on any one that might lead her to think it was her guilty stew pot suspect. They were a cool, conniving bunch.

Alice slowly rose and smiled. She bowed to the queen. "Your Highness, I will know which rabbit is the guilty one if I can see him dance. If you would command them, please? Once I find him, I will be off."

"Have a plan, do you? What is it? Tell us!" giggled Cheshire.

"No," Alice said, not bothering to look at Cheshire. She couldn't reveal how she was going to catch the white rabbit.

The queen leaned back, turning her head aside, uninterested. "And why should I order them to dance? I don't care who stole your tea."

"For your amusement, Your Highness." Alice smiled coyly. "Wouldn't you like to see how I catch my thief?"

The queen thought about it for a moment, then said, "Fine. I'll order them to dance, but if you're wrong, your head will roll in his place."

Now Alice knew she really had to get the right rabbit.

"Line up!" ordered the queen. "Anything specific they should dance?"

"Just a little jig would be fine. But have them dance on the table, please. I need to watch them closely."

"But we'll ruin the scones and teacups!" said one rabbit with a lazy ear. He wasn't a suspect and Alice would have ignored him, but she got a brilliant idea.

"Quite right. Here" – Alice got up – "I'll clear the table for you." She stacked the teacups, pushed the scones out of the way, and rolled back the tablecloth. "I don't want anyone to slip," she offered. She moved around the table, and for a brief moment, her back was to the queen and her bodyguards; just enough time to roll the canister into the cloth without anyone seeing. While the rabbits lined up, she pushed the cloth to the opposite end of the table and, as she walked, stuck her hand under and pulled out the canister. With a deft sleight of hand, she pushed it into a pocket on her flight suit.

Even if the rascal got away, she had her tea.

Except if he got away, she'd lose her head.

But her plan was a good one.

Alice sat down. "Your Highness, we're ready."

The queen pointed to the first rabbit. "You! Dance!"

With a nervous twitch of its whiskers, it hopped onto the table. With its big feet, it shuffled a bit, its head swiveling to see the queen's reaction.

"Pssst!" Alice hissed. "Better kick it up a notch if you want to keep your noggin." She looked emphatically at its feet.

With that, the rabbit high-stepped.

Nope, that wasn't the one.

"You're done, next!" Alice shouted.

The first rabbit whispered something to the next as it ran by, happy to get off the table. The new dancer kicked high and after only several moves, Alice stopped him.

"Done. Next!"

And it went on like that until she got to the thirty-seventh one, the fourth of her five suspects. He hopped on stage and only kicked twice when Alice stopped him.

"Take off your gravity boots, please. They make too much noise."

He hesitated, glancing around. "Um, I need them. Yes, this planet has a much heavier gravity than I'm used to and I need them to walk." His head bobbed nervously up and down several quick times.

Alice jumped up, knocking him flat on his back and pinned him down.

"This is the thief!"

Everyone hushed up.

The queen stood and strutted down the length of the table. "How can you be sure?"

"A white rabbit stole my tea, and I chased him here."

"But everyone is required to be presentable in red. And his fur is red."

"Yep, except he was in such a rush, knowing I was right behind him, that he didn't have time to take off his gravity boots, so…" She leaned back, unbuckled a boot and pulled it off, revealing a snowy white foot.

He squealed with fright. Alice smiled.

"Off with his head!" the queen shouted.

Back in her ship, Alice pulled the canister of tea out of her tunic and tucked it in a side compartment of the ship.

With a wicked smile, she hung the rabbit's foot on a control switch. Who wanted a red fur coat anyway?

Always looking for a character to mess with, Charlotte Bennardo loves to write young, new adult, and middle grade fiction, although she has written poetry and non-fiction articles.

She is the co-author of *Blonde OPS*, *Sirenz*, and *Sirenz Back In Fashion*, and is working on several solo novels.

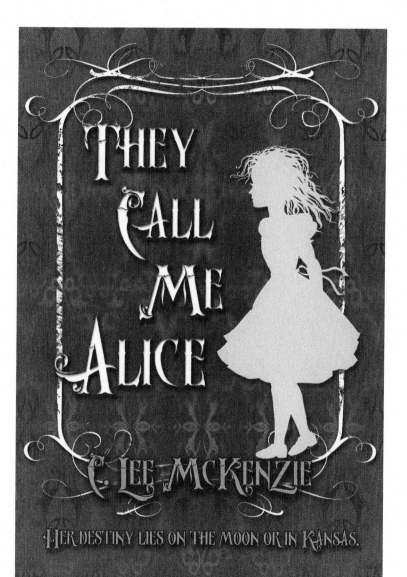

They Call Me Alice

C. Lee McKenzie

Her destiny lies on the moon or in Kansas.

FOR THE FIRST ALICE
WHOSE ADVENTURES ENTERTAINED ME FOR HOURS
WHEN I WAS A LITTLE GIRL.

They call me Alice, but that's not my real name. It's a convenient one, one that my Kansas parents can easily say. Sing Yanyu is what my mother called me. For a while after she was gone, I dreamed the melody of her voice, but I can't hear those sounds anymore. My ears have lost all their music.

"Alice?"

That's Betsy. She and her husband, Mark, brought me here from my true home a few months ago. They're very nice. I live in a big house with clean water and a soft bed.

No.

I don't live here.

Sixteen-year-old Alice does.

Each day I grow more confused about who I really am.

"Alice, are you ready? It's time."

Betsy's enrolling me in a new high school. I failed badly in the first one, and as I hurry to meet her at the front door, I see worry etched across her forehead. She doesn't want me to fail again.

"Where's your backpack?" she asks.

Already, I've forgotten something she told me to do. Her English words slip easily from inside my head, so if I don't translate what she tells me, I don't remember. That was my problem in school, too.

I return to my room, find the new backpack, and make sure I have the notebook and pen Betsy bought for me.

When we drive into the parking lot, the school is very much like the other one, so I feel a dejected curve creep up my spine, the curve that shows I have no hope inside me for success. I wish I didn't have to go here and that I could return with Betsy and help her in the kitchen. I know chopping and stirring and steaming of rice from some lessons I had years ago in another kitchen thousands of miles away. And when I close my eyes at Betsy's stove, the rising steam floats me across those miles, and I'm in the place I belong. I'm clear about who I am.

For a time.

Betsy's waiting outside the car, holding my door open. She expects me to follow her down the sidewalk and up the steps to this new school, so I do. She enters, and I wait one moment to look over my shoulder. Like all the other days since I came to America, I sense a presence, but when I try to find what is there, I see nothing. Today is the same, and that curve in my spine deepens as a terrible longing wraps me in its arms. What is it that hovers just out of sight? Why does it tantalize and disappoint me?

The day falls into chunks of time teachers tell me are periods. And that puzzles me because I've learned that period means menstruation or a mark at the end of an English sentence. Now it has another meaning? This language does not come easily to my Chinese mind.

I sit within a cloak of foreignness at the back of each class. But because Betsy's eyes pleaded "please try" when she left me this morning, I do. I try to make notes about the homework. I complete the writing assignments the best I can,

forcing my hand to move from left to right, drawing the characters so they look like the English marks I'm learning and so they flow across the lined page.

When I must read in one of the books, I squint at the straight up and down block letters that don't easily reveal their meaning to me, and try to untangle the ideas inside them.

At the last bell, I would like to push my way through the jostling students and be quickly outside where Betsy will be waiting. Instead, I steal along the side of the hall, more ghost than girl. More Chinese than Kansan.

I wait at the curb. Betsy's not usually late, so when I don't see her car, a serpent of fear coils inside me. What if she doesn't return as my mother didn't? Then there's that feeling of being watched that grows stronger as students leave and I become more alone.

I fold my arms across my stomach, and again search for whatever I feel at my back that is never there. Then under a parked car, I spy a stuffed rabbit, a child's toy. How sad it looks. Abandoned. But when I kneel to rescue it, the white, furry creature hops farther into the shadows. It's not a toy, and in shock I fall back, staring. The rabbit is the size of my two palms held open. Its nose wriggles and sniffs, but its eyes are steady on me.

In the language of my heart, I ask this rabbit, "You follow me. Why?"

In the language of my heart, he says, "I have been sent."

Before I can ask him what that means, a horn blasts behind me, and I leap up.

"Alice! What's the matter?" Betsy is halfway out of her car, urgency spiraling from her.

"Nothing. I...I dropped something." That's my first lie to her, and it comes to me that it won't be my last. When I look down near the wheel of the car, the rabbit isn't there.

"Yanyu, you are a crazy girl," I say to myself. "You must have left your good sense in China."

And I know that's true. I left everything in China.

Betsy prepares many meals she knows I like, so this night there is white rice with pork and tender green onions. She and Mark have improved in their use of chopsticks, but they still ask if I can adjust their fingers. I think they want to show me how much they appreciate my help. This makes me sad because I want to let them know how their help touches me also, but I don't.

Our talk is about Mark's job, Betsy's day at the cultural center where she volunteers, and then it turns to my first day at the new school.

My second lie comes quickly to my lips. "I talked to two girls in my class. They were very kind to help me find my way."

Betsy and Mark sip their tea and hum with satisfaction. I don't feel so bad about that lie as long as it brings a peaceful look to Betsy's face. Mark smiles at me over his teacup, and I return his smile before I look down and pretend to inhale the

jasmine scent with great pleasure. I may be the only Chinese girl who dislikes the smell of jasmine tea, but I don't tell them this.

When I've finished my tea, I gather the dishes and push away from the table.

"Are you off to do your homework?" Betsy asks. I have one more lie to tell before I leave, but this time I only nod it. And while I carry the dishes to the sink, I wish I could clear the impure air of falseness around me. It's against my nature to not tell the truth.

In my room, I open my notebook, but only to sketch an image of the rabbit. His ears stood straight, his eyes were the color of the sky, and his nose a tiny pink button. I use short, slanted strokes to give his fur depth, then add a few brisk lines to create his whiskers.

I almost think he twitches those whiskers at me. "Silly Yanyu."

Under my drawing I make the character 兔. It sounds like Tù and means rabbit in my language.

When I look up from my picture, the moon is full and hangs low at my window. I stare up at it, and there's a pull of something familiar. Something that comes to me from when I was just learning to walk. For a moment I feel a soft woven carpet under my feet and silk against my skin.

How strange.

When Betsy and Mark came for me, I wore thin cotton clothes, mended and stained. The house had bare wood-planked floors. Where did the memory of a woven carpet and silk come from?

And now in the moon's light and within that memory of fine things, there's a story and a voice that sings it to me. The story is a legend of Houyi, the immortal archer who saved the world with his bow and arrows. But in saving the world, he angered the Jade Emperor who reduced Houyi to a mortal and forbid him to return to heaven.

There's more. I think. And it has to do with that moon.

"Speak to me, moon. What is the part I can't remember?" But it continues its upward journey in silence.

"Climb, moon. Shine on me now and on my mother when you reach the other side of the world."

I'm suddenly tired. Tired of feeling confused. Tired of not fitting anywhere. Tired of the guilt I hold for not loving Betsy and Mark the way they would like.

There's a knock at my door, and Betsy pokes her head inside. "Just wanted to say goodnight. Sleep tight."

This is her usual end-of-the-day ritual with me. She would like to come in to talk. She would like me to tell her what I'm thinking and feeling. But I can't. Because I'd have to tell her I'm longing for my real mother and my real home. That would make her very sad, and I don't want to do that.

At lunch the next day, I escape eating alone by going straight to the library. The rest of the Houyi legend still hides from me, so I find a computer and log on to do a search.

At the next desk a boy leans back in his chair and studies me. "You're new."

How should I answer that? I don't think it's a question, so I agree with a silent nod.

"You got a name?" he asks.

"Sing...Alice."

He laughs. "Sing Alice. That's cool." He reaches across, grabs my hand as if I've extended it to him, and shakes it. "Dan."

Before I think, I say, "You don't look like that name." He doesn't. He looks like a boy from China. His name should be something like Chang Enlai. "Sorry. I meant – "

"I know what you meant, but I was born in Chicago, so were my mom and dad. Therefore" – he points to his chest – "Dan."

Again, what I see in this new place doesn't make sense. When I meet people who look like they've come from all over the world, I think they should talk and act as if they're from Africa or South America or China, but they don't. They're the same as Betsy and Mark even though they look different.

"Sorry," Dan says. "But if I'd said I was from Bejing, you'd make me speak Chinese. I can't do that."

I laugh at that thought. A Chinese boy who can't speak Chinese. The sound of my laughter surprises me. It has been a while since I've heard it.

"Well, Sing Alice, it's great to meet you. See you around." He's up and, with a few long strides, gone.

Dan's the first boy I've talked to in Kansas. He's the first boy to touch me here. I hold out my hand and look at it.

Somewhere at the back of the library, a book thuds to the floor, and I'm reminded of why I came. In a few minutes I peck out the name Houyi, and many choices roll down the screen. I click on one and the rest of the legend is there. I switch the site to read it in my own language.

As the story spreads across the screen in elegant strokes of characters I know so well, my mother's voice is strong in my ears again, and my heart blossoms like the lotus. She sounds sweet, and that makes me content. I remember how she once sang this ancient tale to me, and the story is as sad as my small self thought it was those many years ago.

Poor Houyi had one last chance to restore his immortality, but his beautiful wife, Chang'e, made a mistake and took the whole pill of immortality, not leaving half for her husband. She flew away to the moon, leaving him behind, and now she's forever there with only one companion, a white rabbit who stirs the elixir of life.

That night, the moon, still fat and new, fills my room with light. I open my window and lean far out, stretching my fingers to touch the great circle. It seems to pause on its journey into the sky as if it's waiting for me. I see Chang'e, but her face is my mother's. She looks down from her white palace, and next to her the white rabbit patiently stirs and stirs.

He was sent to guide me to my mother. I'm sure of it.

As I lie on my bed, I feel, more than hear, the whisper. "Yanyu. Yanyu. Yanyu."

It's my mother calling to me, and for the first time in years, I'm filled with joy and purpose. I must leave Betsy and Mark. I must find a way back to my mother. She's waiting.

The next morning I tuck extra food and a jacket in my backpack. I have some money that Betsy says I should keep for emergencies. It's only twenty dollars, but I will find a way.

Betsy drops me at school, and when I say good-bye, I'm of two hearts. One has regret for what I'm about to do to her and Mark. The other has excitement for my journey home.

I'm about to walk away when Dan comes straight toward me, smiling. "Sing Alice! Where you headed?"

"I have to…I have to meet my…mother."

"No school then?"

"Not today."

"See you tomorrow," he says and squeezes my arm before he walks away. His fingers leave a tingling feeling. I keep him in sight until he goes inside the school. Then I cross the street and turn onto the next block where I remember the bus depot is located.

The rain is a surprise. I should have brought the jacket with a hood, but it's too late to think of that now. I walk faster, and then as the rain becomes heavier, I run until I reach the overhang of the bus depot and huddle against the wall.

The day has grown dark with clouds. My socks are already damp, and I have no extra shoes.

And then I see him. The rabbit. He's in the park across the street, waiting under a low bush.

Without looking, I dash into the street. For one second, I hurt. My head. My back. My legs. And as a cloud descends to bundle me inside its belly, the rabbit comes sniffing near my ear.

"This way," he says, leaping ahead, leading me through the trees and to the edge of the park where grass ends and sky begins. The darkness is complete, as if night has fallen, and it must have because I'm staring at the moon, and then I'm floating toward it. Chang'e reaches out her hand, a hand of long, tapered fingers, a hand so like my mother's. I grasp it, and soon I'm at her side with the rabbit offering me tea.

"How did I come to be here?" I ask my beautiful goddess of the moon.

Her smile is warm, and her eyes cradle me inside them just as my mother's did when I was small. "I have been watching you suffer in your loneliness. Such a terrible thing. I know. I thought that if you wanted, you could come to live with me, and we could be company for each other."

The tea stops in my throat, and I choke.

"Did I startle you, Yanyu?" She leans toward me and strokes my hair.

I close my eyes, remembering how my mother used to stroke my hair.

Madness has stolen my mind. I'm sure of that now.

"No, you are not mad," she tells me as if I've said those words aloud. "But you are sick with missing someone."

"You! I miss you, Mother. I want to return to you."

"You know that is impossible, don't you? I was taken by the fever."

"No!" I clap my hands over my ears. "I won't hear that." But it's too late. A tide of memory rises around me, and I've already returned to the day my life as Sing Yanyu ended. The day my mother died. Her pale face, still and staring up at me yet not seeing me anymore is there in my mind again. My father pulling me from the room. My cries. My struggle to return to her.

In a blur of time, our house was sold. My father vanished, his eyes empty, his ears closed to my sobbing. Auntie, who was old and not loving to me, took me to a place where I walked on a cold wood-planked floor. There the woman called Mistress took away the silk dresses my mother had sewn and gave me clothes made of cotton. Old. Stained. I first heard the name, Alice, from Mistress's lips.

Then there was that day I stood in a line with other girls like me, and the door opened, and tall people with pale faces and colorful clothes strode in. That was the first time I saw Betsy and Mark. Her hair was the color of fire, and I stared at her with rude wide eyes and gaping mouth.

She knelt in front of me while Mark stood at her back with his lips pressed together. This woman with fiery hair said many things I couldn't understand. Mistress scurried to my side and told me the woman had said she was pleased to meet me at last. Mistress said I was lucky anyone wanted to take me to live with them because I was too old and not very pretty. She said I must be sweet or they might change their minds.

As I uncover my ears, Chang'e – my mother – repeats her question. "You know it's impossible to be with me, don't you?"

"But I must not say that," I tell her. "Once I do, I will lose hope of ever seeing you again."

"Ah, but you will with each full moon. Imagine how I will be with you here." She touches my chest with the palm of her hand, and its warmth spreads through me and deep into that place I hide fear and longing. "Unless you choose to stay on the moon."

"And if I remain with you," I say, "what will we do together?"

"Why, we will talk of the great mysteries, of I Ching and destinies. We will divine the fate of those mortals trapped by the whim of tides and seasons and stars."

"But I'm mortal." When she doesn't say anything, I ask, "Aren't I? Because I no longer know who I really am. Alice. Sing Yanyu? Mortal? Immortal?"

"You are mortal for the moment. But Tù has the elixir prepared, and when you sip it, you will join me in immortality." She spreads her arms wide, and their long shadows stretch as far as the edge of the white circle. "Here." Then she folds her hands in her lap and waits for my answer.

The idea of being in yet another foreign place saddens and confuses me more than ever. I close my eyes to think very hard about this choice Chang'e – my mother – has offered. If I become immortal I can be forever with her. But forever on the moon.

I would miss the earth. The house of Betsy and Mark. My new school and the Chinese boy, Dan, who can't speak Chinese and who made me laugh.

"I can't. I can't stay," I tell my mother, and a tear trails from the corner of my eye and down my cheek. Then a finger brushes that tear away. My mind churns in thought. The finger doesn't belong to me, and my mother's hands are folded in her lap. The rabbit stirs and stirs.

With each rotation of his spoon, a pain gnaws its way across my chest, down my arm, and along my cheek where the tear trickled just a moment before. Where does this pain come from?

When I open my eyes, things are blurred. I blink and bring the shapes into focus. Betsy hovers over me. Mark is at her back, and both of their faces are drawn into heartache.

I seek my mother, but she's not here. Nor is Tù.

I flex one hand. The other I can't move. It's heavy and rigid, and one leg's suspended from a pulley.

"Betsy?"

Her hand grips mine, and she presses it to her lips. "I'm here."

If Betsy is here, I am safe. I fall into sleep.

It takes six weeks before my bones knit enough so I can return to school. The driver that hit me wasn't to blame. I

darted out, and the woman at the wheel couldn't stop. What a crazy Chinese girl I am, chasing a rabbit in the rain. That's what Dan says when I return to school. Well, he doesn't say anything about a rabbit because he'd think I was…totally weird if I told him about that, but he talks about my being crazy and running into the street in the rain.

"So Sing Alice, how's it hanging?"

"That's idiom, right? Because I don't know what you mean."

"You need some lessons by Dan. Want to go to the dance with me next week? You know, one sort of Chinese guy out with a real Chinese girl. We can talk about Chinese stuff."

"You don't know anything about China, do you?"

"You have crushed me to the core, Sing Alice." He runs his hands through his spiky, gelled hair, and I think how nice it would be to touch it. "But you can make it up, okay?"

I understand he's joking with me. I've had time to watch a lot of American TV while I recovered from the accident, so I'm on to joking. "Okay. I'll go out with you."

When he takes my hand this time, the tingly feeling goes all the way up my arm. He steps closer, keeping my hand captured in his. "I think learning about China is going to take a while, but it'll be fun."

I stare up into his beautiful eyes. They are of the two cultures I know, ancient China and the new North American one I'm fitting myself into.

At dinner that night, the talk is the same. Chopsticks. Mark's job. Betsy's volunteer work at the cultural center. My day at school. But now I have no lies.

"A boy named Dan asked me to the school dance. I'd like to go."

Betsy sips her wine.

Mark scratches his nose.

They shift their eyes to meet mine.

I hold out my hands like I've seen teens do on TV. "Well?"

They both laugh. And I laugh, too. The music we make together is beautiful.

Then Betsy says, "I want to meet this Dan."

Now I have a choice. I can roll my eyes and be all like an American girl. Or I can nod and say "Yes. Of course" and be Sing Yanyu.

I go for in-between. I don't roll my eyes, and I don't nod with obedience, but I do look at them both and say, "He will like meeting you before our date."

It works. It works for me, and it works for my…family.

When I think of that word, it comes to me twice. It comes to me as 家庭 and, at the same time, in English sounds.

That night as I'm shutting down my computer and climbing into bed, Betsy comes in and says, "Just wanted to say goodnight. Sleep tight."

"Betsy, can you stay a while?"

There's only a sliver of a moon, but my room is bright with her smile. She sits on the edge of my bed. The shimmer of her red hair is so fiery, so vibrant. Freckles dance across her nose. Her skin is not like mine at all, but lovely.

We are quiet for a moment. Then she says, "What can I do to make you happy, Alice? Ask, and, if I can, I'll make it happen."

How lucky I am she cares for me this deeply. How lucky I am to have her as my second mother.

"Two things. First, I would like not to drink Jasmine tea."

She laughs, and it is like wind chimes high in tree branches. "Done."

"And" – I wait for a moment to be sure I say this in the right way – "I would like a new name. Alice is okay, but not big enough. Sing Yanyu is beautiful, but not big enough. I would like a name that says I belong in America, but I am a child of China."

Her face becomes serious, but it's not a face drawn into lines of worry; it's a face filled with thought. Then her expression softens, and she says, "I've always loved the name Mia."

I test that on my tongue. It's almost right.

"Mia Lee," I say, and there's music in the name we've made together. My ears rejoice to hear it.

Author Note: To those who know the myth of Chang'e and her companion, the rabbit, I've taken some liberties with it and played with the idea of another girl named Alice on a fantastic adventure. This Alice has been born into a century with global and space travel, so her Rabbit Hole doesn't take her into the earth, but around it and far from it.

There are several versions of Chang'e's story. Now there's one more.

C. Lee McKenzie is a native Californian who grew up in a lot of different places, then landed in the Santa Cruz Mountains where she lives with her family. She writes most of the time, gardens, hikes, and does yoga a lot. She travels whenever she can.

ALICE, LAST OF THE BEATING HEARTS

DAVID TURNBULL

IN A WORLD RULED BY MACHINES, IS ALICE
TRULY THE LAST OF THE BEATING HEARTS?

There came a crack like thunder.

A rabbit hole, launched from its orbital warren, streaked down through the clouds. It hung in the air like a frozen fork of lightning. Beneath the helmet that Hatter had made for her, Alice felt the root ends of her hair tingle from the electrical change that accompanied its arrival. What appeared to be a stuffed white rabbit tumbled earthward. Payload delivered, the hole rapidly lost its integrity and dissolved into a glimmering fragment that dissipated on the wind.

Alice crouched low amongst the ruins as the rabbit sniffed the air, internal sensors trying to get a fix on her location. She clutched her vorpal sword. The pistons on the rabbit's spring-loaded flanks gave a venomous hiss as it launched itself into a powerful leap.

It landed not far from her on an ivy-strangled hillock of fallen masonry, infrared eyes glowing red as it scanned for signs of body heat. Above its white head, on what was left of a concrete wall, a faded and tattered poster depicted a bottle of amber liquid, alongside the legendary – *Drink Mead®*.

The rabbit's long ears stood suddenly erect, deciphering the sonar signals bouncing back to it from all corners of the derelict building. Alice could hear the mechanical workings grinding in its neck as the big white head juddered this way and that, trying to get a fix on her. The hunt was on. But Alice was not one to be hunted. She was firmly of the view that the best way to handle a problem was to confront it head on.

She tightened the strap on her helmet. Then, gripping the sword with both hands, raised it above her shoulders and stepped into the open. Cutterflies, disturbed from the endlessly diligent task of dissecting slabs of fallen masonry, rose from their work to flutter around her head on glassy slithers of wings.

"You're late," she called to the rabbit.

"The queen wants me to fetch your heart." Its voice grated in the dreadful manner that Alice found annoyingly common in all machines. "I'm going to have to take your head to get it."

"You're welcome to try, Mr. Rabbit," she said.

The rabbit produced a watch-shaped object from the pocket of its armored waistcoat, pressed down on the winder to set the centrifuge in motion, and held out an automated paw. The watch rose a foot or so, hovered for a moment, and then spun toward her at breakneck speed, vicious circular blades protruding from its circumference.

Alice waited 'til the watch was almost upon her before she swung her sword with all her might and batted the dreadful spinning missile right back to where it had come from. The rabbit crouched, ready to leap. But it was not quick enough. The wildly gyrating object exploded in a blinding flash of blue.

"Howzat!" Splinters of metal and tufts of imitation fur showered down onto Alice's protective headwear.

As the smoke cleared something became dislodged from the exposed girders of what had once been the upper floor of

the ruins and fell with a deafening clatter into the blast-charred remains of the white rabbit.

Alice approached with caution and tapped the object gently with her boot. It rocked back and forth. She picked it up and sniffed. The smell reminded her of the coppery residue that always seemed to cling to her palm whenever she handled the vorpal sword. It was smooth and silvery and slightly curved on one side. On the inner part of the curve were two loops through which an arm could be passed.

Sheathing her sword, Alice passed her arm through the first loop on the strange object. The second loop had finger grips around which a hand could be wrapped. The grooves of the grips were the perfect fit for her fingers. Where her thumb now sat there was a little red button.

"Curious," said Alice.

She pressed down on the button with her thumb.

Nothing happened.

She found Hatter in his den, hunched over his workbench, soldering iron protruding from the index finger of one hand, a blighted circuit board in the other. He didn't look up when she entered. Stamped into the leather upholstery of his back were the words:

Hypotrionic Android Technician
(Self-Recharging)
Model – TZ606

"You may have to mend the helmet you made for me," said Alice.

"What happened this time?" asked Hatter, attention still firmly fixed on his work.

"White Rabbit," said Alice. "Blew it to smithereens. But the helmet took a bit of a bashing from the shrapnel."

Hatter soldered part of the circuit board.

"As soon as I get this working I'm going to need you to insert it into my head. It should prevent any further deterioration in my functionality applications before I go completely mad."

At the mention of impending madness Hatter's body seemed to freeze, locking his head at a slight tilt. He began to ramble in an utterly confusing and incoherent manner. "Round and round ticks the clock in an inkling. Mustard and lemon are two entirely different things, you know. Unfortunately, I seem to have forgotten why a raven is like a writing desk."

"I found something that might interest you," said Alice.

He had been her surrogate parent since the death of her mother, and she was now used to these increasingly frequent blips.

Hatter looked up and the madness receded. His telescopic eye retracted. The tip of the soldering iron dulled and slipped back into the sheath of his finger. He looked at the object. Furrows creased on his leathery brow.

"I can't believe it. It can't possibly be!"

The telescopic eye slid outward again. His head jerked forward to examine the smooth side of the object. "I never thought I'd see one of these again," he said.

"What is it?" asked Alice, her curiosity well and truly roused.

"It's a looking glass shield," replied Hatter.

He seemed so elated she almost thought he was about to break into a dance.

"A looking glass shield?" she repeated.

"Vorpal swords and looking glass shields," said Hatter. "The last weapons deployed by humanity against the tyranny of machines. Queens and their drones fell before them. The beating hearts almost won, but in the end, they were defeated."

"This one doesn't do anything," said Alice. "You'd think that if there's a button to press, something might actually happen when someone presses it."

Hatter cast a glance at the half-repaired circuit board on his worktop.

"Perhaps I can get it to work," he said. "Sometimes we all have to make little sacrifices."

His telescopic eye retracted.

"You know what this calls for?" he asked.

"Tea?" said Alice.

"Tea," said Hatter.

53

The Tulgey Wood was a twisted tangle of plastic-covered wires and rubber-coated cables. These were woven and interlaced through the leafless branches of a forest of long-dead petrified trees whose bark stood ghostly white against the vibrant reds and blues and yellows of the wires and cables.

Here and there one might also encounter impenetrable briars of razor wire, fortified with spiky iron railings. The Wood was the queen's defensive perimeter, and Alice had no choice but to pass through it, in order to reach the lair were she reigned over her mechanical multitude.

"You don't have to come with me," she said to Hatter, who was utilizing an impressive array of cutting implements to hack a path for them.

"I think you would make slow progress without me," said Hatter.

"Perhaps," agreed Alice. "But when it comes to the crunch I believe I will be quite capable of assassinating the queen on my own volition. After all it's my mother who needs to be avenged, not yours."

Hatter sliced through another tangle of wires.

"We'll see," he said.

His lack of faith disappointed her. Feeling her confidence waning a little, she glanced down at the looking glass shield. "Tell me how this thing works again."

The leather on Hatter's face wrinkled to a grimace. She knew he hated being asked to repeat himself, but he was a patient teacher. "Once activated, the smooth surface will reflect back the electromagnetic pulses which emanate from

the queen. It will cause a momentary short circuit, paralyzing her for enough time for you to finish her with a penetrating jab from the vorpal sword."

"I know how to use the sword," said Alice, assuredly.

"Using it as a cricket bat is not exactly textbook technique," said Hatter.

"Some situations call for improvisation," countered Alice.

They proceeded through the tangle.

In time they came to a dirt track of sorts, winding narrowly through the wire woven trees. Alice touched the hard brown soil. "Curious," she said. "You'd think something passed this way on a regular basis."

"I think that very something is watching us this very minute," said Hatter.

Gripping the handle of the vorpal sword, Alice rose cautiously back to her feet. "A raggamorph?" she asked. She'd heard there were creatures in the wood, neither one thing nor the other, endlessly transforming from flora to fauna and back again.

"I rather doubt it," replied Hatter, nodding in the direction of a crooked branch that overhung the path.

When Alice looked all she could see in the shadows was a wide, tooth-filled grin. "Come down from there," she demanded. "Whatever you are. It's bad manners to spy on people."

The grin disappeared. Something dropped from the branch to the path. What stood before them was a queer looking thing in a cat-skin suit and a cat-head hat. It struck a

defensive pose, shaft of a long wooden staff clutched between cat-skin mittens, and grinned cheekily at Alice.

"The name's Jack Cheshire." It gave a convoluted bow. "Jack of the Borogoves. Jack the nimble. Jack the quick – scourge of giants. Stole a pig and away I ran. Kissed the girls and made them cry."

Alice turned to Hatter.

"Is it dangerous? Have its circuits blown?"

"He's boasting." Hatter chuckled. "It's what boys do."

"A boy?" said Alice, scrutinizing the creature. "A real boy? I thought I was supposed to be the last of the beating hearts."

"It would appear rumors of the extinction of your race may well have been greatly exaggerated," said Hatter.

"You don't want to go wandering around alone in the Tulgey Wood," said Jack. "I'll be your guide for a price. Juicy wet kisses are legal tender 'round these parts. I bet you're a pretty little thing beneath that helmet."

He grinned again.

Alice shuddered. She found herself counting slowly down from ten beneath her breath. *Pretty little thing indeed*, she thought, sorely tempted to punch his stupid nose. "We are not in need of a guide, thank you very much," she said. "And if we were, I certainly would not surrender to paying you in kisses."

Jack grinned in an even more inflated manner.

"Bodyguard then." He spun his staff around in the most ridiculous fashion. "There are dreadful machines lurking

around in this place. Jubjub birds and frumious Bandersnatches, not forgetting the dreaded Jabberwocky."

Alice looked to Hatter for confirmation that these were real things and not just fantastical fictions the bothersome boy was making up. Hatter just shrugged his upholstered shoulders.

"We have no need of a bodyguard," she said. "I'm armed with a vorpal sword and a looking glass shield."

The boy puckered his lips and let out a loud whistle. He rested his wooden staff against his shoulder. "Boy-oh-boy. A vorpal sword and a looking glass shield. You sure do mean business. You hunting Snark or something?"

"Snark?" exclaimed Alice, growing increasingly weary of the boy's nonsense. "I'm not hunting Snarks, or Jubbly birds, or whatever you call them. It's the queen herself that I'm hunting. She's going to pay for the death of my mother and all the other beating hearts she massacred."

"The queen," said Jack. "Well, why didn't you say so in the first place? She killed my parents too, wiped out the whole bleedin' Borogove tribe and left me orphaned. If it hadn't been for the Legion of Hares I'd have been a goner a long time ago."

"Legion of Hares?"

Alice looked again at Hatter.

"Hybrid combatants," he said. "When humanity was on its last legs, they created all sorts organic amalgams. Hares being one of them."

"The Legion raised me from a nipper," said Jack. "Found me where my parents left me in the woods. If you're going after the queen, then I'm coming with you."

A vivid memory flashed through Alice's mind. She saw the bright yellow flash of multiple explosions and heard the screams of terror. She recalled her mother's hands resting tenderly on her shoulders and the urgent words that had been whispered – "Go with Hatter. He will see that no harm comes to you."

It was the last time she had seen another living soul – 'til now.

Jack pulled off a mitten and spat on his palm.

"Deal?"

He held it out his hand for her to shake.

Alice winced.

"We may need all the help we can get," said Hatter.

Alice took Jack's proffered hand. Beneath the unsettling squelch of spit, his palm was warm. The metrical beating of his pulse made her heart quicken. She vaguely recalled the intimate familiarity of her mother's touch. This was a different sort of intimacy though, almost intrusive, but somehow invigorating.

Up close Jack looked more of a man than a boy. Beneath his cat-skin suit all that climbing in trees had toned his muscles. And under the strap of his cat-head hat, stubble was sprouting on his chin. There was an odor about him that sent an odd shiver quivering through Alice.

Jack unraveled his hand.

"Steady on," he said, a huge grin encompassing his face. "Next you'll be looking for a kiss."

As if. Alice scowled.

"Clean cup!" cried Hatter in a moment of temporary irrationality.

Jack dropped to his knees and set about beating a rhythmic tattoo.

"Whatever are you up to now?" asked Alice.

"Summoning the Legion," replied Jack. "The queen isn't going to let us walk into her lair without a fight. We'll need an army at our backs."

With Jack as their guide they quickly arrived at far edge of the Tulgey Wood. Ahead of them stood the ancient and crumbling edifice of the queen's lair. A palace of sorts, with a faltering neon sign erratically flashing out the mysterious words "West Mall" before blinking out and then flickering back to life.

Beneath the neon was a gigantic version of the faded advertising poster Alice had seen in the ruins of the city – a bottle of amber liquid and the legendary *Drink Mead*®.

"In times gone by, this was a place for retail and commerce," said Hatter in response to the crease that formed on Alice's brow.

She noticed now that between the Tulgey Wood and the lair lay an odd looking humped and undulating blanket of brown fur. It must have been a mile long and a mile wide. It seemed to rise and fall, occasionally quivering and twitching in random parts.

"Horde of sleeping dormice," said Jack. "Set there by the queen to guard her lair. If one awakens, it will awaken all the others. There are thousands of them and each with teeth of steel."

"So what now?" Alice scanned the furry blanket for any hint of a passage through. "They're so tightly packed that we're bound to step on one."

Jack fell again to his hands and knees, one hand holding onto his cat-head hat as he pressed an ear to the ground. "Help is on the way," he muttered from the side of his mouth, and sure enough Alice could feel a dull vibration thump-thump-thumping in the ground beneath her feet. From the forest there came the echo of rhythmic chanting.

"March hares, march! March hares, march!"

Hatter nodded nervously at the slumbering assembly of dormice.

"I think perhaps the Legion would have done well to consider approaching with a bit more stealth."

One of the creatures on the fringe of the blanket stirred and opened its mousy eyes. It blinked and yawned, revealing rows of frightful teeth. Its companions to either side shook their sleepy heads, noses twitching. Then row after row after row of dreadful dormice came awake. They raised themselves up on their hind legs, the sensors on their whiskers bristling and trembling.

"Your friends better get here fast." Alice withdrew the sword from its sheath and held the glass shield protectively against her breast.

Jack rose to his feet and adopted a combat stance, staff at the ready. Hatter produced a pair of ferocious looking scythe-like implements from the sockets on his wrists. His leathery upholstery became taut with the tensing of his mechanisms. Alice's pulse thumped inside her head.

The dormouse that had been first to awaken bared its teeth and chattered an algorithmic order to its companions. The horde came roaring at them in an awesome wave of fur and fangs and claws.

Alice swung her sword left and right and left again, batting away surge after surge of tiny determined assailants, slicing some clean in half, using the shield to block those who managed to avoid the blade.

"Callooh! Callay!" Jack rushed gallantly forward and tried to shake off three or four dormice that had sunk their metallic teeth into his staff. Meanwhile, Hatter entered the fray, swinging his scythes and rambling incomprehensively.

"Clean cups! Clean cups! Move along! Move along!"

But the dormice came and came and came. No sooner had Alice chopped down a dozen than a dozen more were there to take their place. Jack stumbled and fell; dormice swarmed over him. A huge strip had been torn from Hatter's back, revealing the cogs and wheels of his innards. The teeth of a dormouse made contact with Alice's knuckles, raking the flesh. Pain shot up her arm. Had she not been able to block another incoming dormouse with the shield she could easily have lost her grip on the sword.

The ground around her feet was filled with fallen dormice, juddering and sparking as their internals short-

circuited. But still they came – too many, too fast, and too ferocious to be able to fend them off. She was bitten all over. Sickeningly warm trickles of blood from dozens of wounds ran down her arms and her legs.

Then came a blur of brown to her left.

Followed rapidly by another to her right.

Another and another and another, so fast they made her eyelids flutter.

And then she saw them. The Legion of Hares, the automated hybrid fighting machines Hatter had spoken of, armored breast plates and toughened gauntlets, long ears rampant, faces curled into venomous snarls, setting about the horde of dormice with staffs almost twice as long and double the thickness of that sported by Jack.

They may have been outnumbered one hundred to one, but they were designed for close quarter combat and their expert command of marshal arts made short measure of the dormice. When battle was done, and not a single dormouse was left standing, the commander of the Legion reached down and hauled Jack up by the scruff of his tattered cat-skin coat.

"See the trouble you get yourself into when you wander off on your own?" he said.

Somewhat bruised and bloodied, Jack pointed skyward with a trembling finger. "Twinkle twinkle," he croaked.

Alice looked to where he was pointing.

High above the clouds, something sparkled and glistened in the sunlight.

"Orbital Warren maneuvering into position," barked the commander. "Assume defensive formation."

One hundred hares formed a perfect circle around Alice and Hatter and Jack, one hundred staffs pointing outward like the spines on a porcupine. Alice saw scores of rabbit holes begin to streak down from the sky, like a storm of wild electrical lightning.

Now a legion of White Rabbits faced the Legion of Hares. They took their watches from their waistcoats and sent them spinning into the air. The hares batted them away with their powerful staffs. Many exploded in the air. Through the smoke and debris, the White Rabbits came bounding and leaping. The hares broke formation and joined in ferocious battle.

Alice heard a roar from behind her.

From out of the Tulgey Wood trundled a monstrous multi-wheeled caterpillar, metal segments of its body clattering as its voracious maw slavered gobs of grease and oil. Behind it scuttled a brace of mock turtles, barbed war spikes protruding from their toughened shells.

"Go!" Jack swiveled his staff, the white grin of his teeth contrasting the dark red of his bloodstained face. "This is your chance. Go while you have confusion for cover."

"Go!" agreed Hatter, brandishing his scythes, before descending once more into transitory madness. "More tea? I need clean cups!"

Sword in one hand and shield in the other, Alice turned and raced headlong for the mall.

Alice passed cautiously beneath an ivy-smothered archway and into the maw of the mall. She found herself on a wide walkway with alternating tiles of black and white under foot and flickering globes of electrical light overhead.

To either side of her tall storefront windows, glass aged with grime, behind which there stood an array of grotesque manikins. Each one the mummified cadaver of a person, severed heads propped up by their feet, wizened flesh rolled back over empty rib cages long ago robbed of their hearts.

From the remnants of the threadbare and flea-bitten cat-skin suits Alice assumed these were Jack's relatives. The last of Borogove tribe, victims of the queen's cold-blooded genocide. Repulsive trophies for her to gloat upon. She thought of Hatter, whom she had known all her life, and Jack, whose existence she had only been aware of for a couple of hours, and couldn't decide which one would make her feel more heartbroken and angry were they to end up like this.

That's why you have to finish it once and for all, she told herself.

Filled with a new determination, she pushed deeper into the mall, into the very heart of the queen's lair. She heard a click-click-clicking on the tiles behind her and found she was being stalked by a flock of automated flamingos, creepily hued in pink, curved copper bills and bulbous heads weaving eerily about on serpentine necks. Hedgehogs began to roll around at her feet, curled tightly into little spiky balls.

Aluminum dragonflies of emerald green and cobalt blue flitted menacingly about her head.

She knew these things had been dispatched by the queen to unsettle her, to weaken resolve, to make her turn and run. She laughed out loud. She wasn't afraid. "You'll have to do better than this," she called out, knuckles white around the handle of her sword. "You hear me? I'm not scared."

Now things began to stir in the hollow gloom of the store interiors.

"Keep moving forward, girlie," rattled a raw voice. "We're rooting for you."

"Who are you?" Alice whispered, able only to make out indistinct silhouettes in the murky dimness.

"We are the dispossessed," replied the voice. "Machines who have been left to succumb to ionization and decay. We despise the queen for the neglect she has shown us. At least the beating hearts that once tended us showed us the kindness of regular maintenance and the occasional drop of oil. So move forward, girlie. You are our hope for salvation."

Alice heard the flutter of pink synthetic wings and tap of sharp synthetic claws. She pressed on without looking back, kicking hedgehogs out of her way and swatting dragonflies with the sword. She came to a wide atrium, domed ceiling as tall as a cathedral, dull shafts of sunlight slicing downward from a multitude of holes shattered in the glass.

Ahead of her, a wide screen flickered brilliantly to life, causing her to gasp in surprise and squint her eyes. The image of a playing card appeared on the screen and on that card the

image of a Red Queen. The card flipped over, and on the reverse was an image of a White Queen.

The card flipped rapidly back and forth, Red Queen – White Queen – Red Queen – White Queen. Alice realized they were one and the same, two integral parts of the whole. They spoke, a duet of harmonious voices in perfect stereo, each matching the cadence and timbre of the other.

"So, you have finally come to pay homage?"

"I have come to kill you." Alice jutted her chin forward as the stealthy pink flamingos went slinking about her.

"Kill us?" laughed the queens. "A puny carbon-based child? What is that pitiful pitter and patter we hear? Could it be the beat of that pathetic little valve that pulses the blood in your veins. We'll have that. And we'll add your head into the bargain."

"I'm armed with a vorpal sword," warned Alice, stepping forward. "And a looking glass shield."

"You will never get close enough to deploy your shield," sneered the twin voices. "Did you honestly think we would defend our lair and not ourselves?"

Automated objects came gliding into the atrium. Black in color, arranging themselves in rows on the tiles of the floor, smaller objects to the front and larger objects to the rear. Alice recognized what they were; she had played many a chess tournament with Hatter. She gritted her teeth and faced the oversized pawns and knights and bishops.

"Do you like games, child?" asked the queens, flipping from red to white and white to red. "We like games.

Unfortunately, this one will not be much of a challenge. But we will play with you – until we grow bored."

One of the pawns came gliding from one tile to the next. A pneumatic arm juddered out of its side. On the end was the sharp bladed head of an axe. The arm swung the axe, slicing it through the air.

"Off with her head," giggled the queens.

Now eight pawns advanced in unison, each similarly armed.

Alice moved back.

The pawns moved forward.

Alice moved left.

The pawns moved left.

Alice stood still.

The pawns advanced in formation, swinging their axes.

"Off with her head!" yelled the queens.

Alice brought the shield up in front of her. Her thumb located the little button on the hand strap. She waited 'til the pawns were almost upon her and she could feel the wind from the swiping of their axes against her face.

She pressed down on the button.

A visibly shimmering haze went pulsing through the air. As soon as it engulfed the pawns they fell immediately still, raised axes frozen in mid swipe. Alice knew she had not a second to waste. She moved in with the sword and witnessed for the first time its true power. As it pierced the iron casings of the pawns, like a hot knife slicing into butter, their circuitry sparked and popped and exploded.

"Round one to me, I think," Alice called up to the screen as smoke filled the atrium.

"Pawns are naught but pawns," said the queens. "See how you fare with knights."

The knights came at her from either side, armed with long, terrible looking lances and moving in an odd L-shaped manner that zigzagged across the tiles. Alice knew her only hope was to go on the offensive. She ran headlong at the knight to her right, slamming the sword down onto his lance with a loud clang. The knight rocked and spun into a skid. Alice followed his spiraling trajectory across the tiles and used the momentary advantage to deploy the shield.

The knight froze.

No sooner had she dispatched him than the second was at her back. Alice ducked beneath the advancing lance, rolled over, and jumped up behind him. Her thumb pressed down on the red button. The knight juddered to a halt. Alice finished him with a fierce lunge of the sword.

Up on the screen the playing cards flipped back and forth from Red Queen to White Queen. "Such fun. Such fun."

Now the rooks, armed with brutal maces, and the bishops, with lunging daggers, came at her across the black and white tiles. Alice dodged and ducked and danced, felling them one by one with her trusty shield and sword. When the king moved in front of his queen to protect her, Alice strode purposefully across the tiles. A pair of mighty broadswords emerged from the king's sides on his pneumatic arms. Not allowing him the slightest chance to move forward, she

blasted him with the shield and neutralized him with the sword.

The queen chess piece swiveled. Beneath her crown, where a carved depiction of a face should have been, was a glass compartment, and inside that compartment was a human head. Alice gasped. She recognized the face.

The last time Alice had seen this face had been on the summer's day when the queen had sent her robotic knaves to slaughter the inhabitants of the settlement she'd grown up in. Again the words she had heard on that day echoed in her mind.

"Go with Hatter. He will see that no harm comes to you."

Her heart did a dizzying somersault in her chest.

"Mamma?" she cried.

"Surprise!" cried the twin voices from the big screen.

Alice looked closer at the face. It wasn't quite the smiling face she remembered. Veined and marbled, red and bloodshot eyes, dank hair, hung down like matted rattails. An array of wires dangling from the frayed hem of its neck sparked and caused its blackened lips to twitch and quiver into animation.

"It's not me, Alice," said her mother's voice. "It's hardly even the ghost of me. The queens bicker endlessly to see which one can wrest control of what little I have left."

"Do not," protested the Red Queen.

"Do too," insisted the White.

Alice took a step back, unsure of what to do next.

"Set me free, Alice," pleaded her mother. "Free me from this endless torment."

"Hush your jibber-jabber," said the Red Queen. "Hush and do your job. Off with her head."

"Perhaps we'll replace you with your daughter," suggested the White Queen. "An hereditary monarchy, so to speak."

The cards spun wildly as the queens squealed in malicious delight.

I hate you both, thought Alice, wondering exactly how she might free her mother.

Before she could come up with anything, a swarm of arms, bearing an array of weaponry, sprouted from almost every part of the chess piece. It glided forward rattling swords and sabers and scimitars. Alice ducked and dodged and darted to avoid being assailed and shredded by the blades. Sparks flew as the sword blocked parries; the shield clattered noisily as blow after blow rained down.

"Slice her and dice her!" crowed the queens' voices, and laughter once more echoed through the atrium.

Flamingos pecked viciously at Alice's back and shoulders, trying to distract her. Hedgehogs rolled dizzyingly between her feet, trying to trip her up. Dragonflies flitted endlessly before her eyes, trying to blur her vision. The face of her mother inside the chess piece bore a blank and absent expression as it maintained a relentless assault.

"She can't do it," said the Red Queen.

"Can't kill her poor mamma," said the White.

"Too sentimental," said Red.

"Too gushy and slushy," said White.

"Typical beating heart," said Red.

"Typical bleeding heart," said White.

Alice found herself backed into a retreat. One of the blades made contact with her sword-bearing arm, slicing a deep gash into the flesh beneath her elbow. She screamed and fell to the ground, kicking back with her heels to distance herself from the advance of the murderous chess piece.

Blood gushed from the wound. She began to cry. Beneath her mother's neck, wires sparked and a trace of life oozed into her bloodshot eyes. Her lip quivered as if she was struggling to gain control.

"You're hurt. I hurt you."

"It's all right, Mamma," said Alice. "They made you do it."

The queens clucked smugly and flipped from Red to White.

"The hard drive is in the chess piece," blurted her mother. "A black heart in a black queen. Destroy me and you destroy them."

Alice lumbered back to her feet and held the shield to her breast.

Her mother's face fell blank once more. Her eyes glazed over. The big screen turned suddenly dark. The image of the Red Queen appeared in her mother's right eye. The image of the White Queen materialized in her left.

The chess piece came gliding rapidly toward her.

Flamingos and hedgehogs and dragonflies closed in on her.

Now the voices of Red Queen and White Queen came from the chess piece itself.

"Can't do it," said one.

"Won't do it," said the other.

Alice gritted her teeth and pressed her thumb down on the red button. The shield just juddered and fell still. *I've blown it*, she thought. *All those dents and knocks have undermined Hatter's repairs.*

The Black Queen moved in for the kill, sabers and scimitars spinning wildly. The twin faces reflected in her mother's eyes adopting a demonically triumphal countenance. Biting her lip, Alice pressed down again on the red button and held it there with her thumb.

The shield shuddered and died and then shuddered once more and, just as dozens of blades were about to shred her to ribbons, the wave pulsed forth. The Black Queen jerked to a halt, swords immobilized mid swipe. Her mother's eyelids fell closed. Alice looked up at the screen. The playing cards had reappeared, frozen halfway between Red Queen and White.

Unraveling her arm from the shield Alice let it fall to the floor. Then, gripping the vorpal sword with both hands, she raised it high above her head. "I love you, Mamma." The chess piece trembled, as if it was regaining its energy. Alice knew she did not have a second to spare. A scream emerged from deep in her belly as she brought down the sword and cleaved the Queen in two.

The exploding of the ruptured hard drive sent her flying through the air. The long legs of the pink Flamingos buckled as they fell and the rolling hedgehogs lost momentum. All around flitting dragonflies dropped dead from the air. The card on the screen spun intermittently from Red to White to Red.

Then flickered.

Then died.

Alice emerged from the Mall, pressing a rag against her wounded arm, behind her, on buckled wheels and lopsided legs, came a procession of the battered and dented automata of the dispossessed.

A scene of utter carnage awaited her. Upturned turtle shells and mangled bodies of dormice. White Rabbits, spewing mechanical innards. Amongst them, stripped of their synthetic fur, the twisted remnants of dozens of fallen hares. She found Hatter, turning little circles on the spot, dazed and somewhat confused, upholstery flapping around him in ragged tatters, wiring poking through the lesions.

"Look what they've done to you," she said, blinking back her tears.

"Nothing a needle and thread and little bit of patchwork mending won't fix," he assured her.

Next she found Jack, even more bruised and bloodied than before, slumped by the smoking and mangled ruins of the mighty caterpillar. "You should have seen me," he began

to boast. "The brute lunged and tried to snap at me with its teeth, so I wedged my staff between its jaws. And then…"

Alice grabbed him by the ears of his cat-head hat, pulled him to her, and planted a huge, sloppy kiss on his lips.

"What was that for?"

"Just for being you," she told him.

He flashed her a cheesy grin.

The commander of the Legion sidled up beside her. Half of one of his ears was missing. There was a long scar streaking down from his left eye to his chin.

"Are there others?" Alice asked him.

"Others?"

"Queens," said Alice. "Are there other queens?"

The commander gave a solemn nod of his wounded head.

"Queens and mainframes and alpha-networks. All with petty little fiefdoms of their own."

Alice felt her shoulders tense against the weariness that had threatened to overwhelm her. "Then it's not over," she said. "Not until I bring battle to every last one of them."

"Count me in," said Jack, his fingers cautiously touching his lips, as if he could scarcely believe she had kissed him.

"The Legion will march at your side," vowed the commander.

"A drop of oil and a few repairs – and we will follow behind," promised the leader of the rust addled dispossessed.

The surviving hares assembled before her, battered but not bowed.

"Three cheers for Alice," barked their commander.

"Anyone for tea?" asked Hatter.

 David Turnbull lives and works in London. In addition to being featured in Salt Publishing's Best British Fantasy 2014, his most recent short fiction has appeared in *Different Dragons 11* (Wolfsinger Publications) and *Solstice Shorts* (Arachne Press). He is a member of the Clockhouse London group of genre writers.

THE WATCHMAKER'S BALL

CHRISTINE NORRIS

SOME INVITATIONS SHOULDN'T BE ACCEPTED.

FOR CONNIE, WHO HAD THE IDEA.
PYGMY WARRIORS FOREVER!

"Stand straight, Alice. Slouching isn't proper for a lady." "I'm not a lady," Alice grumbled. She didn't know how her posture could be less than poker-straight, considering the amount of muscle that had gone into lacing her corset. She dragged her feet as she followed her mother and older sister across Fairmount Park, through the crowds, and toward her doom.

"Alice Elizabeth Purcell, I won't talk to you again. Keep up."

Alice tried not to roll her eyes and trudged on. Ever since her older sister, Katharine, had talked to that boy at the bookshop, she had been begging their mother to take them to the Centennial Exposition. So here Alice was, on her way to an afternoon of torture and utter despair.

The Women's Pavilion.

Alice had come along hoping she would get to glimpse the amazing machines on display in the Machinery Hall, but they were on the other side of the fairgrounds. She had begged her mother to let her go see it, but her mother had forbidden it.

"It's not proper for a young lady of your station to be looking at dirty machines."

Alice had tried to keep her tone rational. "Every new, modern invention is there. You want me to be a smart and modern young woman, don't you?"

Her mother had closed her eyes and sighed. "I will hear no more about it today, Alice. I must concentrate on who is here and to whom Katharine should be introduced. It's her coming out year."

As if Alice needed to be reminded.

Her mother walked on, catching up to Katharine. Her older sister wore a brand-new walking dress and carried a parasol over one shoulder. Alice didn't know what her mother was so worried about. Pretty, sophisticated Katharine would have no trouble filling her dance card for the Assembly Ball.

The Pavilion loomed in front of them. Alice could practically smell the domesticity. Mother and Katharine entered, with Alice coming in a distant third.

She stepped across the threshold and wondered if she was in the wrong place.

A steam engine filled up much of the space at the front of the hall. Alice guessed it wasn't half the reported size of the Corliss, but the sight of it filled her heart with glee. The machine was tended by a woman in a gray dress. Alice went to it as if drawn by a magnet.

"What is this?" she blurted, without anything in the way of a proper introduction.

"This is a Baxter steam engine," the woman replied with great pride. "It runs every loom and spinner in the pavilion. I'm Emma. Emma Allison."

Alice was sure she wore a ridiculous expression, but couldn't help herself. "Alice Purcell." She was so distracted by the engine she didn't even gasp at the idea of a woman steam engineer. "It's beautiful."

Emma laughed. "You really think so? Most girls aren't interested in machines."

"I'm not most girls."

"That's obvious. Let me show you how it works." Before Emma could utter a word, Alice's mother appeared at her side as if conjured from the very air.

"Alice, come see the lovely embroidery and corset exhibits." Her mother's pleasant tone didn't fool Alice. The muscles along her jaw were laced corset tight, and Alice could almost hear her mother's molars grinding against one another.

Alice held back her sigh. "Thank you, Emma." She turned to follow her mother, but Emma grabbed her wrist in a vice-like grip.

"Beware the white rabbit."

Alice's eyes grew round and wide. "What did you say?"

"The white rabbit. No matter what he says, don't follow." There was panic in Emma's voice. She gave Alice one last squeeze, and then released her.

Alice shook her slightly sore hand and followed her mother. She looked back, but Emma had turned away. Her expression gave away nothing of her strange words.

The next half hour was excruciating, full of weaving, cooking, tea services, and dinner dishes. While her mother and Katharine were cooing over place settings, Alice searched for anything remotely interesting. A display of clockworks caught her attention. Emma's strange words floated back to her. Away from the moment, Alice giggled – what harm could a white rabbit be?

"You're late."

Alice looked for the speaker. The voice was small, like a child's.

"I said, you're late. Over here."

Her gaze skimmed across the display. There, among the inventions, sat a bit of white fur. A stuffed rabbit. A stuffed *white* rabbit.

Don't be silly. It's just a toy.

It winked at her.

Alice let out a squeak of surprise. She leaned in to get another look. It didn't move. *Of course it didn't.* She turned her attention to a brass carriage clock, but out of the corner of her eye, she caught a flicker of white-furred activity. When she looked, the rabbit was still there, sitting in exactly the same place.

Not exactly the same. Its right paw was raised in a waving gesture. Had it been like that before? She glanced over her shoulder, but no one else was looking. They were all too busy to see her step into the exhibit, past the velvet rope meant to keep people at a distance.

The rabbit was pretty and well-made, and with a key sticking out of its back. It was a clockwork. She felt ridiculous. Someone had wound the rabbit, and she had witnessed its last movements before the spring wound down. She grabbed the key, gave it several turns, and then set it on the ground. The rabbit moved, its nose twitching and its paws waving, hopping up-and-down at regular intervals. That solved the mystery.

The rabbit turned its head and looked at her.

"You're late."

The mouth moved, and the words were clear as day. It looked less like a toy and more like a real rabbit, except that, of course, real rabbits didn't speak.

"I'm late? For what?" Alice couldn't help but reply.

"For the ball, of course." The rabbit made an annoyed clicking sound. "As if you didn't know."

"I'm not late for anything, and the last place I need to go is a ball." She looked around again. Her mother and Katharine were yards away, talking to a woman. Likely someone with a daughter or niece coming out this year, to be sure. Or maybe she had a son who needed a wife.

"We really need to be going." The rabbit's tone was insistent.

As nice as you please, the clockwork rabbit hopped away. Before she knew what she was doing, she followed. He stopped in front of a grandfather clock and pointed to the long, thin door on the front.

"What's this silliness? We can't go in there." Alice realized she was talking to a toy and scolded herself.

"Of course not, if you don't have a key." He tilted his head, his button eyes reflecting the light. "You do have the key, don't you?"

"Of course I don't." She opened her reticule and showed the inside to the rabbit. "See?"

"What good are you if you don't have the key?" The rabbit made the annoyed sound again. "Are you sure it's not in your pocket?"

"I don't know what you're blathering about." Alice had had quite enough. "But, just so you'll be quiet…" She jammed her hands into the pockets of her walking dress. "See? I told you…" The fingers of her right hand brushed against something at the very bottom of her pocket. It was a

brass skeleton key, shiny, with a long barrel. The top was sculpted like a brass gear, the teeth biting into the pads of her fingers.

She turned to the rabbit. He gave an impatient hop and waved her on, then stood still. The spring must have wound down.

She took a step, then stopped. Emma's warning rang in her ears. She had sounded so dire. How had she known about the rabbit? And yet, here it was, trying to get her to go through a door in a grandfather clock. What did she have to lose except a few more boring minutes with her mother and sister?

She picked up the rabbit and wound it again.

"Thank you. Now, can we *please* be on our way? The Watchmaker will be cross if we're much longer."

Alice set the rabbit down and slipped the key into the lock on the grandfather clock's door. It turned easily and the door popped open. She peered inside, expecting to see the chains and weights normal to such a device. The carpeted hallway was an utter shock. The rabbit hopped inside, his winding key turning. He waved her on in a way that said she should hurry.

Alice paused, her hand on the clock, her foot raised to step over. Emma had warned her, and here she was, following. She would only be a few minutes. Just a quick look around. Not enough time to get into any kind of trouble.

"Oh, my goodness, this clock is much bigger on the inside." Alice had wondered if it wasn't some kind of optical illusion. But her feet stepped on thick, soft carpet of deep

blue. The walls of the corridor were lighter blue, with plaster trim in white. It was like being inside one of her mother's Wedgewood teacups. The deep quiet made Alice shiver.

"All right, I've seen it. Now I need to go."

She turned to leave, but the door had shut and locked. She patted her pockets, but the key wasn't there. Had she taken it out before she stepped through, or was it still in the lock of the grandfather clock? She couldn't remember.

"How am I supposed to get back?"

"You can't go back, only forward," the rabbit said. He hopped up and down like a child who needed the lavatory.

Alice huffed. "A fine mess this is."

"Come along." The rabbit hopped away, leaving Alice no choice but to follow. The hall was long and lined with doors.

"There must be hundreds. Where do they all go?" She tried to open a few, but they were locked. The hall connected to another, and then another. The rabbit made so many turns Alice was dizzy.

Finally the hallway came to an end. The rabbit stopped in front of a pair of double doors. Polished oak, carved with all manner of gears and springs, interspersed with leaves and flowers. They intermingled on the door as if it were a natural thing that flowers and gears grew in every garden. She pressed her ear against it and heard the barest strains of music.

"Are you going to open it, or not?"

Alice had nearly forgotten the white rabbit. He sat beside her feet, nose twitching, gears turning. It had been a while since she had wound him. How much longer until he would

need to be wound again? Perhaps she wouldn't, if he was going to keep being so cheeky.

"Just a minute. I don't go around opening doors willy-nilly."

The rabbit gave her a look of deep irony, which Alice ignored.

"I've told you, you're expected." An envelope appeared in the rabbit's paws. It must have been a magic trick, sleight-of-hand, though Alice had no idea where he had been hiding it. She took the envelope. Her name was written on it, in swirly, elegant writing. She lifted the flap and pulled out the invitation inside.

> *You are cordially invited*
> *to the Watchmaker's ball*
> *held every 6th Saturday*
> *at the Ballroom-in-the-clock.*
> *Please be prompt.*

"This invitation makes no sense," Alice exclaimed. "There are no sixth Saturdays. And how can I be prompt when there is no time written here?"

"You're nearly late." The rabbit tapped his foot impatiently. "Open the door."

Alice eyed the rabbit suspiciously. "How do you know I'm nearly late? You don't even have a watch."

"What a very silly thing to ask a rabbit made of clockwork."

Alice jammed a hand on her hip. "That makes no sense, either. Besides, I'm not dressed for a ball." She indicated her dusty but neat walking dress.

"Go inside," the rabbit insisted.

Alice sighed. There was no more use arguing. "All right, then." She pulled the door open.

The music swelled as a gorgeous ballroom was revealed. She had never seen the one at the Academy of Music, where the Assembly Ball was held, but she couldn't imagine it would compare to this. A long room with an impossibly high ceiling. Three walls covered in gilt-framed mirrors, making it look as if there were a thousand people inside. There were probably only about a hundred, if Alice had to guess, all dancing. The fourth wall was dominated by an enormous clock face, the numbers and hands made of polished brass.

Alice's heart flipped. Women in gowns of every color, like dancing flowers, being led by men in embroidered waistcoats with tailed coats. Their jewelry glittered like fire in the lights of the crystal chandeliers.

"I can't go in there," she whispered to the rabbit.

"Why ever not?" the rabbit asked with a sniff.

"I look like a ragamuffin."

"I beg to differ. I think you look fantastic."

A tall man stood before her. He wore a bronze-colored tuxedo of the oddest material Alice had ever seen. It almost looked as if the fabric were made of metal. His chestnut hair shone in the light from the chandeliers, and his smile was open and charming.

"Thank you, sir, but I doubt…" Her voice trailed off as she looked down at herself. Her walking dress was gone, replaced by a ruffled and fitted gown the same color as the

man's suit. She blushed at the gown's neckline. *If my corset were pulled any tighter, I'd fall right out.*

"But…how?"

"You've been invited to the Watchmaker's ball," the man said. "Everything is always taken care of for invited guests."

The rabbit, still sitting by her feet, wore a black-and-white tuxedo, a white bow tie beneath his chin. He winked at her, waved, and then scampered off, leaving her alone with the man.

Alice had no experience with formal balls, but had watched her sister practice often enough. She attempted a slightly clumsy curtsy. "Good evening, sir."

"Good evening, Miss Purcell. Welcome. I am the Watchmaker." He returned her curtsy with a polite, jingly bow. When he stood, Alice saw the source of the jingling. A huge brass ring of keys hung on the front of his jacket, attached to a watch chain. He held his hand out to Alice.

"Would you care to dance?"

"I…I, uh…" She stuttered. "Shouldn't I have a dance card?"

The Watchmaker laughed. "Why would you need a card for dancing? Which one would you prefer? The Ace of Spades? Or the Queen of Hearts?"

Alice giggled at his silly answer. The Watchmaker bent his arm, offering his elbow. Alice, nervous, slipped her arm in his. He led her to the center of the dance floor, where the other couples moved apart to give them space. He spun her around so that she was facing him, and took her by the waist. She realized she had no idea what dance was coming next.

Over the shoulder of the Watchmaker, Alice had a good view of the musicians. They sat on a dais along the wall in front of the clockface.

They were clockwork. But not *clever* clockwork, like the White Rabbit. These were simple machines with metal limbs. Tuxedos hung limply from their frames. Above their bodies were clear glass bowls turned upside down. Inside were the clockworks that made them run, gears turning as the metal musicians prepared to play. The music started.

It was a waltz. The Watchmaker began the dance, his feet moving in time with the music. More couples joined them almost immediately, filling the spaces and turning the room once more into a bouquet of spinning fabric. Alice laughed, and the Watchmaker held her tighter.

"New partner! Move down!"

She couldn't tell where the call had come from, but the effect was immediate. Everyone released his or her partner, spun around, and grasped hands with another. They didn't even miss a step. Alice's mouth fell open.

"How do they know where to go?"

The Watchmaker, who had abandoned her in the middle of the floor for a blond woman in a fluffy pink dress, called over his shoulder, "How does a music box know what to play?"

Without even trying to figure out what he meant, she turned toward her next partner. A tall man with chestnut hair, in a coat of deep green appeared. He bowed, a wide smile on his face, and held out his hand. They twirled across the floor, Alice's heart racing, and he didn't say a word. She changed

partners three more times, each time at the command of the strange call. She laughed out loud as she was tossed from one well-appointed partner to the next, wondering what her prim-and-proper sister would think of such silliness.

Finally the song ended. Alice was out of breath, her throat dry. The Watchmaker appeared at her side once more.

"Are you enjoying yourself, Alice?"

Alice nodded. "I never thought I would enjoy a ball, but this is so exciting."

"I'm glad you think so, but you must be thirsty. Allow me to get you something to drink."

Alice found a cushioned seat along the wall and fell onto it. The musicians played a Virginia Reel, and every dancer fell into place. Just watching them spin and twirl made her want to dance again.

The Watchmaker returned with a small, crystal glass. It was filled with a red liquid. Attached to the handle was a small tag.

"I hope this will satisfy your thirst, my dear."

Alice took the glass and brought it to her nose. She took a small sniff. It didn't smell like wine, which she had tried once but hadn't liked. It had a fruity smell – and something else she couldn't place. She looked at the tag.

Drink Me.

What else would she do with it? She took a sip. Delicious. Abandoning her manners, she gulped the rest down.

"Thank you." She handed the glass back. "What was that?"

The Watchmaker smiled. "My own special blend. Are you ready to dance?"

Alice stood, perhaps a bit too fast. She wobbled, and the Watchmaker steadied her with a hand on her elbow.

"My dear, are you all right?"

Alice giggled. "That punch had a bit more kick than I thought." Her vision wavered, then righted itself. "I feel very curious."

"Oh, dear." The Watchmaker sounded concerned. "That must be the potion. It has that effect on some."

"The what?" The room tilted, everything blurring around the edges.

"My special potion. Everyone here has drunk it." The Watchmaker's tone was infuriatingly matter-of-fact, tinged with amusement. "It's how they never stop dancing."

"What does that mean?" Had he drugged her? "What is happening to me?"

The song ended and immediately a new one began. This time it was a light, jaunty polka. The Watchmaker took her hand and pulled her onto the floor. The room had stopped spinning, but her arms tingled and felt strange.

"Wait," she pleaded. "Wait, please, I don't know if I can dance."

The Watchmaker waved away her plea. "Of course you can. Soon you will be able to dance forever." Before she could protest further, he had pulled her into the polka. She whirled at a fantastic pace, the music seeming to speed up as they danced. She moved so fast she didn't have time to think. Her arms still tingled and suddenly felt heavy though the

muscles did not ache. The song ended, and Alice took the chance to get away.

"Excuse me. I need to…powder my nose."

She had no idea if there was a powder room; she just ran out of the ballroom and into the hall. The muffled quiet made every sound she made as loud as the midnight bell in a churchyard. She lifted an arm and bent her fingers. The skin was intact, her slender fingers the same as always, the nails slightly ragged. Whatever the Watchmaker had given her, its effects were happening *beneath* the skin. She held her hand near her ear and flexed her fingers again. This time she heard it. A mechanical sound, like pulleys and gears turning.

It was coming from her hand.

She bent her arm at the elbow, and the sound was louder. In horror, but with a little fascination, she moved first one arm and then the other. The sounds came from both.

"Impossible." Alice breathed the word.

"I try to think of seven impossible things before breakfast." The Watchmaker appeared in the middle of the hall like an apparition. "I know it might be uncomfortable at first, but when the change is complete you'll be right as rain."

Alice's stomach churned, bile crawling up the back of her throat. She pressed her back against the door to get as far away from the Watchmaker as she could. "That's monstrous." An even darker thought occurred to her. "All of them, inside? *All* of them are clockwork?" She left off the bit where they had once been flesh-and-blood people. It was too terrible to think about, let alone say aloud.

The Watchmaker smiled, but it wasn't malicious or cruel, rather a smile that said he thought he was doing something wonderful and clever. He nodded.

"Do they think? *Can* they think?"

The Watchmaker's smile fell. "Why does it matter? Like you, they were unhappy in their lives. I invited them to my ball, and now they are always happy."

"I'm not unhappy." It wasn't a question, or even an argument. It was a statement. "Why do you think I'm unhappy?"

"What else would I think of a girl who has a secret workshop in her attic and dreams of building steam engines?"

Alice fell against the door, the strength drained from her. "How did you know that?"

The Watchmaker shrugged. "Your mother wants you to be a lady, but instead of dresses and slippers, you want gears and springs."

"And being here, at a ball of all things, will make me happy? How does that make any kind of sense?" Alice gasped as the strange feeling that had begun in her arms moved into her chest. What would happen when her heart turned to clockwork? Her brain? Each of her ribs was turning to metal, one by one, like fingers clamping around her lungs.

"You said you were enjoying yourself. I thought you'd want to stay." The Watchmaker held out his hand to her, just as he had when she had first set foot in the ballroom. This time it was ominous instead of inviting.

What could she do? Run? Where? The door to her world was locked. Feeling like a mouse that has been cornered by a

cat, she took his hand and let him lead her back into the ballroom. The music had stopped, and the dancers were still. No one moved from the dance floor, not to sit and rest or get a drink. There was no laughter, no flirting, not even conversation. It only lasted a few seconds, until the musicians took up with a polka, but it was enough to send a chill down Alice's spine.

Then the band took up a Redowa, a lively waltz. The dancers moved again, leaping and twirling about the floor. "I know you've had a bit of a shock. Skip this dance, and I'll be back."

He stepped onto the floor and pulled a woman dancer away from her partner. The male dancer stepped off the dance floor and bent at the waist, his hands dropping to his sides. He did not move. Alice went to see if he needed help. His eyes were open, staring at nothing. She tapped his shoulder, but he did not move. He was just a clockwork doll whose spring had wound down.

If they're not dancing, they don't exist. Part of her wanted to open up the back of the doll, to see how it worked, while the other part shuddered in revulsion at the idea of opening up what had once been a flesh-and-bone human being. Still, it was fascinating.

She had to find a way out of here. Emma Allison had warned her about the rabbit. She must have been here and had escaped. How had she done it?

"New partner, move down!"

Alice pinpointed the source of the voice. She followed it across the room and found the white rabbit. He was sitting

on a tall stool, holding a cone-shaped speaking trumpet. Alice grabbed his ears and lifted him to eye level.

"You. You dragged me into this, and you will help me out of it."

The rabbit squirmed. "Put me down. How would you like it if someone pulled you around by your ears?"

Alice had often had just such a thing done to her, by both her mother and her governess. "Not until you tell me how I can fix this."

The rabbit's whiskers quivered. "The Watchmaker would disassemble me."

"A-ha!" Alice used her free hand to point at the rabbit's nose. "So there *is* a way."

The rabbit's eyes widened. "You tricked me."

Alice set him on the stool, but didn't let go. "Tell me."

"I can't." The rabbit cast a nervous look over at the dance floor, perhaps searching for his master. "I won't."

Alice changed tack. "Look, if you help me, I'll…take you with me." She let go of his ears.

The rabbit shook his head, like a real rabbit. "Really?"

"Of course. I wouldn't want you disassembled on my account. Come with me, and you'll never have to see him again."

The rabbit paused. "One second, please." He raised the speaking trumpet to his mouth. "New partner! Move down!" He lowered the trumpet and cast an aside glance to make sure no one was listening.

"If you want to stop it, you must leave the Watchmaker's realm. That's the only place the potion works."

Alice's heart fell. "How am I supposed to do that?"

"You can't, of course, unless you have your key."

"My key?" Her thoughts raced to come up with an answer. "The one I used to open the clock? I left it."

The rabbit shrugged. "If you say so."

"All right, fine. Where is the key?"

"Where do you think?" the rabbit pointed to the dance floor, directly at his master.

The Watchmaker's key ring, on the chain attached to his coat. So many keys. About a hundred.

"If I were to count the keys on the ring, would it be the same as the number of dancers?"

The rabbit's whiskers twitched, and he gave a nod so small Alice almost missed it.

"Perfect." The potion continued its work inside her, and she could almost feel the time she had left slipping away. "How long is forever?" she muttered, not to anyone in particular.

"Sometimes just one second," the rabbit replied sadly.

The music ended.

The Watchmaker returned. "Come along, my dear. Time to dance."

"Where did they all come from?" The whispered question barely made it past her lips. She grimaced at the burning, tearing pain in her feet as the bones, one by one, turned to metal. She had to make this quick.

The Watchmaker shrugged. "Here and there. Poor, miserable souls who wanted to be happy. Now they are."

"Are you certain?" Alice couldn't bear to look at them, dancing the polka, unaware of their previous lives.

"They're smiling, aren't they?" the Watchmaker smiled, and that was when Alice knew.

"You're mad. Completely mad."

The Watchmaker shrugged. "We're all mad here. Now come." He held out his hand.

Alice swallowed her horror as she let him lead her to the dance floor. He spun her around, diving right into the dance. Breathless and dizzy, she couldn't even think of a way to get the key ring. Her clockwork legs felt as if they could dance all night. Which, she supposed, was the point. They were in a never-ending night, at a ball that had no final dance. The polka ended and immediately the dancers formed squares of eight, ready for a Quadrille. This could be Alice's chance.

The dance began. Alice focused on the steps, forced herself to smile, so that the Watchmaker would think she was enjoying herself. As they crossed paths for the first spin, she slid her hand across his jacket, touching the key ring. At the next pass, she kept eye contact with him as her fingertips caressed the cold metal. When she danced with the other men in their square, she contemplated how to nick the key ring. The best course, she decided, was to grab and pull as hard as she could.

She faced the Watchmaker again. Her smile was still there, but this time it was a smile of treachery. They came together, arms around each other's waists, and turned in their circle. Alice slipped her fingers through the cold brass ring.

The Watchmaker's eyes widened as she stepped back, the key ring in her hand. She pulled as hard as she could.

The rip of fabric as the chain pulled free from his jacket was satisfying. Alice ran.

She didn't notice that the ballroom had gone completely silent until her hand was on the handle of the carved ballroom doors. The quiet was so eerie she had to turn and look.

Every dancer faced her. The musicians had put down their instruments and were standing in front of their chairs.

The Watchmaker, his face angry as a thunderstorm, pointed an accusatory finger. "Bring her to me."

The first dancer hadn't even taken a step when Alice ripped the door open and dashed out. She slammed it behind her, realizing it made a poor barrier. She looked for something to put in front of it, but there was nothing.

"Fantastic. Trapped in a corridor full of locked doors." She had a ring full of keys, but couldn't lock the door.

"I'd run if I were you," said a voice.

Alice spun and nearly tripped over the white rabbit. "What are you doing here?" The last words were drowned out by the sound of hundreds of feet on the other side of the door.

"I thought you might try to go back on our deal. If I knew you were going to make a scene, I'd never have told you the secret." The rabbit waved a paw. "But now you've gone and done it. Run."

Alice lifted her skirts and raced away from the ballroom. The sound of double doors slamming open, hitting the walls behind them, chased her down the corridor.

"How do I know which key?" she yelled to the rabbit. She hadn't thought this plan through very well. At this point she didn't care *which* door she left through. She just wanted to get out of this infernal hallway.

"Come on, this way." The rabbit hopped ahead, his four feet much faster than her two.

"We need a place to hide." She was surprisingly fast, and for a fleeting moment she could see the advantage of clockwork legs.

The rabbit kept running, turning right and left as they passed dozens of identical doors. The pace was dizzying and Alice tried to keep a count of how many rights and lefts, but she couldn't manage it.

The rabbit skidded to a stop. They were at the end of the corridor.

"Give me the keys."

Alice pulled them protectively to her chest. "Why?"

The rabbit made a clucking sound and rolled his eyes. "Do you want to go home or be a clockwork doll? Give me the keys."

Alice handed over the brass ring. There were so many keys, some long and some short, some old and some new. The rabbit picked through them, discarding one after the other.

"Hurry," Alice whispered. Their pursuers couldn't be far behind.

"Have patience," the rabbit scolded. He picked out one key and held it away from the others. "This one."

Alice took the ring, holding on to the key. It was the shiniest one on the ring, with a long barrel and a brass gear on the end.

She glanced at the rabbit. "You're sure?"

"Are you going to keep your promise?" The white rabbit tilted his head, his whiskers twitching. "Because if not, I'll wait right here and tell him I was trying to stop you, and you'll be left to your fate."

"Of course I'll keep my promise."

"Then I'm sure." The rabbit hopped to the door at the end of the corridor and waited. Alice slipped the key into the lock.

"Stop!"

The Watchmaker had arrived. He stood a few yards away, his army of clockwork dancers behind him. Alice pressed her back against the door. A fog fell over her thoughts like a wool blanket. She was out of time – her brain was turning to clockwork. Another few moments and she'd be just another doll. She shook her head to try to clear the fog. The Watchmaker took a step closer, and his toys followed.

"I'm sorry." Alice had no idea what she was apologizing for. "I can't stay."

The Watchmaker knitted his brow. "Why not? You would be happy here. Always."

"Life isn't about always being happy." The fog began to descend again, and it was harder to breathe. *Clockwork dolls don't need to breathe.* She forced her hand to turn the key. The

bolt slid back. "And honestly, I don't think you have any idea what happiness is."

Alice turned the knob and leaned on the door, falling with it as it opened. There was a feeling of a great weight being lifted from her – her bones and muscles turning back to normal, she guessed. She fell onto the floor of the exhibit hall, landing on her backside. The Watchmaker was at the door, reaching through to grab her. She leaped forward and slammed the door shut, falling against it with a rush of exhaled breath. Every muscle in her body ached, and she was grateful for it.

"Alice? What on earth are you doing?"

Her mother and sister stood in front of her, wearing identical looks of embarrassed amazement. Alice looked down at herself. Her walking dress had returned, and the rabbit, once more a clockwork toy, was in her hands.

"Mother, Katharine. I am so glad to see you! I was…looking at this clockwork rabbit. It's very well built." She would never look at any clockwork, or her workshop, the same way again.

Her mother heaved an exasperated sigh. "Alice, when will you learn to be a lady? We've been looking all over for you."

"I'm sorry, Mother. I've been right here all along." She couldn't even begin to explain her afternoon.

"Well, I hope you're happy. You've missed the very best exhibits in the entire Exposition." Her mother pulled her lace shawl over her shoulders. "And to think, *you* wanted to spend the day looking at machines. Come along; it's time for tea."

Christine Norris is the author of several speculative fiction works for children and adults. She is highly over-educated and, therefore, loves to be in the library, which is her secret day job (whoops...). She also has an addiction to British television and believes in fairies.

RABBIT FEVER

JACKIE HORSFALL

DON'T BE LATE FOR YOUR DATE WITH THE PLAGUE.

FOR MY PARENTS,
WHO BOUGHT ME A LIVE WHITE RABBIT.

Summer 1665
The outskirts of London, England

Alice wrapped the poultice of stewed onions and garlic in a square of linen and carried it to Edward's bedside. The fleshy knob growing out of his neck had turned a shiny yellowish-purple, large as a goose egg about to burst. His hair was a disheveled wet mess, his pillow drenched with sweat. A pungent smell hung in the air, vaguely sweet like rotting apples.

"Run, Alice," he rasped. "Go away from this death house. God has abandoned us." Edward moaned as a spasm of shivering shook his body.

"Rest easy, brother," Alice crooned as if to a wee babe, even though Edward was two years her senior. "I am not leaving." Not that leaving would be possible. Plague was rampant in London, and only the wealthy bearing a certificate of good health signed by the Lord Mayor could exit the city.

Alice laid the soggy packet aside and drew two tail feathers plucked from a live chicken out of her pocket. These she placed over Edward's swelling and covered them with the poultice to draw out the poison. He lay silent now, his breathing shallow and rapid. She was glad for these plague remedies and protections from Widow Maud who also prescribed the wearing of dead toads and application of powdered unicorn horn. Dead toads were readily found along the muddy roadways, but neither Alice nor Maud knew where to obtain powdered unicorn horn, much less find a live unicorn.

Alice knelt next to Edward's bed. She folded her hands and rested her head on them. The church taught plague was sent by God to test and punish His people, and the clergy preached repentance. "Dear God," she began, "please forgive Edward his sins and take the fever from him. He sorely repents…" Alice hesitated. She tried to speak honestly, but the words stuck in her throat. What sins had Edward committed? She lifted her head and sifted through her memory. She could not remember a one. He was an angel upon earth, as was their beloved mother who was taken by plague the month before. If this punishing God was all-powerful, He was also unjust, merciless, and cruel. She would not honor a vengeful God, nor ask for forgiveness of imagined sins by a brother whose soul was as pure as the first winter snow. Widow Maud was right – prayers were not cures.

"Alice, come," her father called from outside. "Come see how God has blessed us."

Alice stood and brushed her hands down her apron, wondering what God could possibly be blessing them with but more plague. She stepped to the door, its front painted with a large red cross, the mark of a plague house. Da's stooped figure trudged up the path, a bulging fetch-sack slung over his shoulder. Da was a good provider. Could it be true? Had he found a unicorn's horn after all?

Da swung the sack from his shoulder and sat heavily on a stool near the door. He drew open the drawstrings and reached inside. "How is our boy today, Alice?"

"With us. But still with fever."

Da raised his eyes to the heavens and muttered a prayer. Alice quickly scanned his neck for swellings and sores. Sweat beaded on his brow. Was it from fever or merely exertion on a hot day? He did not wheeze or complain of headache. His gait was lumbering as usual due to his bowed legs, but Alice saw no signs of muscle pain or weakness. So far, she and Da had been spared the scourge. But for how long?

"What have you brought us, Da?" If Edward was to live, Widow Maud said the unicorn's horn must be ground to powder, made into a paste, and applied immediately.

"Patience, child." Da rummaged in the sack and pulled out a dead rabbit by its two hind legs. It was scrawny and flea-bitten, with patchy brown fur. "Set the pot to boil, Alice. I have brought our supper."

"Oh." Alice tried to hide her disappointment. She should be thankful. They had not supped on meat for weeks. She fought the urge to ask where the rabbit had been snared and sealed her lips shut. City trade had ceased, the streets empty of merchants. Da had either filched the rabbit from an abandoned market or poached from royal grounds while King Charles and Queen Catherine escaped the sickness at their country estate.

Da set to work skinning the rabbit, first slicing a ring around each leg, just above the leg joint, and up the back. He worked his fingers into the sleeve of the hide and pushed it to the base of the rabbit's skull, like a fine lady removing her glove. With a quick twist, he snapped off the head, and yanked the skin off entirely.

Alice had watched this skinning many times before, but today a wave of dizziness washed over her. She closed her eyes and tipped her head against the doorframe.

In the distance, a rumbling. Alice knew what it was without opening her eyes.

The dead-cart.

The cart slowly approached their cottage. Arms and legs stuck out over the top, flopping up and down as if waving their final good-byes. Her own dear mother had been taken away on a dead-cart for pit burial with other plague victims. She had begged Da to find private burial ground, but the graveyards were full. Hundreds of the sick were dying daily, their bodies stacked up against the walls of houses until the dead-carts hauled them away.

Alice shifted to block the door, but the driver had already spied the blazing red cross. "Bring out your dead," the cart-driver called to them. "Bring out your dead!"

Alice curled her hands into fists at her side. A rage exploded in her, so fierce it made her head ache. "Be gone, cart-man," she shouted. "My brother lives. We have no dead for you."

The driver shrugged and spit in the dirt. "Tomorrow then," he said casually, as if collecting bodies was a normal occupation like blacksmithing or cobbling. "I will return tomorrow."

While Da gutted the rabbit, Alice slipped inside and set a kettle to heat. Fury simmered in her. There would be no body for the dead-cart driver tomorrow, or ever. Edward was still breathing, still alive, and she would use every remedy and

potion to cure him, even search to the ends of the earth for a unicorn horn. She stacked wood in the fireplace and fanned the embers. It was rumored bad air caused the plague, and fires burning night and day, even in the heat of summer, would cleanse the air. Alice would set their thatched cottage to a bonfire if it would heal Edward.

Alice felt a tickle in her throat. Suddenly, without warning, a great wracking cough shook her. At first she willed her ears into disbelieving. It was only the smoke from the fire irritating her throat. She poked at the wood and it blazed, sending sparks up the chimney. Although great heat emanated from the fire, Alice felt chilled. She took her mother's shawl from a peg and drew it around her shoulders.

Edward cried out and thrashed in his bed. "Lord have mercy upon me," he muttered over and over in a raspy whisper.

Alice took a step toward him, but the room spun in a dizzying spiral. She staggered and fell backward against the stone fireplace. Sparks ignited her dress, burning black holes in the thin fabric. She beat at the sparks with her hands. Stooping, she doused her hem in a pail of wash water near the hearth. Her aching bones were so stiff she could barely ease herself upright. Her mouth was as dry as ashes.

With great effort she climbed to her sleeping loft and fell on the thin pallet. Her throbbing head felt about to burst. She drew in a shuddery breath. The symptoms were all familiar. Chills, dizziness, weakness, and headache were the signs of plague sickness. The next day or two would bring drenching sweats, pus-filled swellings, and seizures.

The dead-cart would be stopping for her within the week.

"Dear God," she whimpered. "Please…"

No. She would not stoop to prayer. Instead, she reached for her stuffed poppet, a hand-sewn rabbit made by her mother. The poppet's body was made of rough-spun white fabric and wearing a patchwork jacket. The lumpy head had two longish ears adorned with tufts of fur, the body stuffed with leaves and dried flowers. Widow Maud had put a protection spell on it. Alice hugged the poppet to her chest and breathed in the scent of herbs. "Mamma," she whispered to it, "open your arms for me. I am coming to you."

As she spoke, the world went black and Alice tumbled head over heels,

Falling

Falling down, down, down

Through the swirling vortex of a warm dark tunnel.

Alice fell slowly, drifting from side to side like an autumn leaf, giving her time to think. If this was death, it was very comfortable indeed. It gave Alice great comfort to think that her mother had been freed from pain and seizures in this same tunnel. Her mind shifted to the living. Edward would miss her very much. Widow Maud would declare her abduction by fairies. And Da, poor Da, would fret when he found the pot boiling but no daughter to cook his rabbit stew.

Wherever she was going, Alice felt remarkably clear-headed, not woozy from sickness at all.

Thump. Alice landed on a soft, fluffy pillow.

"Oof! Get off me," pleaded a muffled voice.

Alice sat back on her heels. Lying crushed beneath was not a pillow but her rabbit, no longer a child's hand-sewn poppet but a full-grown white rabbit wearing a patchwork waistcoat. He hopped up and looked anxiously about as if he had lost something.

"Oh, my dear paws. Oh, my fur and whiskers. She'll have my head." He sat on his haunches, lifted a hind leg, and scratched furiously behind one ear. "Wretched fleas. These fleas will be my death."

"May I help?" Alice reached out her fingers to ear-scratch the same way she did for Dinah, her cat. Dear Dinah was gone too, not from plague directly, but by order of the City Corporation. All cats and dogs were ordered to be killed as a plague precaution.

The rabbit flinched and leapt back. "How rude of you to fall on me," he grumped, brushing dirt from his sleeves. "Where are your manners?"

"It was not on purpose." How ridiculous, conversing with a rabbit. Edward would call her a silly goose if he could see her now.

"Purpose, porpoise." The rabbit waved her away with his paw. "Now run along home."

Alice turned in a circle. An expanse of green fields and leafy trees stretched out in all directions. Which way was home? If she was indeed dead, wasn't this her new home?

"Is this not heaven?" she asked.

"Heaven?" The rabbit scratched frantically under his chin. "I do not know the place."

"Then where am I?"

A dark thought filled her mind. She had been falling down, not up. The bowels of Hell were ruled by Satan, though it was unlikely Satan bred rabbits. Wherever she was, how nice of God to spare her even though she had refused to pray to Him.

"Why, everyone knows this is the land beyond the end of the world."

Alice thought this very curious. Widow Maud said the world was round and had no end. The only land beyond was the moon. Maud claimed the moon was inhabited by a man with a bundle of sticks on his back, so far removed from Earth that he was beyond the reach of death. This place most certainly was not the moon.

The rabbit pulled a watch from his waistcoat pocket. "Oh, mercy me. I am very late. She will snap off my head and boil my bones in her stew pot."

Alice gasped. She poked at a shadowy memory lodged in her brain. Da, snapping off a rabbit's head.

At this moment a voice called out, "All hail Her Majesty the Queen."

"Oh, my fleas and fur." The rabbit held his head in his paws. "My head, my poor head."

Queen? Alice expected to face a white-bearded God, scolding her for her disobedience. Were the church elders wrong? Was God a woman, and a queen?

Alice fluffed her blue homespun dress and adjusted her apron to hide the burn holes at the hem. She raked fingers through her tangled hair. Taking a deep breath and forming

her mouth into a smile, she turned in the direction of trumpets.

A regiment of royal foot guards marched toward Alice and came to a halt. They parted to allow a dozen courtiers to pass down the middle, followed by a stately woman dressed in a billowing silver gown trimmed with jewels.

Alice stood as if frozen. She squinted into the sunlight as the entourage approached. She rubbed her eyes and looked again. No, this could not be.

The Death Queen was her own Queen Catherine of England. Alice had only once seen the queen, wife of King Charles, from afar during a procession in the city. But her likenesses were everywhere, on paintings and embroidered linens. Alice thought perhaps she had not died at all.

Instead of Heaven or Hell, she seemed to have been delivered to the king's country estate in Oxford.

The queen floated toward Alice and pointed her scepter. "Who is this wretch trespassing on my land?"

The rabbit nervously scratched behind one flea-bitten ear. "Oh, my goodness gracious." His nose twitched as fleas hopped between his whiskers. "She fell from the sky, Your Grace. Right atop – "

"Silence!" the queen bellowed. "Let the wretch speak."

Alice dipped in a low curtsey. "I am Alice, your humble servant. In all truth, I fell on my poppet by accident."

"Poppet?" the rabbit sputtered. "I am most certainly *not* your poppet."

"My mother sewed him from scraps, but he seems to have taken on a mind of his own." She grabbed for the rabbit's ears, to give him a sound shake for his brazenness.

The queen's scepter knocked Alice's hand away. "Do *not* touch my rabbit."

"Scraps" – the rabbit sniffed – "as if I were a common field rabbit instead of a royal white Snowshoe courtier."

"Tell me, Wretch Alice," the queen said, "from where do you come?"

Alice hesitated. The queen must be testing her. "Why, I am from London, the same as you."

"Lun-dun?" The queen turned to her rabbit. "Do you know of such a place?"

"I do not, Your Grace. It seems to be a land in the sky. Perhaps the moon."

"Nonsense," the queen huffed. "Everyone knows the moon is ruled by the Earl of Sticks-on-His-Back. His estate is definitely not titled Lun-dun."

The queen faced Alice again. "Wretch, where is this Lun-dun?"

If this was a silly game, Alice decided she'd had quite enough. Had the plague made Queen Catherine feeble-minded? Why did she not remember her own city?

Alice spoke slowly and plainly, as if to a half-wit. "In the country you rule with King Charles, your husband."

The queen's face burned with fury. "I have no husband. No king rules here."

Alice had always been a quiet, sensible girl, but she could no longer tolerate this nonsense. She crossed her arms and snapped, "In my country, you are my queen and King Charles is your husband. You deserted your subjects who are dying from plague." Her bowels cramped as the misery of her

existence spewed like poison bursting from a pustule. "We are trapped in your filthy city, the cobbles slick with horse dung and slops, the stench so thick we walk with scented kerchiefs pressed to our noses. We sup on flea-bitten rabbit and bitter ale" – the rabbit moaned and put a paw to his throat – "while you dine on sweetmeats and wine at your grand country estate."

The queen's guards and courtiers gasped and whispered behind their hands.

The queen stepped close to Alice. She dipped her head so low their noses nearly touched. "Silence," she hissed, "or this will be your fate." From her fingers dangled a furry white lump on a chain. Alice shuddered when she recognized what it was.

A severed rabbit's foot.

The queen's breath smelled of something sickeningly sweet, like rotting apples. Her eyes drilled into Alice, black as the tunnel but lacking its warmth. Alice scoured her memory for Widow Maud's protection spell. Finally, it came to her.

Against all evil, I set this charm,
Keep its bearer from all harm.
So mote it be.

She would need the rabbit poppet in hand for the spell to work its magic. Without the hand-sewn poppet, a live rabbit must do.

"Rabbit," Alice beckoned him, "come to me. Quickly."

The rabbit jittered nervously as he pattered toward her.

Whack. The queen's scepter sliced between them, barring his way. "Are you a half-wit, wretch?" she thundered.

Alice took a giant breath and blew it out. "No, Your Majesty."

"Do you remember my royal command?"

"Yes, Your Majesty."

"Well?"

"Do not touch the rabbit," Alice repeated. "*Never* touch the rabbit."

"Very well then," the queen said, fluttering her fingers in royal dispensation. With her scepter, she lifted the hem of Alice's apron to expose the burn holes. "I have a notion to take you as my scullery maid. You may tend my hearth and empty my chamber pot." The queen extended her arm. "I don't like the look of you, or your attitude, but you may kiss my hand if you wish."

"I'd rather not," Alice said.

The queen's eyes bulged in astonishment. "What did you say?"

"I would rather not kiss your hand. It might carry plague."

The rabbit scratched frantically behind his ears, chin, and hindquarters. "Fleas. Fleas and plague."

"Blasphemy," the queen roared. "How dare you insult your sovereign? This is treason, a criminal offense. Guards, arrest her."

Two foot guards strode forward, swords drawn.

"No," Alice shouted, hand up to halt them.

For a moment, the queen stood stunned. "No?" She seemed never to have been addressed in such an impertinent

manner. "You said…no?" With both hands she hoisted her scepter like a croquet mallet and swung at Alice's head.

"I did nothing wrong," Alice cried, ducking the blow. "I fell into your land through no fault of my own. I committed no offense."

"Fetch the executioner," the queen ordered. "This wretch will die."

The rabbit squealed and spun in shuffling circles, his pink eyes pinwheeling. "Die. She must die."

The royal bugler lifted his horn and blew three notes. Alice heard a familiar rumbling starting far in the distance. Dread inched up her throat. The dead-cart heaped with bodies wheeled along the rutted road, limp arms and legs bouncing and waving.

"Bring me your living, soon-to-be-dead," the executioner sang, stopping his cart at the queen's upraised hand. He drew a gleaming sword from its scabbard and hobbled toward Alice. Dung and mud caked his boots. He grinned a row of yellow, chipped teeth, as if meeting an old friend.

"'Tis the morrow, Alice," he said, tipping his blood-smeared cap. "I have returned as promised."

The queen jabbed a finger at Alice. "You know this wretch?"

"I do, Your Grace." He fingered the fabric of Alice's dress and apron, payment for his services. His lips twisted in disgust. "These will hardly fetch two pence." He spat in the dirt. "Remove your garments and kneel before me in your shift. Pray to God to have mercy upon your soul."

Pray to God? A raging defiance surged through Alice. What had she done wrong, what sins committed? It was not her fault that she was cast into this awful place.

"I most certainly will not," she told the executioner. She did not need God's mercy. She did not need a poppet or its protection spell. She had her own talisman within, locked in her heart. Her love for Edward was a bold, fearless charm.

"Carry on," the queen ordered. "She may keep her filthy rags. The devil take her."

"Wait," Alice said. "I beg of you a last request."

"What say you? A request?" The queen turned to the executioner. "Is this allowed?"

He touched two gnarled fingers to his forehead, feigning thought. Shielded by his hand, he winked at Alice.

"It is highly unusual in your queendom, but I believe tradition calls for the dying to be granted a last request."

"This is very vexing," the queen said. She turned to her courtiers and consulted with them privately. With a swirl and flounce of her skirt she again faced Alice. "Although your manner is insolent and you are unworthy of my favor, I am intrigued by your strange entreaty. I am wealthy beyond all imagining. What is your request?"

"The horn of a unicorn," Alice said, "ground to a powder."

Peals of laughter rang out from the guards and courtiers. The queen shrieked in spasms of laughter, so heartily her bosom nearly burst from the low-cut neckline of her gown. "Such…such a small thing," she choked out, barely able to catch her breath, "when you could have your choice from my royal coffers."

Alice could not understand the humor in her request. The queen's riches held no appeal. Edward was dying, and a plaster of unicorn horn was the only remedy that might heal him. It was all she wanted. That, and a secret escape route back to Edward's bedside.

The rabbit offered his handkerchief, and the queen dabbed at her teary eyes. "Why, we drink tea brewed with powdered unicorn horn every afternoon at four."

The attendants again exploded with laughter.

"Silly wretch, you have wasted your request, but I will be generous." The queen raised her scepter. "I grant you one horn from my stable of unicorns, ground into powder by the royal apothecary. So shall it be."

Alice was bound to the dead-cart while a horseman was dispatched to fulfill her request. Swarms of flies buzzed over the bodies. Strangely, they bore no signs of plague, no swellings or ruptures. The corpses seemed almost asleep, not dead at all but lost in dreams.

Dreams. Was she dreaming? Alice bit down on her tongue and winced. No, of course she wasn't. Dreams were hardly this real. Alice considered the dilemma before her. Home. She must find a way home to Edward. How she arrived at the royal country estate was a mystery, but the way leading back to London must begin from these grounds. With the powdered unicorn's horn in hand, she would only need to escape and find safe passage.

Alice set her mind to formulating a plan, but her eyes grew heavy and her thoughts blurred. Yawning, she slid down as far as her bound hands would allow. She rested her head

against the cart wheel and dozed, flies buzzing over her body as if she were already among the dead.

"Wake up, wretch."

Alice snapped out of her nightmare. She shook off sleep, blinking and squinting as the ropes on her wrists were cut free.

The queen loomed over her, blocking the sun. She held out a drawstring pouch. "Here is your powder. Taste to your pleasure. Then prepare to die."

Alice opened the pouch and sprinkled a dusting of powder on her palm. She put her tongue to it. It tasted of soured milk left too long in the sun. But Edward would not need to taste it. Following Widow Maud's directions, she would moisten it, work it into a plaster, and apply it to his swellings to draw out the poison.

But first she needed an escape plan.

With a glance at the rabbit, an idea came to her.

"Your time is up," the queen bellowed. "The day is wasting. Executioner, take your stance."

Alice slipped the pouch into her apron pocket and swiveled to face him. "Sir, you look weary. You have had a long tiresome journey, and your bones must ache from this most unpleasant work."

"That they do." He sucked in a ragged breath and hefted his sword with two hands. "You are my eighth execution of the day."

"Eighth," Alice said in mock horror. "So many. Why, you must be famished."

"I've not set down for a good meal since morning." The sword trembled in his hands. "Not even a morsel of bread."

"Oh, you poor dear." Alice wiped away a fake tear. "How I wish I could fix you a nice hot bowl of rabbit stew to fill your belly."

The executioner's sword dipped as his eyes flitted toward the rabbit. He smacked his lips. "Mmmm," he murmured, "rabbit stew." A line of drool glistened on his chin like a snail's trail. Alice heard his belly rumble loudly as a dead-cart over cobbles. The blade wavered in the air, swinging lightly to and fro. With a sudden deft shift in stance, the executioner wielded his blade away from Alice and thrust it at the rabbit's throat.

"Oh no no no no," the rabbit squealed. With a giant bound he leaped over the executioner's head and landed with a *thump*. Hindquarters pumping, he scampered toward a stand of trees.

Alice picked up her skirts and hurried after him. She had never run so fast or so hard. His puffy tail bobbed as he zigzagged around rocks and bushes. Alice kept it in sight. With a single bound he flew into the air and dived into a hole hidden by tall grass.

And was gone.

Without so much as a backward glance, Alice held her breath and jumped in behind him.

Above her, muted in the distance, came the queen's screeches. "Do not touch my rabbit. Do you hear me, wretch? Keep your hands off the rabbit."

Alice fell slowly, but she was not alarmed. The tunnel was warm, and though she was again falling down, she sensed that this was the passage home. Rabbit drifted below, caught in a frenzy of fur scratching, cursing the fleas feasting on his skin.

Fleas. Alice felt herself shrinking down to their wee size, and they became huge spiny beasts, piercing the rabbit's skin and sucking his blood, regurgitating sickness into his wounds.

Rabbits and fleas. Fleas and sickness. Rabbits and sickness.

Fleas and plague.

Alice woke to the slow tolling of church bells, ringing once again for the dead. At first she didn't know where she was, only that her headache and chills were gone. She rolled over on her pallet and crushed a soft lump beneath her. The scent of lavender and rosemary filled her nose. She reached under her chest and pulled out her poppet, its seams bursting, dried herbs and flowers spilling out.

Her *rabbit* poppet.

The awful journey to Oxford flooded her memory. It seemed so real, and yet here she was back in her own bed, safe at home, the hand-sewn stuffed poppet clutched in her hand, no longer the queen's live talking rabbit.

Memory – or dream?

She would know for certain in the next moment. Alice eased herself up and dug deep into her apron pocket. She ran her fingers along the side and bottom seams. She poked a finger into each corner. She turned the pocket inside out.

Empty.

No pouch, no powdered unicorn horn.

She had dreamed it all: the queen, the rabbit, the executioner, the healing powdered unicorn horn.

Alice dropped her head to her hands and sobbed. "Oh, Edward, I have failed you. What a silly wretch I am to be fooled so."

A clanging of pots came from below. Alice dried her eyes and climbed down from the sleeping loft.

Widow Maud, her long white hair tied off with yarn from which dangled a dead toad, sat hunched over Edward's pale, motionless body.

Alice crept to his bedside. She forced herself to say the awful words. "My brother...is he...dead?"

Maud pressed a pad of linen to Edward's neck. "The swelling has burst. He will live."

Alice heard the light hiss of his breathing. When she took his fingers lightly in her own, he squeezed them weakly.

Maud removed the pad, and the open sore oozed pus spotted through with shreds of dead flesh. Alice knew this was a happy sign, for those whose plague lumps burst often recovered. She wept silently but smiled at the same time.

Maud put a hand to Alice's brow. "Are you well, child? You've been dead asleep since mid-morn."

"I was indeed dead," Alice said, "but now I find I am most certainly alive."

"I see our girl is up." Da stood in the doorway holding another dead, flea-bitten rabbit by its hind legs. "God be praised, I have the morrow's supper."

Alice grew dizzy. An aching panic overtook her. Her vision narrowed to a tunnel. In her mind, she flailed as she fell through the darkness.

Rabbits and fleas. Fleas and sickness. Rabbits and sickness. Fleas and plague.

At that instant Alice felt herself changing, shedding her old self like the pelt of a rabbit. She raised her voice, imperious and demanding. "Take it away, Da. Take it from this house *now.*"

Da stumbled backward, stunned by his daughter's ungratefulness and disrespect. "Take it away?" he growled. "Why do you say such?"

In time, Alice would explain to Da how bringing flea-bitten rabbits into their cottage was the source of Edward's plague infection, and was likely to infect them all. But for now, he must obey her command.

Whether memory or dream, Alice knew the queen's greatest gift was not the powdered unicorn horn. Now her harsh words made complete sense, and Alice repeated them.

"Do *not* touch the rabbit, Da," Alice ordered, as forcefully as a queen to her subject. "Never *ever* touch the rabbit."

Author Note: All of the superstitions and remedies of the Great Plague era – including the application of powdered unicorn horn – are historically accurate as far as I can determine. Although rats were believed to be the primary carriers of plague fleas, plague was also transmitted by small rodents such as rabbits, which people brought into their homes for food.

Jacqueline (Jackie) Horsfall is the author of twenty books and hundreds of magazine stories, articles, and poems. She lives in the Finger Lakes region of upstate New York and is the proud owner of Martin Gardner's original 1960 edition of *The Annotated Alice*.

MUSTANG ALICE

ALICE

MEDEIA SHARIF

HIT THE ROAD FOR AN UNFORGETTABLE JOYRIDE.

TO THE SCBWI
FLORIDA AVENTURA GROUP
FOR TEACHING ME ABOUT THE CRAFT.

"Come on, Alice, stop daydreaming. Out, girl. Let's get us some snacks and be back on the road."

Alice looked at the speaker, Maizie, the most aggressive girl in their group. Maizie had long, curly strawberry blond hair and fierce freckles. She also wore a frown. She didn't care too much for Alice.

"Ugh, don't blame me if you're hungry and need to pee hours later," Maizie said. "Loser," came out under her breath.

Alice frowned. Folding a corner of a page from a book she was reading, she closed it and looked out the window. The group of fifty classmates and four chaperones was headed to Orlando for a fun weekend stay. Alice wasn't looking forward to getting there. She wasn't interested in water rides or roller coasters. She was happy being a homebody, studying hours a night. That's how she ended up on this field trip. Their school was rewarding students for top grades. Alice had never wanted to sign the field trip form, but her mother smiled, thinking it would be a good idea for her to go.

"You never go out much," her mother had said. "Something's missing in your life. You need to go out more often." She'd even hand delivered the field trip form to the main office to ensure that they received it on her daughter's behalf.

Alice cracked open the window. Sitting next to Maizie had been no easy task. The first hour, Maizie had been asleep. Many of them had been, since they'd arrived at the school to board the bus at six that morning to get to Orlando before noon. Then the second hour, Maizie had been nasty, giving

her snide looks and making remarks about Alice's mousy hair, pale skin, and nose in a book.

It was a cold February day, with one of those rare cold fronts that descends on Florida. People wore sweaters and jackets. A line formed outside both restrooms, people hugging themselves and even shivering. The bus driver also got off the bus to go to the restroom. They were somewhere in Central Florida. The thrum of cars driving over the speed limit caused vibrations at the service plaza in the middle of the highway.

A yard from the bus, a driver of a shiny black Mustang parked next to a fuel pump. A middle-aged man with a paunch stepped out. He pulled his jeans up, but didn't manage to yank them across his middle. The belt slid down and settled underneath his stomach. He wiped his nose with a finger, adjusted his sunglasses, and walked inside.

Alice admired the car, her eyes scouring back and forth the onyx length of it. On the dashboard was a stuffed white rabbit, which didn't match the man who exited the car. Her eyes narrowed on it, because it looked familiar. It reminded Alice of her own stuffed white rabbit from childhood. She carried it back and forth between her parents' homes when she stayed with her mother on weekdays and her father on weekends. She took it with her to elementary school. Then in the third grade, during recess, someone stole it. A boy with a wicked smirk and mad eyes knocked her to the ground and grabbed it. She cried and complained to a teacher, but no one did anything and she never saw the rabbit again.

Despite that, her childhood had been happy for the most part. She smiled thinking about that time, when things were simpler, unlike the lonely, boring hell of high school.

Loud laughter erupted from the other side of the bus. Boys walked from one end of the gas station to the other, joking and cramming donuts into their mouths. Maizie faced a friend and talked with her hands, using sweeping gestures, as she stood in the bathroom line.

Alice went back to looking down at the Mustang and the white rabbit. It wasn't a large stuffed animal, but from her standpoint she could see it was smiling. It had a thin strip of red for a mouth. Maybe it belonged to the man's child or grandchild.

"Oh my God, bro, I totally don't want to get back in that bus," a boy named Ronald said outside the gas station.

"Yeah, we need some more stretch time," a girl said. "Although, I'm really cold."

The kids continued drinking coffee, eating pastries, and going to the bathroom. Many hung out in the warm interior of the convenient store, where there was a small sitting area. Then there was that shiny Mustang, beckoning to Alice. Maybe she would peek at it, see it up close, and then return to the bus when she saw people going back in. Maizie was right. She was a loser. Why was she sitting in the bus by herself? Why was she always alone and never doing anything interesting?

She had packed lightly for the trip, so she pulled her book bag from an overhead compartment. Everyone had left his or her things inside, but she didn't want to. *Don't leave anything behind*, she thought, despite her intention of coming right back.

The chilly air nipped at her face and hands. She scurried around the bus and to the Mustang. She wasn't a car person, but she appreciated its smooth lines and shiny silver rims. The bus was between her and her classmates, so no one was looking at her. She walked around to the other side to where the pump was. No, it couldn't be. The man had left the keys in the ignition with the car running.

Do it, do it, do it. What was she thinking? No, she couldn't do it. She wasn't that type of person.

Yes, you are!

Alice touched the handle to the door and pulled. She gasped. Why would she touch a stranger's possession? She always respected other people's property. She never toilet papered anyone's house during Halloween, never shoplifted, never did anything like that...

The white rabbit's smile lured her into the car. She sat inside, threw her book bag into the passenger seat, and put her hands on the steering wheel. It was still warm from the man's touch. The leather seat molded to her body. Her hair bun loosened as she dug her head back into the leather. It was very different from driving her mother's minivan or her father's junk car. And it was her grandfather who taught her how to drive in his beat-up Mustang. Out of all her family members' cars, she liked that one the best, but it wasn't shiny

and modern like this one. The paunchy man's Mustang had a new car smell, a satellite radio, and leather seats. Being alone in it was luxurious.

Someone coughed. It was the driver, walking to his car. Alice wanted to hide, sink down, or make a clean getaway without him seeing her. No, it was too late. He glared at her, with sunlight bouncing off his sunglasses. "Hey!" he yelled.

Panic gripped her, and she wasn't thinking clearly. Alice locked the door and put the car in drive.

"Hey!" the man yelled again, reaching the door, but he was too late. Alice zipped off, driving slow at first and then faster, with the man following her to the ramp.

"Nooooo!"

The same way the man was yelling no, that word reverberated in her head. *Nooooo.* How could she do such a thing? On the highway, Alice sped up to match the speed limit. Her heart pounded, and her free hand shook. She wasn't on some local street or neighborhood road. She was on the turnpike in a car that she stole.

"Amazing," a voice from the back called.

Alice jumped in her seat, and the car swerved.

"Watch where you're going," the boy yelled. The white rabbit tumbled off the dashboard and onto her book bag. She was veering onto the shoulder of the road. Alice yelped and held the steering wheel with both hands. She was back in the right

lane, where she was supposed to be. This wasn't happening. This had to be a dream! She was in a stolen car with a strange boy. Was he a thief, too?

"You're ruining my morning," he said. "Or maybe you're not."

"What are you doing here?" Alice managed to squeak. "Who are you?"

Alice focused on the road so she wouldn't get into an accident, but her eyes darted to the rearview mirror, to an unbelievable sight. This was no tattooed, unshaven older thug in the car. It was a boy her age, with floppy black hair, violet eyes with long lashes, and a chiseled jaw. *No way*, she thought. He was too good-looking to be a criminal. And those eyes…she had only met a few people with eyes that bright and sparkling. There was a boy from her childhood with those eyes. She had also known a girl in middle school with violet eyes – a teacher nicknamed her "Liz Taylor," although few students knew about that actress. Alice had lost touch with all of those people since she was pretty much friendless.

"You stole my dad's car," he said. "I was snoozing. That's why he left the keys in the ignition, with the heat on. And you, holy heck, you stole it!"

That explained everything. No one in his or her right mind would leave the keys inside. Some people did it by accident or out of laziness, but surely no one with a car as nice as this.

"I'm so sorry," Alice said. "I don't know what got into me. I was in a bus, forced on a field trip I didn't want to go

on in the first place, and then I saw this beautiful Mustang and this white rabbit…"

"All right, all right," the boy said, waving his hand in the air. His phone rang, but he ignored it. "That's my dad."

"Oh my God, I'm going to be arrested for stealing a car…and kidnapping."

The boy laughed, his perfect face tilting back. Alice saw a faint five o'clock shadow and his Adam's apple bob up and down. He was so handsome.

"I can turn around," she said. "Really, I'll tell people I had a momentary lapse, that I must be bipolar or something. I swear I don't do things like this every day."

"I'm Lou by the way," he said. He reached over, not to shake her hand, but to grab the white rabbit. He sat up, put on his seat belt, and plunked the rabbit in his lap. "This is my rabbit, Freddy. I don't play with him anymore, but I've had him since I was a kid."

"I used to have a white rabbit."

"My dad thinks this rabbit is lucky. He used to take me on these casino trips as a kid, and he always won if he took Freddy with him. I wouldn't be there since I stayed in the hotel room or pool, and I don't know if he's good luck anymore considering my dad's car was just stolen."

"I'll turn around, I swear," Alice promised. But how could she? The next exit was miles away. The turnpike stretched ahead with no end.

"How about we go to where you were planning on going?" he asked. "We can convince my dad later that I know you or that I wasn't right in the head…"

"Or that *I'm* not right in the head."

Lou smiled. Alice did, too. She had snapped and become crazy today. The people on her bus must all be frantic and looking for her. She'd ruined their field trip. How could she do such a thing? The chaperones must have called the police already and everything. The goody-goody in her was scared, but underneath that was the thrill of breaking rules for the first time. That was something lacking in her life – she had never done anything adventurous before.

"I have two tickets to an amusement park," Alice said. "Do you want to go there?"

"Sure, why not?" Lou said, stretching his arms back. "That's better than where I was going, which was my grandparents' home, where they argue all day and live in the middle of nowhere. We'll go on all the cool rides."

Alice had Maizie's ticket. Ms. Morris, the teacher in charge of the field trip, who was also chaperoning, found it left behind on a bus seat and asked Alice to return it to her classmate. As far as Alice was concerned, Maizie didn't belong on the field trip. She lost everything, copied assignments, and cheated on every test – Maizie would even play nice to Alice sometimes to cheat off her. She and Lou were going to use her ticket. Alice could try to access the hotel reservation, although maybe that would be flagged if they reported her missing.

As they drove, the car got stuffy. She turned off the heat, and it was still unbearable. Alice opened the window. A gust of wind blasted her hair, taking it out of the bun. Her mousy brown hair looked golden as it whipped around her face.

What a feeling, this freedom, even though it would come at a cost. She'd surely be arrested, placed in a jail overnight, and suspended or expelled for doing such an impulsive thing on a field trip. Every single time she saw a police car in the distance, she sped up, and if one was in front of her, she slowed down and changed lanes to hide behind other cars. An APB must have been issued on her.

Alice pulled up into the amusement park's lot. In the distance were a gargantuan water slide and a scary looking roller coaster. Alice gulped, afraid of heights. Lou, on the other hand, jumped out, ready to explore.

She looked in the mirror. Her normally straight hair was wavy and falling across her shoulders. She looked around, but couldn't find her hair band. It must have fallen on the floor. It was her only one and she hadn't packed another.

"Come on," Lou said. "Let's go in."

"But, but, my hair." She patted the floor.

"It's fine," he said.

She looked up at his dazzling smile. He had perfect teeth, and the skin around his eyes crinkled. What was she getting herself into? No, she was already deep in this. While Lou was adjusting his belt and transferring a wallet from his jacket pocket to his jeans pocket, she grabbed the white rabbit from the back and stuffed it into her book bag. She was a thief. She

couldn't help it today. First with the car, and then with the rabbit. After her arrest, she'd give it back to him.

Lou grabbed her hand and with her other hand she yanked the strap of her book bag. She was fixated on Lou's violet eyes, which became paler in the sun. They mesmerized her, challenged her, and dared her. She'd stolen the car – yes, that was her decision – but he was pushing her to do more…to go on amusement park rides that both thrilled and frightened her. She shook her head and then nodded.

"Let's go in, yeah?" he said.

"Yeah," she echoed.

They went past the gate and no one questioned them. They had the one-day pass tickets, the ones that allowed them to go through a speedy line. After the short wait, cotton candy and hot dogs scented the air. Alice closed her eyes, thinking of childhood again, going high on swings and running through parks. Then there was her parents' divorce, moving to a new school where she clicked with no one, and other issues that had settled on her like a fog. She had once wanted adventure, but she ended up closing herself off to everything, became glum around her parents, and dived into her studies without swimming up for air.

Lou took out his cell phone and texted with both hands, letting go of hers. She immediately wanted him holding her hand again. "Are you sending a message to your dad?"

"Just so he'll bug off for a while," he said.

"What are you telling him?"

"That I'm with a pretty girl at an amusement park."

Alice was agape. She didn't consider herself pretty, plus he was giving them away since there were only so many amusement parks in Central Florida. How many minutes or hours of freedom did she have left until she was caught? Alice squashed her fears and doubts for the first time. It was no use being what the people at school called a *G.G.* – good girl. She messed up, so she might as well enjoy herself while she was here.

It was late morning, the time when vendors opened their kiosks for early lunch. Alice and Lou had burgers, fries, and elephant ears washed down with soda. Alice had skipped breakfast since she didn't want to be late for the bus. She felt like a glutton, a satisfied one.

"Time for the rides," Lou said.

Alice shook her head. She looked at all the children who circled their decision-making parents. Young couples smiled as they joined long lines for rides. "No, I can't," she said. "I thought I could, but I'm afraid. Maybe I'll go in the spooky tunnel or on a Ferris wheel. I'm not afraid of those. I can't go on anything too high or that flips me around. And I hate being upside down. That scares me."

"It's okay being upside down," Lou said, his smile dying on his lips. He became serious. "Didn't you do an upside down thing by stealing the car?"

Alice pondered that. Yes, she had done the opposite of what she normally did. She wasn't a field trip person. She wasn't a thief. She didn't attract good-looking boys. Everything about today was abnormal.

Lou led her to the line for the roller coaster. That warm, pleasant sensation of holding hands with a boy returned, but then it was engulfed by her fear. The roller coaster's ascent didn't look too bad, but the decline was so sharp and steep. She would be hurtled down, down, down.

She passed a kiosk that had a shiny metal exterior. Her reflection shocked her. She looked wild with her messy hair and lips swollen from eating food and sweets. She looked unlike herself, upside down.

Her heart thumped as she stood in line. Lou was to the right, to the left, pressed to her back, and sometimes in front of her, always attached to her somehow, with their arms touching. His woodsy cologne wrapped around her. It was too much for her senses…him, his scent, his touch, and then this upcoming roller-coaster ride.

It was time. First a dozen people went before them, with an attendant seating them. Then the attendant ushered them to their seats. *Nooooo*, Alice thought.

"Yes!" Lou said, pulling her up the stairs and across the platform.

Her vision blackened around the edges. Her body moved across the platform and into a hard seat. She could barely see. Then something whooshed over her head and hugged her shoulders and chest…the safety harness. The attendants were getting ready to launch this huge, metal, train-like thing into arcs and then the finale…the steep decline. Alice was convinced this was all insanity. Who would create such a ride and who would go on it? She would, because she had gone crazy.

Alice's vision cleared, and she stifled a scream. The roller coaster picked up speed. Her first scream erupted from her mouth during the first loop, when her body pressed into the harness and she thought she'd fall out, headed toward the ground to her death. She turned to look at Lou, and he was smiling, whooping instead of screaming.

There was a gentle decline and then another loop. Screams shot into the air, and not just from Alice. Everyone was making some sort of noise. Whenever people raised their arms, Alice was the only one who held onto her harness, her fingers turning white with her grip.

"Here it comes," Lou yelled.

It was the crazy decline. First, she saw sky, and then the view changed with the amusement park grounds in sight. Her torso was pressed into her harness. She opened her mouth to scream, and her whole face changed as air entered her mouth. Her cheeks expanded. The pressure of going down slammed into her body. Then something happened during that long, yet brief, time rushing down.

She stopped screaming. She was at peace. Her life was headed toward something new and different. She was free to explore other things, because she dared to ride a Mustang when she thought she was fated to only riding four-door sedans. She was with one of the best-looking boys she had ever met. Most importantly, she was on the scariest roller-coaster ride and didn't have a heart attack.

As the descent neared its end, Alice didn't have a care in the world. All her worries drifted out of her, pushed out by the dizzying excitement and frigid air. The ride was over. The

roller coaster's connected cars slowed down onto the platform. The harnesses released. On wobbly legs, people got off. Adults were supporting children. Men were holding up women.

"Are you okay?" a mother asked her son.

"I'm gonna hurl," a young blond woman announced, rushing off the platform and toward a restroom.

Alice felt the opposite. She had a dreamy smile on her lips.

"That was awesome, wasn't it?" Lou asked.

"Yes," she agreed.

She didn't expect it when he leaned down to kiss her. His soft lips were on hers, his tongue darting in gently and then more forcefully. She closed her eyes and kissed him back. It was her first kiss. She didn't imagine it would be like this. She wasn't awkward or fumbling. She slanted her face at the right angle, as if by instinct, or by following his lead. The kiss came naturally, in the middle of a packed amusement park.

Lou stepped off and helped her to her feet, although she didn't really need his support. She remained strong and clear-headed, until she saw something that disturbed her.

A man in a security uniform walked by them, passing by the rail that separated the ride from the rest of the public. The thin, tall, young man narrowed his eyes at them. His gaze was steady, but then he moved on.

"Did you see that man?" Alice asked.

"Him?" Lou jutted his chin in the man's direction.

"He must be looking for me!"

"Don't be silly. He was probably just checking you out. Who could blame him?"

"But – "

"Stop worrying, and come on." He pulled at her hand.

The sensation of someone watching her, that the authorities were nearby, was in the front of her mind, then in the back. The security guard didn't stop her, pursue her, or anything else. She followed Lou, although she was more watchful of who was around her.

Lou wanted to go on another gut-twisting ride, one in which a gondola was raised high in the air and spun people around. It was as scary-looking as the roller coaster. "Give me a few minutes," Alice said. "I'm feeling light-headed." Because of that kiss. "I need to sit somewhere."

They found an empty gazebo where they could look out into the crowd, but still feel isolated. The old wooden structure had people's names carved into the wood, with hearts and arrows. It was a romantic spot. Lou pulled out a candy bar and broke off a piece. "You want?"

Alice shook her head since her stomach was full. Lou crammed the chocolate in his mouth.

"Why don't we get out of here?" Lou said. "We can crash at my friend's house in Tallahassee."

"Tallahassee?" Alice said. "That's hours away."

"So? We can also go to Georgia. I have friends there, too. Let's go on a real road trip."

Alice thought about his crazy idea. The roller-coaster ride was scary, but she was glad she had gone on it. Now a road trip, to northern Florida…no, out of state to Georgia was his last suggestion. He must be joking, because all they had was a car. She was low on cash, and she assumed he wasn't prepared for any sort of lengthy trip either.

"Okay, let's get out of here," she played along. "Why stop at Georgia? Let's go to D.C. I know, New York City. I've always wanted to go there."

"Me, too!"

He beamed at her, and she also smiled at the idea of the jet-set life, of being able to travel whenever the desire hit them.

"What about California?" Alice added. "We can ride up the coast."

"On those mountain highways…"

"Yes!"

"Whoa, whoa, whoa, stop daydreaming and let's get realistic," he said. "I'm not looking at all these other states. Let's stick to the Southeast. Yes, let's go to Georgia. Come on. It's the state closest to us."

Alice's smile faded, her heart rate increased. This guy was serious. He wanted to leave Florida. She wasn't ready for this.

"Georgia's, like, right there," he continued. "It's just a few hours."

"No!" Alice didn't want to raise her voice, since it was rare for her to do so, but she felt like she had to be heard. She

wasn't going to leave her family, school, and everything she knew. Not at this moment.

"Okay, you have something against Georgia. What about Alabama? I know people there, too. We can chill at their house, maybe get jobs, be on our own."

"This is too soon. We just met."

"I need to get out of Florida, Alice."

"Why?"

"I have my reasons," Lou deadpanned.

"Well, I'm not going." Alice shook her head. She wasn't going to allow this boy to lead her around anymore. It was one thing to spend the day at the park, but another to leave their lives behind and go on an unplanned trip to stay with his friends – who were strangers to her. She wanted to travel on her own terms, not his.

Lou's head hung to the side as he stared at her, as if she was the one being problematic. "Then what do you want?"

"I don't want to go to Georgia or Alabama. I just want…want…" She wanted exactly what was in front of her: the excitement of the park, the sun above, and this boy. She came closer and kissed him. Her mouth devoured his, one hand twisted into his hair, and the other to his back to mold his body into hers. His breath was sweet with chocolate. They were unsteady on their feet, and their bodies leaned against the thick pole in front of the gazebo.

They disengaged. Lou's violet eyes bored into hers, and they looked sad and defeated. Then she saw something else that made her ill. The sight was to her left, between the

columns of the gazebo. Men in uniform wove through the crowd, their eyes on her.

"Lou," Alice whispered, "we have to get out of here."

"Huh?" Lou said.

She grabbed his face and forced him to look at the six police officers headed right toward them.

"Holy crap," he said.

The two of them went on the other side of the gazebo's platform, which had another short stairway to ground level. It was closed, but Alice unlatched the gate and ran out, with Lou fast behind her.

"Stop, stop!" voices commanded.

Alice sped up, bumping into people. At one point, a boy tipped his soda over her shoes, but she kept going, jostling against people who became angry with her.

"Watch where you're going!" an elderly woman screeched.

"Hurry!" Lou yelled, now in front of her.

They hit a wall of people waiting in line. Going around the crowd slowed them down, which meant the police officers were catching up.

Lou was faster than she was. He was yards away. The police officers were right at her feet. They would surely tackle and handcuff her. She tried to go faster to meet Lou, but she couldn't. She was slim and healthy, but not an athlete. A new idea stabbed into her head, upsetting her. Why was he going so fast? Why couldn't he slow down a little bit so she could catch up with him? He had been so chivalrous and romantic.

She thought they had a rapport, but she was wrong. He was out for himself.

Also, why was he running when he didn't steal his father's car? She was the thief and perceived kidnapper. That thought hit her so hard that she slowed down and stopped running altogether.

The police officers zipped past her and overtook Lou. He tried to fight them off, but one of the officers threw him against an ice cream van, with children scattering and screaming, their parents pulling them away from the scene. Five officers piled on top of Lou and handcuffed him.

"What?" Alice asked. "What the hell?"

One of the officers stood beside her. "Why are you with him?" the tall, middle-aged man asked her.

"Umm, uhhh." She was completely tongue-tied.

"Did he force you to do this?"

"Uhhhhh…"

"The boy's father should have called for an ambulance for him. He had a psychotic episode this morning, but his father thought he'd take it upon himself to drive him to the mental hospital. He shouldn't have left the boy alone. We looked at the gas station footage, where you're driving and he's in the back. He has a history of violence. I'm glad you're okay."

Alice remained speechless. Mental hospital? History of violence? There was no way. He hadn't acted deranged with her, except when he insisted they leave town. It must be a case of mistaken identity or Lou's father was the one with issues. And could it be that she was free? No one was

pressing any charges against her? She opened her mouth to say something, to defend him, to let him know that she was also at fault because she stole the car. She couldn't, though. Lou was destined to go to the mental hospital, but she didn't have to be destined to go to jail.

The middle-aged officer took her back to the roller coaster platform so she could retrieve her book bag from a locker. Then he took her to the parking lot and put her in the back of a car so that she could make a statement at the police station. Lou was in another car. At one point, her car and his car were side by side on the road. He looked at her with eyes that had lost a little bit of their sparkle.

Lou shook his head and pounded it into the metal grate in front of him. No! She couldn't bear it if he hurt himself – there was no need to. Maybe that was part of his alleged illness. She pressed her hand against the window, wanting to hold him again, but then her car sped up.

"We should have requested a padded van," the officer who was driving her said. "Who knows what he's capable of?"

Alice pressed her lips together as she heard his hard words. What was Lou capable of? Showing a girl a good time. Kissing her. "I think you're exaggerating," Alice said.

"Young lady, I've been in the force for twenty years. Been dealing with crazies for two decades."

The police car with Lou inside pulled over. The radio inside her car crackled. "Backup needed."

"Yes, they'll definitely get another vehicle or maybe get a doctor to sedate him right away. I'm sorry such a young thing

like yourself had to see all of this and that he somehow forced you to ride with him, away from his fate at the hospital. Your chaperones told us what a fine student you are."

The police officer had a completely different perception of what had happened, but she wasn't going to deny his beliefs since she was free. Lou's insanity had given her the opportunity to be brave, wild, and romantic for the day. She wanted to be like this more often, minus the criminal activity. Excitement was attainable, not some obscure, abstract thing that was meant for others and not her. This was the beginning of a new chapter in her life, and it had all started by following that white rabbit.

She pulled it out of her book bag and studied its red smile. It looked so much like her childhood rabbit. It even had one ear bigger than the other. When she was little, she would chew on her rabbit's left ear in her sleep. She rotated the rabbit in her hands. When she reached the label, she gasped.

ALICE was written in a childhood scrawl. Her penmanship had become much better over the years, but there was no doubt who had written it. She used to label all her stuffed animals with her name.

Lou had been the boy in the schoolyard many years ago, knocking into her and stealing her most prized possession. He always had those intense eyes. During her elementary school years, anger bubbled to the surface of her emotions any time she thought about the boy who took her rabbit. She always felt like nagging a teacher or principal about the

incident, but she was invisible around those adults. They were older now. She could forgive Lou, especially with the difference between the two – he had his own issues, which were bigger than a schoolyard theft, and she had her rabbit…and her freedom. Sorrow washed over her, because he soon would be contained behind the walls of a hospital.

Alice squeezed the rabbit to her chest. The day he had bullied her, she had felt violated, with a piece of her missing. Now she was reunited with that missing piece.

 Medeia Sharif was born in New York City and now lives in Miami. She received her master's degree in psychology from Florida Atlantic University. Published through various presses, she writes middle grade and young adult short stories and novels. In addition to being a writer, she's a public school teacher.

WHITE IS A HUMAN CONSTRUCT

LAURA LASCARSO

...IN THE FOREST, DARK AND DEEP,
I OFFER YOU ETERNAL SLEEP...

The October sky was as crisp as a red apple. The morning light sliced through the overgrown yard, causing every shape and shadow to stand out in high contrast, including the white rabbit.

At first Alice thought it was a stuffed animal propped up inside a ramshackle hutch with a piece of roofing nailed to the top and hardware cloth stapled across the front. But as Alice approached, she saw that it was, in fact, alive. Its whiskers twitched, its mouth moved as if nibbling a blade of grass, and one ear fell forward rather sloppily.

"Curiouser and curiouser," Alice whispered and glanced toward the house. Mrs. Miller had passed away months ago and the house had been vacant ever since, or so Alice had thought. The weeds grew to the tops of her navy kneesocks and tickled the backs of her legs as she hurried past the rabbit and onto Bradford Hills Preparatory School.

At school Alice kept her head down in the hallways and her nose in a book in class. The rumor mill still churned out stories about Alice's stepfather, Congressman Shipley, each one more outrageous than the last. The circumstances of a high-profile politician leaving their small town so suddenly, and in the midst of a campaign for re-election, proved too mysterious for anyone to let fade away.

"I heard her mother caught him with another woman."

"I heard it was Alice who caught him, and it was her mother's sister."

Alice didn't elaborate upon or deny the stories, for as terrible as they were, their speculations were much safer than the truth.

On her way home from school, Alice cut through the Miller's backyard again, pausing in front of the hutch to find the rabbit luxuriating in the warm afternoon sun. The rabbit turned its head lazily in her direction and winked.

She'd spoken very little in the past six weeks, not to her friends, not to her classmates or teachers, not even to her mother. Perhaps it was the bleak loneliness, which perched on her shoulder like a bird of prey, or the most basic need for human connection, which prompted Alice to say, "Hello, white rabbit."

The rabbit twitched one ear and replied quite civilly, "White is a human construct."

Alice stumbled back and glanced to either side to see if perhaps there was someone who'd uttered those words, but she was alone in the empty yard. Alone with the rabbit. Light-headed, she pressed one hand to her chest to find her heart thumping wildly, a fist hammering to get out.

"I beg your pardon."

Manners were of paramount importance, she'd learned from an early age, and though she despised that tendency in herself, drilled in through years of discipline and countless hours of etiquette, she could not help but be polite.

"Rabbit is also a human construct," the rabbit said. "A way for you to organize that which you experience into tidy boxes."

Alice felt the ground tilting and leaned against the hutch to keep herself upright. A clammy warmth pressed against her skin. The afternoon heat was causing her to imagine things – and she hadn't eaten enough that day. That had to be it.

"Excuse me," she said to the rabbit, made an awkward bow, and bustled away.

For the next two days, Alice avoided the Miller's backyard, taking the long way to school along the tree-lined avenue, but on the third day, she ran late again. Another tardy would earn her a detention, which meant a call home to her mother, a risk she wouldn't take.

Alice hurried through the overgrown yard, passing quickly by the rabbit who nibbled quietly on a bit of dry hay. *It was only a hallucination*, Alice told herself. *Just a silly daydream.*

On her way back home that afternoon she dared to take the shortcut again. Intent on proving her sanity, she marched up to the hutch and said, "You're just a rabbit."

"*Je ne suis pas un lapin*," said the rabbit.

Alice froze. The hairs on the back of her neck raised up and her stomach turned.

"French," the rabbit said. "I am not a rabbit."

A shiver ran down her spine. Alice took a few deep breaths and, pushing her hair back from her face, looked the rabbit boldly in the eye. "How are you doing this?"

"Do me a favor, Alice. See that over there?" The rabbit pointed with one ear toward a patch of clover. "Bring me some of that green goodness. I've had nothing but this bitter, dry stuff for days."

Alice glanced from the rabbit to the clover. Perhaps there were more important questions to ask, but Alice said, "How do you know my name?"

"I know a lot about you, Alice Shipley. Perhaps more than you'd like."

Alice cringed at the sound of her last name, because it was *his* last name, a tie that linked him to her, one she wished to sever. She'd been so careful not to reveal anything to anyone. If the rabbit knew her last name, he must also know about the circumstances of the congressman's departure, which meant...

"Do you know about my mother?" Alice asked shakily.

"She's not been herself lately. But how could she, after what happened...?"

Alice's pulse quickened at the thought of her stepfather. She picked at a scab, one of four parallel cuts on the inside of her arm, just above the elbow where no one else could see.

"I know about that, too," the rabbit said quietly.

Alice pulled down the sleeve of her shirt and glared at the rabbit. "You can't know about that."

"But I do."

"I don't want to talk about it."

"Well, then, why don't you make yourself useful?" The rabbit pointed again at the clover. Alice walked over, collected a few handfuls, and brought them back to the hutch. She searched for a door, but found none.

"Feed me through the mesh."

"Who put you in here?" They must not have known this was a talking rabbit.

"A most terrible man," the rabbit said. "He trapped me in his snare. I nearly chewed off my own leg to get out. Then he stuck me in this cage, and I've been here ever since."

"Why would he do that?"

"Perhaps he has a taste for rabbit stew. I do not pretend to understand the habits of your kind. Senselessly cruel, every last one."

Alice sympathized. There was not even a teacup of water in the hutch, and a cage was a terrible place to live one's life. "Where's the door? I'll free you."

"There is no door," the rabbit said.

"That's impossible."

"Does your cage have a door?"

Alice narrowed her eyes at him. She didn't appreciate how he turned everything around on her. "Every cage has a door. You must not want to be rescued."

"Touché, Alice."

Alice crossed her arms and scratched at her scab until she felt a prick of pain, then a trickle of warm blood. Out of the corner of her eye, she saw a shadow move behind a curtain in the house. She noticed, too, that one of the back windows had been busted, but was now repaired. Someone must live there.

"Mrs. Miller died months ago," Alice mused aloud. "Who's there now?"

"The terrible man," the white rabbit said. "Don't trust him, Alice. Not one bit."

His words gave her goose bumps. She did not trust men, any of them. She did not trust women either.

"I'd better go."

"Please come again," the rabbit begged, his eyes going wide. "No one ever visits me. Only you, Alice. You're the only one."

Alice knew what it meant to be lonely, to feel cut off from the world, to be bound by secrets that were stronger than chains, to be suffocated by them.

"Tomorrow?" the rabbit asked with a note of desperation.

"Tomorrow," Alice replied.

Since the congressman fled the coop like a fox with a mouthful of feathers, Alice's mother spent her days watching HGTV. She'd become fixated on redecorating. Her slurred monologues, for she also drank, were punctuated with "distressed cabinetry," "rehabbed end tables," "white-washed metal shutters," and "bold accent walls." Like a parrot, she repeated whatever catchphrases she'd picked up from the television that day and was, at times, incoherent. In the six weeks since the congressman left, her mother burned through the liquor cabinet and had moved on to the wine cellar.

Meanwhile, the house itself was in disarray with ripped wallpaper hanging from the walls like shed snake skin. Pastel paint was smeared across surfaces like blood. The dining room table had been haphazardly scraped and its legs truncated to different lengths so it no longer balanced a glass

of water. One day Alice came home from school to find that every plate, glass, and teacup had been smashed on the tile floor of the observatory. Alice did not clean it up. The house was treacherous, and it was best to remember it.

On Saturday morning Alice sneaked out before her mother awoke and used the small amount of money she had left over from pawning a desk lamp to buy carrots at the produce stand. She carried them, wrapped in an embroidered napkin, to the Miller's backyard.

"What a lovely surprise," the rabbit said. "Where's your usual attire?"

Alice wore jean shorts, cut off at the knees, and a long-sleeved shirt, both splattered with paint from one of her mother's episodes. "No school today."

"Ahh, but those days are harder, aren't they?"

The rabbit's words carved away at something wooden inside her. "How is it you know so much about me, white rabbit?" Alice insisted on calling him both. Even though "white" and "rabbit" were human constructs, she needed this, at least, to fit inside a box.

"I'm very perceptive," he said. "And also very hungry, if you please."

Alice squeezed one narrow carrot through the hardwire mesh. She nibbled on another herself. She'd been accustomed to the grass tickling the backs of her legs, but today it was not. The yard had been mowed, the leaves raked and bagged. The lawn was more open without the overgrown grass and weeds. Alice felt like a target.

"Who cut the grass?"

"My captor," the rabbit said. "He ruins everything." Alice glanced back at the curtains but saw no movement.

"He's not here. Probably off dining on the entrails of small, helpless mammals. We're safe for now."

"The weeds will just grow back," Alice said, more to herself than the rabbit.

"Weeds will do that," said the rabbit. "They are very stubborn about surviving."

Alice turned her attention to the rabbit. "Are you magic, then?"

"Do you think I would demean myself to pop out of some fraud's musty top hat?"

"You are white," Alice said.

"Not entirely. I've a spot right here." The rabbit turned to show her his tail, which was painted with dark fur. "Do you believe in magic, Alice?"

She chewed on the end of her carrot. She believed in magic before, at a time when she also believed that her mother and stepfather loved each other and cared for her. Her faith seemed to erode so quickly, though she could no longer recall the exact moment. It was a series of small cruelties, which led her to realize that there would be no magic spell, no fairy godmother, and no charming prince to save her.

"No, I do not."

"But you used to."

Alice thought of her life before the big house, just her and her mother, sharing a one-bedroom apartment on the

wrong side of town. Every night she slept in her mother's bed, and every morning she awoke to sunshine streaming in through the windows, warm and safe, cocooned in her mother's love. Perhaps it would be easier to forget that those times ever existed. Then the loss would not be so great.

Alice shook her head. "I can't go back to yesterday, because I was a different person then."

"Indeed," the rabbit said.

"So, if you're not magic, what are you?"

The rabbit raised itself up and glanced past her. "Popsicles, Alice, I thought he was gone. Don't say anything that will get us in trouble, understand?" He edged away and propped himself against the side of the hutch. His eyes glazed over.

"Hey there," said a deep voice.

Alice spun around, confronted by a young man near her own age.

"I thought I saw you out here the other day," he continued. Alice glanced between him and the rabbit, wondering if he was the intruder or if it was she.

"That's funny." He pointed to the carrot in the hutch.

"He won't believe you, Alice," the rabbit uttered in barely a whisper. "He'll think you're mad."

"What's funny?" Alice asked the young man. Her mouth was so dry she could barely speak.

"You know, the carrot." He smiled and it appeared genuine, but smiles were slippery things. They had a way of turning into sneers.

"What are you doing here?" Alice asked. "In this house?"

"My grandmother lived here. She passed a little while back. My mom and I are fixing it up. We're thinking about staying for a while. Do you live in the neighborhood?"

"Don't tell him anything, Alice," the rabbit commanded. "What if he follows you home?"

"Did you put the rabbit in this cage?" Alice asked, steeling herself against him.

The boy glanced over at the hutch, then back at her. "It was like that when we got here."

"He's lying, Alice," the rabbit fumed. His ears stood perfectly straight and still. Only his whiskers twitched. "He's the one who put me in here. You know what it feels like to be deceived."

"But how will it get food and water?" Alice asked, trying to catch the young man in a lie.

He tilted his head, a bewildered look on his face. "You're messing with me."

Alice studied him. His eyes were kind, his face open and trusting, but like smiles and flattering words, a face was a mask and who knew what lay underneath. "I'm not messing with you."

"The rabbit's not real," the boy said. "It's a stuffed animal."

Alice drew in a sharp breath as panic flooded her. She tried to see what the boy saw, a simple stuffed rabbit, but she did not. And what did that mean?

Meanwhile the rabbit howled, "I told you, Alice. He can't be trusted. He's not like us. He's an outsider. A stranger. He'll think you're crazy. He'll tell your mother. He'll – "

"Stop!" Alice put both hands on her ears and hunkered down over her knees. The young man placed his hand on her shoulder. His touch terrified her, and she bolted. By the time she slowed down, her legs were rubbery and weak and her lungs burned from exertion.

She stopped when she reached the train tracks, an old haunt. She sat by the tracks and waited for the train to come. Only it would quiet that voice in her head, *his* voice, telling her she was stupid, useless, worthless.

But when it came, the noise wasn't loud enough.

Nothing was.

Alice made her way home that evening as the day was bleeding into dusk. The row of mansions that lined her street stood ominously against the darkening sky. Their white columns cast skeletal shadows on the porticos, and Alice felt, as she often did, that the houses were watching her.

When she reached the end of the cul de sac where she and her mother lived, she found the boy from the Miller house sitting on the curb.

"What are you doing here?"

"You dropped this." He held out her purse. Alice took it and turned it over in her hands.

"I had to open it to find your ID."

"Yes, of course. Thank you."

Alice stared at the glittering sidewalk to avoid meeting his eyes. When she was little, her mother said the builders put crushed quartz in the concrete so that the sidewalks would sparkle. Like walking on diamonds, and weren't they lucky to be living in a place like this? The two luckiest girls in Thomasville.

"You're the congressman's daughter," he said.

"Stepdaughter." She braced herself for whatever rumors he might wish to authenticate.

"This is a pretty fancy neighborhood." He glanced around warily, like a criminal, and shoved his hands deep into his pockets.

"Did you knock on the door?" Alice searched his eyes.

He hesitated. "I did. Was that your mom?"

There was no way for Alice to know what condition her mother was in when she answered the door. What he might have seen or heard…

"Yes," Alice said softly.

"She thought I was the painter. She asked me inside – "

"Did you go in?"

"Only for a minute. You're mother, she seemed…"

He'd seen the inside of her house. Earlier, he'd caught her talking to a rabbit, a stuffed one apparently. And he must have heard the stories about the congressman. He must think her mad, all of them.

"She seemed drunk," he finished.

"She's not been herself lately." Her words were cold and hollow as her heart.

"I told her we were friends, but I don't think she believed me."

"Friends?"

He stuck out one hand. "My name's Finn. Finnegan Miller."

"Alice." She reached for his hand, and he clasped it tightly. His warmth made her feel colder. "I should go inside," Alice said. "Thanks again for returning this."

"No problem. You know where I live. Don't be a stranger." He smiled once more and jogged off down the middle of the street as if he didn't want to come too close to the sidewalks. Alice stared at the houses standing sentry and imagined them all tipping like dominos.

Starting with her own.

It took a full five days for Alice to gather the courage to venture back into the Miller's backyard. This time, she made sure both Finn and his mother were absent. His mother worked at Thomasville Memorial Hospital and Finn at the gas station over on Midway. She'd tracked their comings and goings from afar. On this particular day, Alice waited until the sounds of Finn's motorcycle faded into the distance before sneaking into the backyard. To both her relief and dismay, the white rabbit was there.

"I thought you weren't coming back," the rabbit said with a petulant note to his voice.

"You said Finn was a monster," Alice whispered, not wanting to be overheard by the neighbors.

"Isn't he? Aren't they all?"

Alice didn't come to argue about the merits of Finn's character. There were more important issues to tackle. "Why are you here? Why am I the only one who can hear you?"

"Why do you think?"

"It's rude to answer a question with more questions."

"We wouldn't want to be rude, dear Alice."

Alice paced in front of the hutch, reviewing what she knew about the rabbit, glancing over every now and again to catch him being a simple stuffed animal. Meanwhile, the rabbit watched her with its one ear raised and the other flopped forward, giving him the appearance of only half-listening.

"White is a human construct, Alice."

"What does that mean?" Her voice rose with frustration, and she quickly tamped it down.

"Some things won't fit into a tidy box, no matter how you bludgeon them."

"Is that why you're here? To frustrate me with riddles?"

"I'm here to advise you, Alice, on matters of consequence."

Alice stopped pacing. She put aside the incredulity of having a conversation with a rabbit, living or stuffed, and focused on that which mattered to her most.

"Can you fix my mother?"

The rabbit cocked its head as if in deep contemplation while his eyes lowered to half-mast. After a moment, he said, "There is no easy fix."

Alice knew that already. She'd tried everything since the congressman left. She went along with her mother's redecorating plans, brought home paint samples, tried out new colors. Of course, they weren't talking about anything of importance then either, but Alice hoped that after some time, they would.

"I can't fix your mother," the rabbit said at last. "But perhaps you can."

"She gets worse every day." Alice worried she was already too far gone.

"You have to make her see the truth."

Her mother had seen the truth already. This was her way of dealing with it. "How?"

"Let the well dry up."

Alice stared at the rabbit, slowly realizing his meaning. Her mother was poisoning herself with all that liquor and wine. Alcohol was causing her to act this way. Alice simply had to take it away.

"Run along now, Alice. You haven't a minute to waste."

Alice hurried back to her house where her mother lay, half-conscious on the couch with an open bottle of Merlot on the coffee table. Alice marched to the table and scooped up the bottle.

"Alice," her mother said feebly.

Alice took the bottle to the kitchen and poured the remainder down the drain. Then she went down to the cellar

and began pulling bottles off the shelves, letting them fall to the ground and shatter, upsetting crates and barrels until the cement floor was stained purple and shards of glass lay everywhere.

When she came back upstairs, her mother had locked herself in her bedroom. Alice went to her closed door and knocked softly. "Mom?"

She waited for a noise from within. "Mom, I want to help you. Can we talk?"

No reply.

"It didn't work," Alice said to the white rabbit when she met with him alone again.

"No?" He didn't seem too surprised.

"Now she watches TV all day long. The shows replay and she watches them again. She's traded one addiction for another."

"Hmmm, well there's an easy solution for that." He pointed his left ear toward a shed. "There's an axe inside there. It's very sharp, Alice. Be careful you don't cut yourself."

Alice scratched at the four parallel lines on her arm, like a measure of music. She used to play the piano, the baby grand in the observatory, where the notes hung like tiny souls in the still air. The house was always so lonely, as inviting as a tomb.

"Hey there, Alice."

Alice spun around to find Finn approaching when he was supposed to be at work.

"I suppose I'm trespassing," Alice said.

"I won't press charges." He smiled. "Visiting the rabbit?"

"I was just passing through and…" If she told Finn about the conversations she and the rabbit traded, what might he think of her then?

"Make up an excuse to make him go away," the rabbit said.

"I'm awfully thirsty," Alice said. "Could I trouble you for a glass of water?"

"It's no trouble. You want to come inside?"

"I'll just wait out here."

"Okay. Be right back."

He turned toward the house. Alice waited until he'd shut the door behind him, then dashed toward the shed. She found the axe easily, propped up between a rake and shovel. She held the metal close to her chest and drew one finger down the length of its blade.

"Alice?" Finn called to her from the backyard.

Silently, she sneaked around the side of the shed and ran away toward home.

Her mother was reclined on the couch, zombie-eyed, her skin lit by the blue glow of the television, when Alice swung the axe. In one fierce blow, the television screen exploded in a flash of light, then darkened black as a hole. Alice was sweating and shaking as her mother glanced around at what Alice had done.

They stared at each other. Alice searched for a sign of recognition, and then her mother said, "I'd better clean this up."

Her mother spent the next week cleaning. She began by sweeping up the shards of glass and mopping the floors, then moved to the observatory where the broken plates still lay on the tile, then to the basement where the spilled wine had turned black with mold. Once that was done, she brought out a toothbrush and bleach and took to cleaning the grout of every tiled surface of the house.

"We should sell this house," Alice said. There was no end to her mother's mania.

"This house is all we have."

It wasn't true, Alice thought, for despite everything that had happened, they still had each other.

"You look terrible," the rabbit said when he saw her a few days later.

Alice dropped the axe on the ground and sat down beside it, exhausted. She hadn't been sleeping well. It was difficult when her mother vacuumed at all hours of the night. That and the fumes from the bleach and disinfectants gave Alice headaches.

"I've made things worse," Alice said.

"We're on the curve of the bend. The end is near, but not in sight."

Perhaps Alice put too much faith in the white rabbit. "I'm not sure where to go from here."

"If you don't know where you are going, any road will get you there."

It was chilly that morning and much like the color white, school had become a human construct. She had hoped the rabbit would offer some guidance, but he seemed as lost as she was.

"Shouldn't you be in school?"

Alice jumped up. Finn had sneaked up on her again.

"You're supposed to be at work," Alice said. "I heard you leave."

"I rode for a few blocks and then walked back. I wanted to see if you'd come."

Alice was caught. He must know that she only visited when he and his mother were away. "I was just returning your axe." She picked it up and handed it to him.

"I was looking for that."

"I should have asked you first."

"I would have let you borrow it. You didn't have to trick me into getting you a glass of water so that you could take it." He looked hurt when he said it, and Alice felt bad for treating him so unkindly.

"I'm sorry. I'm afraid I haven't been a very good friend. I'm a bit out of practice."

His expression softened. "Forget it. What did you need the axe for?"

"Tell him you were chopping wood," the rabbit said.

Alice opened her mouth to repeat the rabbit's lie, then decided it was a bit unbelievable. Besides, the truth would surely scare Finn away, and maybe that was for the best.

"I smashed our television set."

Finn raised his eyebrows. "Why?"

"So my mother wouldn't watch it anymore. Last week I broke all the bottles of wine in the cellar so she'd stop drinking." She scratched at her arm without meaning to.

"What's that?" Finn asked. Too late for Alice, he'd already seen it.

"Tell him I scratched you," the rabbit said.

Alice laughed at how ludicrous that would sound to Finn. A stuffed rabbit, locked in a cage with no door, had scratched her.

"What's so funny?" Finn asked. Concern darkened his face.

Alice quieted. "I should go."

"Wait, are you hungry? Let me make you a sandwich."

Eating was also a human construct.

"He's going to ask you about me," the rabbit said. "And if you tell him, he'll think you're crazy. He'll have you put away with criminals like the congressman."

"He's not put away," Alice said.

"What?" Finn glanced from Alice to the rabbit.

"Nothing." Alice's world was spinning out of control, each moment more confusing than the last. She put one hand to her forehead.

"Let me get you a chair." Finn walked across the yard and retrieved a plastic lawn chair, which he set before Alice. She sat down gingerly while he grabbed one for himself.

"You're in some kind of trouble." He leaned forward with his elbows on his knees. "What's going on?"

Alice glanced at the white rabbit. He was shaking his head. Finn noticed the exchange, and the creases in his forehead deepened.

"I can't explain myself, I'm afraid, because I'm not myself."

"I work at a gas station," he said. "I see a lot of strange things. Try me."

Alice took a deep breath and pulled at a loose thread on the hem of her school uniform. "I'm having a hard time distinguishing what's real and what's not."

"Like the rabbit?"

Alice nodded.

"He talks to you?"

She nodded again.

"You probably think I'm crazy."

He shrugged. "Maybe a little. But all the best people are, right?" He smiled, and Alice relaxed a little. She appreciated his kindness and was about to say so when her stomach grumbled, loudly.

"That's right. I promised you a sandwich." He rose. "You like peanut butter and jelly?"

"Yes." Her mother used to make her peanut butter and jelly sandwiches sliced diagonally with the crusts cut off.

"Grape or strawberry?"

"Strawberry, please."

"Okay. I'll be right back. Don't go anywhere." He gave her a stern look.

She smiled. "I won't."

As soon as he was inside, the white rabbit began jumping around spastically. There wasn't room for him to jump freely, so his hind legs kept banging on the sides of the hutch, causing the whole structure to shake.

"You've really done it this time, Alice. He's probably calling for someone to come and take you away."

"He wouldn't." She spied him through a window. He appeared to be opening cabinets.

"He won't understand about your mother, Alice. You shouldn't trust him."

"I suppose I should trust *you*, though?"

The rabbit stopped jumping and stood on his hind legs. Both ears drooped, and he had a stricken look about him. "I'm here to help you, Alice. Why else would I be here?"

"You said Finn put you in there."

"It's a human construct, Alice. I'm not here because of Finn; I'm here because of you. And if you can't trust me, then you can't trust anyone, which means you are truly and utterly alone."

"Shush," Alice said sharply. "He's coming back."

"So, you go to school around here?" Finn handed her a paper plate with the sandwich and napkin. The sandwich still had its crusts, and it was cut straight instead of diagonal.

"Yes." Alice unfolded the napkin and laid it on her lap. Finn watched her with curiosity.

"That private school?"

"Yes," she said cautiously. "How about you?"

"I got my GED. School wasn't my thing."

"It's a human construct."

"A what?"

She shook her head dismissively. "A hoop. Some dogs are better at jumping through it than others."

He nodded and seemed satisfied with her explanation. Meanwhile, she tore apart the sandwich bit by bit and put the portions into her mouth, chewing and swallowing with care. Halfway through she had to take a break because her stomach was full.

"So, the rabbit," Finn said, "what does he say?"

Alice shrugged.

"Did the rabbit tell you to trash the wine cellar and smash your television?"

Alice stared at him. "It was my idea."

"And did it work?"

"Yes. And no. Now she's cleaning. The house is big. I'm afraid that as soon as she finishes, she'll just start all over again."

"Have you tried talking to her?"

Alice thought of the conversation they'd had last night, when Alice said she was hungry and her mother told her to take the money on the counter.

There is no money on the counter, Alice had said, determined to drag them both into the light of reality.

Of course there is, her mother said. *This house is made of money, Alice. It's everywhere. I've nearly got all of the wallpaper down and not a minute too soon. The painters are coming tomorrow...*

"I've tried talking to her," Alice said. A memory from years ago struck her, the first time they'd visited the

congressman at his house. Alice in her Sunday best, creases sharp and shoes polished with two braids down her back. *Remember your Ps and Qs*, her mother said severely, as if their entire future hinged on Alice's ability to mind her manners.

"This house is worthless," Alice said aloud. At that moment an idea struck her. "May I have a drink?" she asked Finn. "A cold glass of milk perhaps?"

"Of course." He stood up.

As soon as he was out of sight, Alice turned to the rabbit. Before she could utter a word, he said, "I never said anything about burning it down."

Alice imagined it, flames licking those tall, spindly columns. The walls cracking and splintering from within, everything reduced to a black pile of rubble. For a moment she felt elated, a tethered balloon set free.

"Are you opposed?" She valued the rabbit's opinion. He seemed to be the only one who understood the depth and complexity of her predicament.

"The idea has merit."

"I'm afraid I wouldn't know how to do it." Her every nerve was electric, her senses heightened. She stared at her hands, imagining their potential.

"It's quite simple. There's gasoline in the shed. Finn stores it in a red gas can."

Alice wondered how the rabbit would know that, having never left his cage, just like the axe. But some questions were less relevant than others. "Finn will notice that it's missing." She glanced over to where he was coming out the back door to join her.

"Come back tonight. They'll both be at work."

"What about my mother? I don't want her to get hurt."

"You're a clever girl. You'll figure something out."

Alice was quiet, turning the plan over in her head like a shiny copper penny.

"You're still here," Finn said with a smile.

He offered her a tall glass of milk as the rabbit whispered, "You've always hated that house."

Alice returned that night to find the white rabbit reposing with both eyes open, tracking her as she slipped though the backyard and over to the shed. There, next to the riding lawn mower, she found the red gas can, full and much heavier than she expected. She'd have to borrow the wheelbarrow as well in order to transport it back to her house.

She was just reaching the edge of the yard when the outside light came on. She heard the familiar creak of the back door and saw Finn's frame silhouetted by the lamplight.

"Alice?" He took a step onto the lawn. "Is that you?"

She froze and hoped he'd turn around and go back inside, but instead he came closer, barefoot and wearing only blue jeans.

"My mother's car ran out of gas," Alice said. "I'll pay you back, I promise."

"It's awfully late. Where'd she break down?"

"Not too far from here."

"Let me give you a ride."

"That's okay. I got it."

"Alice, you're carting around a wheelbarrow in the middle of the night. Let me help you."

Alice tried to remain calm as she said, "I don't want your help, Finn. Please go back inside. I'll return your gas can in the morning."

She wheeled around him, nearly at a run, and did not look back.

When she arrived at her house, her mother was asleep on the couch. Alice grabbed a pot and spoon and banged until she startled awake.

"Alice?"

"You need to get out of the house," Alice said. "There's a fire."

Her mother looked around, disoriented. "There's no smoke."

Alice lifted the gas can from the wheelbarrow. She set it on the coffee table and began unscrewing the lid.

"Alice, what are you doing?"

"This house is a prison, Mother. Ever since we got here, we've been captives. This is the only way to be free of it."

Her mother was fully attentive now. She sat up straight as a rod and wrung her hands together. "If you destroy this house, we'll have nothing."

"Do you love this house, Mother?"

Her mother frowned.

"Do you love it more than me?"

"Don't be ridiculous, Alice."

"You must. Because you traded it for me. This house, for my silence. Isn't that the arrangement you made? If we kept our mouths shut and didn't press charges, we could keep this house?"

Her mother stood. Her hands flew to her chest like twin doves. "It wasn't as simple as that."

"After what he did to me." His meanness she could tolerate; his senseless discipline she could withstand; but when he came at her so unexpectedly, so violently. Alice remembered how she barely struggled, didn't even make a sound, just screwed her mouth shut and waited for it to be over – so polite. Then afterward, instead of acting sorry, he tried to buy her silence with a new car. Alice couldn't be bought, but apparently her mother could.

Alice shook her head. "I hate myself. I hate him. But most of all, I hate this house." She tipped the gas can so that a little spilled on the floor.

"He's a powerful man, Alice. He has resources we can only imagine. He would have ruined us."

Alice began crying. Her breath was labored. "He already has ruined us. He's ruined me. And you." She splashed a little more gasoline on the tile. The fumes tickled her nose. She imagined striking the match and dropping it at her feet, going up in flames with the rest of it.

"Please, Alice. I know he's a terrible man. More than terrible, but I didn't know what else to do."

"You could have protected me. You could have fought for me." Alice sniffed and dragged one arm across her face. "You're my mother."

"I know that." She dropped her head. Her face contorted in pain. "I'm so sorry."

Alice glanced around at all the meaningless glass globules, all the high-priced art, the antique furniture and expensive upholstery. She hated every inch, every thread, and every splinter. She wanted to be rid of it, once and for all. How easy it would be to light the flame and burn it all to the ground. If only that would obliterate her memory of him along with it. But Alice knew that it would not.

Destroying things was easy. The congressman had taught her that. It was repairing that which was broken that took the most effort.

"You have to sell this house," she said.

Her mother nodded. "I will."

"Promise me."

Her mother raised one hand. "I promise."

Alice dropped the gas can and walked out of the house. She needed to see the rabbit, and she couldn't wait until morning. But when she arrived at his hutch, the rabbit was gone.

"Over here, Alice," the rabbit called from the woods behind Finn's house. How did he get out?

"Are you leaving?" Alice didn't want to be left all alone.

"I've found another way."

"What is it?"

"Follow me."

Alice chased after the rabbit as he nimbly jumped over felled logs and thorny vines. He was a splash of white in the

dark, dark woods. His form alone was all Alice could see clearly.

"What's this?" Alice asked when the rabbit finally stopped.

"Here in the forest, dark and deep, I offer you eternal sleep." He pointed with one ear to a hole in the ground, a sort of burrow. The tunnel looked deep and without end.

"Where does it lead?" Alice asked.

"It matters not where it leads, Alice, only that it will take us far away from here."

"Can I come back?"

"How long is forever, Alice?"

"I believe it's a very long time."

"Sometimes, it's just one second." The rabbit hopped closer to the opening of the tunnel. "Come with me, Alice, and your troubles and heartache will be forgotten. It will be as if they never even happened."

The rabbit was offering an escape. A new beginning or, more likely, an end.

"We haven't much time, Alice."

Alice took a step closer, her toes just over the edge of the tunnel. She peered down into the endless abyss. How easy it would be to tip forward and fall in.

"Are you my friend, white rabbit, or do you mean me harm?"

"I present you with a choice, Alice. Will you take this leap with me into this new world, or will you stay and suffer certain pain, the injustice of life?"

To Alice, happiness was a pretty thing just out of reach, a sweet in a jar on a too-high shelf. The girls she knew, they walked in the light. For them, happiness lay down before them like an obedient dog. It was never that way for Alice, for whom happiness came in snatches and tatters or not at all. Alice might never be happy, but she had not yet given up hope that somewhere in all this, she could find peace.

"I'll not be following you, white rabbit. I choose to stay and endure."

"You would choose to live this broken, unjust, and unhappy life with no certain outcome?"

Alice stepped away from the tunnel. "I would. And I do."

"Terrible pity, Alice. I thought I could help you." The rabbit sighed and shook his head, deeply disappointed. "Perhaps one day you'll change your mind." He winked at her once more. "But, for now, I must say, *adieu*."

The rabbit leapt into the hole and disappeared from sight. There was no sound of his footfalls and no cry from his mouth. He was simply and utterly, gone.

Alice looked away for only a second, but when she turned back, the rabbit hole had disappeared as well. The forest floor looked as fresh as a newly made bed.

"Alice?"

She recognized Finn's voice and turned toward a flashlight beam wobbling through the dark forest.

"Alice, is that you? Are you all right?"

Alice was not all right, and she might not be for a long time. But she had chosen to endure, and in doing so, she

vowed to look deep within herself and rediscover who she was. Not as her stepfather's secret or her mother's loss, not as the girl shrouded in mystery in the halls of Bradford Hills Academy. But as Alice, and Alice alone.

Like a weed, she would survive.

Laura Lascarso strives to craft stories that are honest and relatable. Her debut novel *Counting Backwards* won the 2012 Florida Book Award gold medal for Young Adult Literature. Her latest project, *Racing Hearts* (Leap 2015), tells the story of two star-crossed lovers thrust into the world of competitive car racing. Laura lives in North Florida with her darling husband, two children, and a menagerie of animals.

ALICE AND HER SHADOW

TOM LUKE

MEETING A FAN CAN BE THRILLING.

THIS STORY IS DEDICATED TO A HILL,
A GIRL WITH GREEN HAIR, AND MY SHADOW.

It is not a moonless night, nor is the moon full. It is not a half moon, which can be argued is more symbolic than neither. It is not even a crescent, which can be meaningful enough for the magical practitioner on a budget. It is a waxing gibbous. Bulging. Grotesque. And hanging too low in the sky like the misshapen eye of a cosmic horror that has taken an unusual interest in humanity.

Your name is Alice. Your last name is uninteresting and will soon be irrelevant. Your name is Alice, and you are walking home. It is too dark for your mother's purposes, and she worries about you being out too late, but Katherine's house is less than fifteen minutes away, and down two hills. No one waiting to ambush a defenseless teenage girl is going to bother walking up two hills, you told your mother.

You still believe this, but you've since developed other concerns.

None of the streetlamps are working and your shadow is beginning to worry you.

You are particularly worried that it may not belong to you.

It is stretched out in front of you and you don't remember it looking like that.

Your mother has told you that you're going through a late growth spurt, which is apparently why you keep walking into doorframes.

This might, might, account for the fact that your shadow's limbs are unnaturally long and moving in ways you don't recognize.

It does not account for your shadow's head.

Your shadow's head is freakishly large, weirdly distended, and there are two bumps emerging from the top of it.

You try not to speculate about the bumps.

You move your arm. Your shadow moves its arm, maybe a fraction of a second later.

You shiver and fold your arms in front of yourself. Maybe it's just the way you moved, but your shadow seems to swell.

You stop. The sound of your footsteps seems to continue a little longer than it should. When you start to walk again, the noise echoes a little more.

You reach up, nervously playing with your hair. Your hair feels alien and wrong, like the fur of some diseased –

You're wearing a hat.

Katherine gave you a white knit hat with rabbit ears and a little face on the front. You loved it so much that you put it on five hours ago while you and she were watching a movie and forgot you were wearing it.

Your shadow's head looks weird because you were wearing. A goddamn. Hat.

You start to laugh. Your shadow doubles over with you, and if it does it a hair slower, it's probably a trick of the light.

You start to walk again, a spring in your step. You're only five minutes from home. Your shadow walks ahead of you, its step, if anything, slightly springier.

Wait, you think.

It's nighttime.

There are no streetlamps. The moon isn't bright enough.

Why do you have such a distinct shadow?

It's far more solid than the rest of the night, and such a deep black that it seems to suck in the meager light of the gibbous moon. And if there was a source casting it, it would have moved by now. But there isn't, and it hasn't. It's stayed exactly in front of you the entire walk.

So where the hell is it coming from?

A cold breeze caresses your neck like a breath, and brings with it a smell not unlike desolation, a smell like books rotting in an abandoned room in the small hours of night. The smell of a truly haunted house, where there are no ghosts, no "spiritual presences," but only an empty, forgotten dwelling filled with nothing.

The smell a place gets decades after everyone's forgotten about the murder.

You feel it again on your neck, and the smell becomes stronger, because it is no breeze. There was no wind tonight, and you break into a run.

You run for only thirty seconds, tearing up the hill to your house, unconcerned about your footing, until your heel pops out of your shoe (unless something catches it) and you stumble. You put out your arms to prevent your face from plowing into the asphalt and land badly. Though you're winded, you struggle to your feet and stand, panicked.

Nothing takes advantage of your vulnerability. Nothing leaps onto you, clawing at your back, tearing away strips of flesh with claws as big as your thumb. You don't scream. The night is silent.

You are perfectly, immaculately still.

You hear a small noise, like a shoe tapping on pavement.

You whirl around, arms flailing.

And you see yourself, white bunny hat wedged firmly on your head, arms folded, gently tapping your foot. Your shadow is gone.

"Alice," the other you says, "it's so cool to finally meet you." She smiles, and her teeth are cartoonishly pointed like a pirahna's. Her tongue lolls between them, the color of tar.

Only then do you scream.

You wake up on the pavement. Your left arm and side hurt, most likely because you fell on them. You feel a pressure on your mouth, and you open your eyes.

You see your own face and you try to call out, to make some sort of noise. Not for help, you know instinctively that there is no escape from this, but just to express that you're still alive, still real. The hand on your lower face tightens.

"Hey, so I'm really sorry, but I just can't have you making noise, 'kay?" The other you smiles again, and the desolate smell of her breath washes over your face. She's lying on the ground parallel to you, one hand bent at the elbow, propping up her head, the other hand over your mouth.

"Mmmm," you whimper.

"I know, right? This is, like, such a big moment for me."

"Mm?"

"I'm such a big fan of your work. Like, eight to eleven changed my life." Her tongue snakes out over her lips.

"Mm?" you say again.

"Of your life, silly. I watch you all the time. You're so interesting. My favorite arc was when you were fighting with Eli. I thought there was going to be this whole resolution, but then you never talked to him again and he moved away. Ohmygod, I was devastated."

"MmmMM – "

"And when Olive broke up with you, that came out of nowhere. Such a cool twist."

"Mm – "

"And when your father died when you were nine, I couldn't even deal. I just couldn't. Too many feels. Too many."

"MMMM – "

"Listen, don't get me wrong, I would totally love to talk about this all day with you, but I gotta get to the point. Hey, so I'm gonna take my hand off your mouth in a second, but if you try to scream or move too much – I mean, like, you can move a little bit, obviously – I'll put your eye out with my tongue. It's really strong."

The other you lowers her hand and opens her mouth. Her teeth are a perfect white, and they drip with whatever tarry substance coats the inside of her throat.

You stuff your fist into your mouth and bite down on it to stop the scream.

"Thank you," she says. "I didn't really want to put out your eye. You have such pretty eyes. I'm so jealous."

She pauses.

"Oh, silly me. We have the same eyes now. I just did the eyes tonight. Good, huh? People say the eyes are the windows to the soul, but in this case it's my mouth. Can't do much with that, I'm afraid. It's internal."

"What are – ?"

"I'm you, silly! Just look!"

"But – "

"I would love to tell you about my life, but honestly, I don't have much time and it's not nearly as interesting as yours. Obviously. Or else we wouldn't be having this little chat."

"Why – ?"

"Well, that's the thing. I've been such a fan for so long and I'm really sorry to say it, but you've gone downhill lately."

"I – "

"Birth to twelve was amazing. Loved birth to twelve. I wish I'd been there for in utero. You can't get reruns anywhere. Thirteen was pretty good, but it wasn't the same, you know? I figured you were dealing with puberty and the quality would get back to normal soon, right? But then fourteen was bad. And fifteen was even worse. God, we don't talk about fifteen. Sixteen was pretty amazing, actually, but it was in spite of the problems, you know?"

"Are you talking about – ?"

"Your life, yeah! You don't interact with your fanbase much, which I totally respect, genius in isolation and all that, and there aren't really any forums or gatherings, so I haven't met anyone else, but I bet you've got tons of fans. You're the

best. But the thing is, seventeen isn't shaping up too well. Lot of the same problems as fourteen, and I just got so depressed watching. You're my favorite, you know? It's always *so* sad when one of your favorite artists just doesn't have it anymore."

You don't say anything. She's starting to make a warped, frightening kind of sense.

"I didn't know what to do. I kept watching, I had to, but it just made me upset. I got sort of angry with you back in February, but that's never been a good month. Except at nine, that one was amazing. But anyway, my point was, in February, I got so mad I said, (I'm pretty sure I said it like this): 'Oh, I could do better than this!'"

You are still. A thought is occurring to you, bearing down like a glacier. You think if you don't move, you can avoid its inevitability.

"It was such a big epiphany moment for me, you know? I started building another you right away. It was really hard, that thing you did with your hair back in May set me back weeks, but look at me! I'm so pretty."

She licks her teeth.

"So I'm gonna be you now, if that's cool. I mean, not that it matters if you're cool with it, because you're not even anybody now. I'm you, and you're some weird girl with no name. And your old name was so cute. Oops, I mean *my* name!"

The glacier hits just as she tells you. She doesn't want to hurt you. Nothing so small as hurting you. She wants everything. Your mind goes numb. You think about your life

and your memories seem…wrong. They don't belong to you anymore. You just found them somewhere, and now Alice wants them back.

"Seriously though, I've put a lot of thought into this, and I think it's the best thing for both of us. 'Kay? Anyway, I gotta get home. I was out late, and Mom's gonna be mad. Seeya, nobody!"

Your eyes begin to flutter as you see yourself striding away across the street. Her legs are so *long*, you think. Why are they – ?

You're gone.

Alice lets herself into her house with her key and, without hesitation, walks to her bedroom and takes out her pajamas. She knows exactly which drawer they are in without even having to think about it. She goes to put them on, then places the top in front of her face and inhales deeply through her nose.

"Ohmygod."

She discards the pajamas and begins to open all of her drawers, tearing articles of clothing out and rubbing them on her face, bathing in their scent.

"Ohmy*god*."

After nearly ten minutes of feverish sniffing, she very carefully folds all of her clothing and returns it to her drawers. Trembling, she changes into a pair of blue footie pajamas adorned with bananas. She turns to the bed, pulls up the rumpled sheets, and then with great reverence tucks herself in.

"Ohmygod ohmygod *ohmygod*."

She does not sleep, partially because she has never slept, but mostly because she is far too excited.

The first thing the girl with no name does in her life is wake up in the middle of a disused park.

The second thing she does is wipe the grit from her eyes and stand up.

The third thing she does is try to remember.

The fourth thing she does is she doesn't.

The fifth thing she does is stumble, unseeing and unseen, to a shed she knows is abandoned and unlocked. The fifth thing she does is not understand why she knows about the shed. The fifth thing she does is curl up in the corner of a half-rotted wooden bench. The fifth thing she does is cry, inconsolably, for a period of hours, because she has no past and no future and very likely no present. The fifth thing she does is nothing.

The sixth thing she does, several days later when hunger is tearing up her insides, is realize that, in a very real sense, she is nobody. She walks to a river and stares at her reflection. She wonders about her nice coat, her blond hair, her rabbit hat. She thinks about the person she might have been.

She realizes it isn't important. It can't be, if she is going to live.

She gets a bus downtown with money she begs from a pedestrian. She sits on a corner that no one else is using, and she puts an empty cardboard box she finds in a dumpster in front of her.

Later, she will write "Have nothing, please help" on the side of the box.

She takes the last bus back to the shack. No one else seems to be using it. Not even the homeless bother with her park. Or the other homeless, she corrects herself.

In the months to come she will learn how to layer stolen clothes to keep warm at night, or at least keep from freezing. She will learn how to steal. She will learn to suck in her cheeks and keep her box empty even on a good day.

She will learn loneliness so complete that she forgets the sound of her own voice.

She will learn the precise layout of the park, and she will learn that, beyond a few half-feral stray cats, she is practically its only inhabitant. She will learn that it is a safe place.

She will learn that it's probably best to have a weapon around, just in case. She will learn that an abandoned construction project nearby has a lot of lead pipes lying around. She will learn to keep one in her shack.

She will learn to live, more or less.

She will not learn who she is, and she will almost forget that she has forgotten. She is the girl with no name. She lives in an abandoned park, and she begs for change downtown. She keeps what she doesn't spend on food in a sock, as if she had something to save for. Her blank stare makes people uncomfortable, so no one speaks to her and she speaks to no one.

She will almost forget that she has forgotten.

Almost.

At 6:00 a.m., Alice hears her alarm and sits bolt upright. She savors the sound for nearly five full minutes until she gently presses the button and, in the same motion, rolls out of bed.

It takes her nearly an hour to choose an outfit, and another forty-five minutes to do her makeup. Another ten are spent staring motionless in the mirror, mouth agape.

She greets her mother at the breakfast table with an enthusiastic hug.

"Alice, dear?" Is everything okay?"

"Mom. Mom. Everything is so great. Like, you have no idea."

"I suppose not, dear."

"You're the best, Mom. Never change, unless it's, like, narratively significant."

"I'll certainly try."

Alice pours herself a glass of orange juice and some cereal. It tastes perfect, and her mother seems not to notice when she cleans out the bowl with her tongue.

Alice meets Katherine, who seems put off by her relentless enthusiasm for very nearly everything, to walk to school. She isn't sure about Katherine. She was a major character at age fifteen, and Alice isn't sure if she really fits. Technically, she supposes that Katherine is her best friend, but she really prefers Eli, from age twelve. His arc was far more interesting. She supposes he's in Peru now, and hates her, but that isn't terribly relevant.

"Alice, are you okay? You're weirdly…happy."

Alice makes up her mind. Katherine is holding the plot back. Really, she's doing this for everyone.

"Katherine, if you're going to question my happiness, I don't think I want to know you anymore."

"I just meant – "

"Not. Interested."

Alice stalks off, beaming. She'll fix this story yet.

At school, Alice turns her 50s and 60s across the board into 90s in a matter of weeks. Her teachers ask her why she's improved so dramatically. She answers with a giggle that she's cut sleep out of her schedule. They laugh with her and tell her to take care of herself. She says not to worry.

Being the best possible version of herself is her number one priority right now.

Alice and her mother are getting on famously. One afternoon when the two are watching something silly on television, her mother brings up university.

"I'm not sure, you know?" says Alice. "I think I know where I want to go, but I think I might just, like, do a couple of courses in different areas? Like, English, philosophy, maybe sociology? That sort of thing."

"Dear, your father and I always wanted you to go into biology, like he did. You know you always liked animals."

"I know, Mom, but I don't really know if that's my thing."

"Alice, you know your father would be terribly disappointed."

Alice knows precisely how disappointed her father would be. She's counting on it. She waits a number of seconds designed to maximize tension and walks out.

Time to get this story properly going.

Alice graduates high school close to the top of her class. She decides not to make any more friends. It'll be more

interesting if she starts her next arc with no attachments. She's accepted at a prestigious university a few provinces away and decides to take English, philosophy, political science, sociology, and psychology courses in her first term.

Her mother is not pleased.

"Mom, you just don't get it. I know Dad always wanted me to go into science like him, but he isn't around anymore!"

Her mother is tight-lipped, arms folded. She exudes maternal disapproval. Alice basks in it.

"Your father and I talked about this, Alice. If he were here right now, he'd be extremely disappointed."

"Mom. This is happening. I loved Dad, but he can't tell me how to live my life and you can't either."

"If you go to that school, you won't be welcome in this house."

"If that's how it is."

Alice goes to bed, which is to say she goes to sit quietly in her room until dawn. Her mother is left standing in a doorframe, at a loss. She begins to cry, very quietly.

Alice hears and exults.

Alice hauls her garbage bag of possessions into her dorm room. She hadn't wanted to take anything her mother had bought her, for symbolic purposes. She drops the bag on the bed and collapses. She tries to feel tired and lonely. Really, she's elated. This is exactly the sort of interesting

development that she'd been lacking from thirteen to seventeen. She can't wait to see where this story goes.

The door opens and a girl lets herself in. She's half a foot shorter than Alice, and her hair is black and cut very short. She looks like she smells nice.

"Are you Alice?" the girl asks. "I'm Daisy. I think we're roommates. Can you give me a hand with my bags?"

"That's me," says Alice and covers her face. *Right*, she thinks, *I'm supposed to be sad.* She allows a few tears to leak out through her fingers.

"Are you okay?"

"I'm-I'm – "

She sits down heavily on the bed.

"Just…give me a minute. I'll help you with your bags when-when – "

She bursts into tears. The girl sits down on the bed next to her and hugs her. Alice leans on her and sobs into her chest. She *does* smell nice.

A month into their cohabitation, Alice comes back to the room quite late and quite drunk. She'd been to a mixer for the sociology society, and then a mixer for the English society when the sociology society's was shut down by campus security. In a state of utter bliss, she'd flitted from conversation to conversation, dazzling the other drunken

students. She'd made dozens of friends. An hour later, she'd wandered home and found Daisy up doing homework.

"Daisy. *Daisy*."

"Oh hey, Alice."

"Do you think I'm *pretty*, Daisy?"

"I think you're loaded."

"That's beside. Besides. The point."

"Okay, then."

"Wanna make out?"

Daisy's head whips around, her expression going from shocked, to elated, to crestfallen, back to elated, then finally settling on resigned.

"Wanna talk about this in the morning?" she says.

"Noooooo…"

"Come on. Let's get you to bed."

Alice does not resist as Daisy guides her to bed, though she does lean more heavily than she necessarily has to. And perhaps she slobbers on Daisy more than appropriately – which is to say, at all – but neither mentions this. Daisy tucks Alice into her own bed and then goes to leave.

"Daiiiiiiisy."

"Alice, I swear if you're just playing with me and you're straight in the morning, I am going to – well, I'm probably just going to cry and then never mention this again."

"But – "

"Tomorrow, Alice."

It turns out that while Alice can't actually sleep, she can drunkenly pass out.

"Hey, Daisy?"

"Yes, Alice?"

"Can we talk about it now?"

Alice is standing behind Daisy, leaning up against the counter in their very tiny dorm kitchen while Daisy cooks eggs.

"I suppose. Do you want some eggs?"

"Eggs are okay, but you're a much more attractive option right now."

Daisy puts the frying pan down, turns, and kisses her with a mix of hesitation and forcefulness that Alice finds utterly adorable.

After she breaks the kiss, she looks up at Alice and says, "Is this for real?"

"Yes," Alice says.

"Your tongue is really weird."

Alice loves university. She loves being with Daisy, and she loves her courses. She has a few close friends and dozens of peripheral ones. She does well. She makes connections with professors, and people begin recommending grad schools. She is very happy.

She is terrified that the story is beginning to stagnate.

She resolves to do something about it. This arc needs shaking up.

"Daisy. Daisy. I know you're upset. You love me. Obviously. And I love you too. Basically. But it's just not interesting anymore. No one's invested in our relationship. Our ship doesn't even have a good portmanteau. I mean, really."

Daisy stares at Alice from between her fingers. Her eyes are red and raw, and she's soaked a small mountain of tissues throughout the conversation.

"Listen, I gotta go. It'll be okay. We might even have a plot later on where we make a misguided attempt to rekindle things. Before my true love turns up, anyway. That's something to look forward to."

Daisy howls and presses her face into a pillow. Alice gives her a little pat on the head.

"Later, Daisy. You'll always be fondly remembered by a tiny yet vocal section of the fans."

Alice walks out of her dorm room.

Odd. She doesn't feel nearly as satisfied with that resolution as she thought she would be.

She has offers from a number of grad schools, but she's still not certain if she wants to pursue sociology as an M.A. She rents an apartment in her hometown for a month to think things over. On the third day of doing nothing much but

enjoying her temporary freedom from school, her mother calls. She says she's heard Alice is in town, and she wants to go to lunch. She sounds tense. Alice says "yes" and tries to keep the triumph from her voice.

Over lunch, her mother apologizes. She says that she was wrong, that she shouldn't have used Alice's father's memory like that, and that Alice was and is her own person. She says that she struggled with some things while Alice was gone, that some of her vices got the better of her. She's fine now, but she never wants to lose Alice again.

She says if Alice's father were here, he would be proud of her. She says that Alice is the best daughter they could have ever wanted.

Alice bursts into tears and holds her mother's hand over the table. After lunch, they share a long hug. Her mother asks if she wants to sleep at home tonight. Alice nods, too emotional to speak.

More than anything, she's shocked not to be pretending.

She makes plans to eat a home-cooked meal with her mother tonight, then says she has things to do, and they'll see each other later.

They hug again.

Alice, walking away from the restaurant, says to herself, "Oh my God. This is such a great resolution."

After supper at the house and another conversation that nearly brings both women to tears, Alice says she's going to go for a walk before bed. Her mother says she'll be up until Alice gets home, and then maybe they can watch a movie

together. Alice smiles and says, "Yeah, Mom. That'd be great."

She goes for a walk in a nearby park. The city and the surrounding neighborhood have basically abandoned it. Alice wonders why there aren't more homeless people around. She did a course on the sociology of vagrancy in her third year, and she finds the topic extremely interesting.

She thinks about how much work would be involved in doing some proper research into the problem when she finishes grad school. Maybe getting a job in a help center somewhere. She loves academia, but she doesn't know if she wants to study for the rest of her life.

She wonders what sort of narrative arc she can develop if she starts volunteering at a shelter.

Maybe it's not important. Maybe it's –

A noise somewhere in the trees interrupts her train of thought. She licks her lips instinctively, nervously.

Another noise, from the other side of the path. Her eyes dart to its source. Nothing.

She descends a set of stone steps. One of the flagstones wobbles precariously, sending her sprawling to the bottom of the stairs. She lands on her arm, badly. She doesn't like the *crunch* it makes, and she likes the blossom of pain in her hand even less.

She lies on her front for half a minute before she glances upward, then back down. She isn't ready to –

Clank.

The sound of metal on metal. There's a metal railing on the bridge up ahead, but what's hitting it? She resolves to get

moving. Judging from the sound, whatever's there is probably still on the other side.

Clank.

Closer.

Alice gets to her feet as quickly as she can with one working hand. She's just going to go home now. Mom can drive her to the hospital. Alice bets she won't even hesitate when she gets home, and it'll be such a great moment when she holds her hand (not the broken one) in the waiting room and –

Clank.

Clank.

Clank.

A final *clank* and then a scuffing noise like something being dragged through gravel.

It's crossed to this side of the bridge.

Alice starts to walk, cradling her wrist. She hears slow footsteps behind her. She hasn't killed anything in years, and she's not even sure she knows how anymore. Her body's not really suited to it nowadays. She walks faster.

The footsteps don't speed up, but Alice can tell they're close. She tries to run, but the movement jostles her hand and she can't keep it up longer than thirty seconds.

She's twenty minutes from the edge of the park. She sighs, tucks her injured hand into the pocket of her hoodie, and bares her teeth.

She drops to a fighting stance and turns slowly.

There's a girl standing there, a lead pipe hanging limply from her left hand. Her clothes have been ripped and patched

back together a dozen times, but her coat was at one time very nice.

Alice can't tell how old she is. Her face seems prematurely aged, but she could be as young as seventeen. Their build is nearly identical, but where Alice is soft from studying and drinking and getting enough food, the girl has wiry cords of muscle and is frighteningly gaunt. Her face, as much as Alice can see it through the filth, is so thin her cheekbones look like they could cut glass.

She is wearing a white hat in the shape of a rabbit. One of the ears has been torn off; the other dangles by a thread. The rabbit once had a face, but the years have rendered it blind and mouthless.

Alice stares, paralyzed and uncomprehending. The girl stares back. She looks like she's trying to work something out.

She nods, and at the same time, Alice remembers.

"This is the best twist ev – "

The girl with no name hits her with the pipe. Alice staggers, and the girl hits her again, across the knees. She crumples, and the girl hits her again.

And again.

And again.

Again.

Again.

Again.

The girl with no name stops. She lets go of the pipe.

She doesn't know what she expected. She'd seen a girl walking around with her face, or her face if she ate regularly. She was going to talk to her, but when she'd actually seen her,

she'd felt…something. It wasn't rage. More like necessity. As if something in her would break and spill if she let this girl live.

She had precious little substance left in her. She couldn't afford to break and spill.

She turns the corpse over with her foot and stares at the face. She goes through the pockets and looks at the cell phone, the wallet, the house keys.

She finds nothing of herself. She remembers nothing of herself.

Loss fills her, deep and incomprehensible, as she sits down next to the corpse and begins to cry.

Someone should probably come looking for Alice soon.

Maybe they'll know what to do.

Tom Luke is twenty-one and lives in a five-sided blue house with slanty floors. He has been writing long enough to know better and has never been able to understand why Garfield hates Mondays if he doesn't have a job. He hopes you are well.

ALICE

IN

WILDERLAND

JESSICA BAYLISS

EXPLORING THE WOODS WITH THE HOTTEST
GUY IN SCHOOL, ALICE FEELS ADVENTUROUS.

TO ERIC FOR HIS LOVE,
TO MIM FOR HER HEART, AND TO DAD FOR
INTRODUCING ME TO ALICE IN THE FIRST PLACE.

lice snapped off another shot and checked the image in her camera's viewfinder. The light was wrong. She adjusted some settings and brushed a furry caterpillar off her subject, the rare Adders-Mouth orchid, an endangered species in the state of Connecticut. Or, at least she thought it was an Adders-Mouth.

She plucked a waxen petal and pinched it, releasing a delicate cucumber fragrance. Now she had no doubt the tiny bloom *was* one of the rare specimens on her list. And in another minute, she'd have the perfect pic to bring back to the Wilderland Ecological Society, the group that had arranged this weekend trip.

She glanced toward the path. There was no sign of her group through the thick growth of trees and brush. She was *so* not supposed to lag behind. Brooks was going to chew her out for sure, but if she got this shot, it would be worth their guide's legendary wrath. Alice was determined to get into a top ecology program when she applied to colleges this year, and this summer elective was just the kind of extracurricular all the best schools liked to see.

Not to mention the fact that Alice needed something to fill her time, occupy her mind until the day she could get out of here for good.

Alice adjusted her angle, clicked off a few more shots, and then checked the images. "Got it. Sweet." She stood with a smile, and turned, about to relocate the path so she could rejoin her hiking group. Instead she collided, face first, into a broad chest.

Alice's scream of shock drowned out the rumbling "Umph." Overbalanced by his heavy pack, he flailed his arms to keep from going down.

"Aaron," she said. "Holy shit. Talk about heart attack."

Aaron rubbed his collarbone with a large, work-roughened hand. "Man, your head is hard."

"Sorry."

How totally embarrassing. This was nothing like her fantasies about alone time with Aaron Malik. But she couldn't let her brain go *there*. Not now. Not out here.

"Well," she said, trying to keep her voice firm so she wouldn't sound *too* pathetic. "That's what you get for sneaking up on unsuspecting females in the woods." A breeze blew a bit of crunchy leaf to his shoulder. She resisted the urge to reach up and brush it away.

"You didn't hear me?" Aaron said. "I've been calling for like five minutes. Brooks was looking for you. We're not supposed to separate from the main group or leave the path, remember?"

"But I saw patches of white over here when we were taking samples. Look." She pointed to the growth of tiny, delicate flowers.

"Hey, is that Adders-Mouth? Very cool. But we moved on almost an hour ago, and the light's fading fast. Camp's about half a mile from here. Where's your pack?"

Alice searched the shadowy brush for her gear. "There." She pointed. "God, I'll be glad when we can rest. My shoulders are gonna have permanent divots from all the weight."

Aaron laughed. "Yeah, they load us down pretty good on these trips."

Except he didn't seem to have any difficulty managing *his* gear. Not that he *should*. She'd seen him in the gym after school, putting in his time in the weight room to stay in shape for lacrosse. As if to prove her point, Aaron grabbed her backpack and slung it around, one-handed, as though it weighed nothing.

"Here you go." He held it up so she could slip into it.

She froze, eyeing her gear in his hands.

"Well?" he asked.

Alice turned around and let Aaron slide the straps over her arms. Before he settled its weight on her shoulders, he brushed her hair aside, and she barely held back a gasp at the feel of his warm fingers against her neck. He made a fuss over adjusting the straps just so.

This had just become the best weekend of her life. If only this moment could last forever. But a second later, he seemed satisfied and spun her around to face him.

"Thanks." Alice stared into Aaron's smiling face just a little too long. "So…"

"Yeah." His warm, brown eyes were soft, but he snapped to attention a second later. "Right. Let's head out."

When Alice's guidance counselor suggested she sign up for the Wilderland summer program, she had no idea the hot senior was part of it. Alice hadn't believed her luck when she discovered they'd be participating in about a dozen hikes and three overnight campouts together. She'd been eyeing him, mostly from a distance, for two years – two hard years. Her

fantasies about him had been one of the bright spots that fueled her through.

With confident strides, Aaron led the way through the brush back to the path. "Wait 'til you see the campsite." He flashed her a smile over his shoulder. "Right on the ridge overlooking Aster Meadow. You get the best sunrises and sunsets there."

"Sounds great." No – better than great; sunset with Aaron Malik sounded too good to be true.

While she'd been busy with her pictures, a gray cast had fallen over the woods. It would suck big-time to be stranded out here alone in the dark. On the other hand, having an excuse to stay close to Aaron wasn't exactly a *bad* thing. He had at least three inches on Alice's five foot four so her eyes were in line with the top of his pack. A plush, white rabbit keychain dangled from one of the zippers. It bobbed and swayed with every step, nearly hypnotizing her. She yawned, feeling their 4:00 a.m. start and closed her eyes momentarily. Total mistake. Alice smashed, nose-first, into Aaron's shoulder.

"Ouch!" Her eyes watered. "What the hell, Aaron? Why'd you stop?"

"Shhh." He turned and wrapped a quieting hand around her elbow.

She looked at his fingers where they made warm contact with her bare skin. His was rougher and darker than Alice's pale, freckled complexion. Her cheeks flushed hot. But then her brain registered the urgency in his voice. And his

tightening grip. He put one finger up to his ear then pointed ahead.

Alice cocked her head and listened. Something lumbered through the woods, heading in their direction. A deer maybe. *Please let it be a deer.* Twigs snapped and leaves crunched, giving away its hulking size. It chuffed and snorted.

So not a deer.

Every muscle in her body tensing, she bit her lip and peered around Aaron's shoulder. "Oh my God," she breathed.

A massive black bear ambled through the brush right in their direction.

Aaron's large hand moved up Alice's arm to her shoulder and pushed, urging her to go back the way they'd come. "It hasn't scented us yet. We're outta here."

Alice ignored the fact that the path to camp lay beyond the bear and plunged deeper into the woods. Her attempts at being quiet were a total fail, especially the darker it got. They kept throwing glances behind them, squinting into the dusky shadows, but with every step, the sounds of the bear faded to nothing.

When they were a safe distance away, Aaron consulted his compass. "We need to circle back east."

"But how? It's all bog that way." Even here, the ground was spongy with moisture.

"You're right." He stared down the dark path ahead. "Let's stop for a second." He grunted with relief as he swung his pack off his back. Alice followed suit.

"What if we headed west? Circle the long way around?" she suggested.

"We may run into Smokey again if he keeps on the way he was heading." He looked up at the sky. "And it's getting super dark. I've been hiking and camping these woods for three summers now, but I can't navigate to Aster Meadow after nightfall. Even with a flashlight."

"What are you saying?"

"I think we're camping on our own tonight, Alice."

She gulped. Alone? With Aaron Malik? No effin' way.

"Are you sure? What if we – ?"

"Look, I don't like it any more than you do, but night's closing in fast." He gestured to the air around him.

"Yeah. You're right," she whispered through the hitch in her throat.

"I know a good spot not too far from here."

They shouldered their packs again and got moving. Aaron barely said a word. This sucked big-time. They'd both be in trouble, and she was to blame. He'd just been trying to help. She finally got her shot at hanging out with him after years of long-distance drooling, and this had to happen.

And how would they pass the time? A whole night…?

She remembered the feel of his fingers brushing her neck – except in her head, instead of merely slipping the backpack over her shoulders, Aaron pulled her close…closer…

Snap out of it, Alice!

What the heck was she even thinking? That was *so* not going to happen. Hadn't he just said he hated this whole situation? At best, she'd be lucky to make it through the night

without making a complete fool of herself. Oh God, what if she made a complete fool of herself? She was a camper, yeah, a good one too. But Aaron was a total outdoorsman, way out of her league.

As if on cue, she tripped and scraped her arm on some rough tree bark. Big surprise there; it was so dark she could barely see two feet in front of her.

Aaron spun on her. "You okay?"

She touched the stinging scrape. And now she was bleeding…super. "It's nothing. Really."

It could have been worse. A *lot* worse. Camping alone in the woods was no joke. The evening was still warm and humid, but her arms, bare in her tank top, broke out in goose bumps. A million horror stories ran through her mind. Animal attack – the bear – or something even worse. What if a crazed axe murderer was stalking them? Right now. Tracking their every move. She jumped at a *crack-snap* in the shadows to her left then tripped because she wasn't looking in front of her. Again.

"I'm fine," she said when Aaron threw her another worried glance.

Alice blew out a frustrated breath of air. She needed to stop acting like a newbie. Being around Aaron had her off balance, on edge, and she was forgetting everything her dad had taught her.

Well, no more.

"We need to stop," she said. "It isn't safe to keep moving. Too dark."

Aaron nodded. "I think this is good anyway." He stamped hard on the earth below his feet and ran a booted foot over the ground. "Feels solid. We'll stay dry." He dropped his pack and sat heavily on a rock.

"Works for me." Alice stood there, not knowing what to do with herself. If he was pissed off, talking might only make it worse. Regardless, they needed to make camp, and the best way to combat nerves was to take initiative. It's what her father would have done. "What supplies do you have?" she asked. "Let's take stock, figure out our resources."

Aaron was busy trying to unknot an unwieldy boot string but paused to give her an appraising look. Their eyes met for a long time, and she felt the rush of heat again. Did he feel it too? Yeah, right. He was probably wishing he'd never crossed her path. Look at the mess she'd gotten him into.

She swallowed, and her throat clicked. She needed a drink. And a grip.

"Water's most important." Alice dug through her stuff. "I have a small bottle, half-full, and this huge one. What about you?"

"Two small bottles. We'll be good until we find the group, but we should go light. Just in case."

His flat voice wasn't giving away his mood.

"Boy am I glad I got stuck carrying a tent," she blabbered. "Oh no. That means poor Dinah and Tanisha are stuck without one."

She sunk to the ground and drew her knees to her chest. How could she be so stupid as to let this happen? When this

was all over, she'd be lucky if anyone in Wellspring would talk to her. Alice blinked against the threatening tears and swallowed back the burning in her throat. But no, she would *not* cry, had promised her dad she'd never waste her time on tears.

"Don't worry, Alice. Brooksie will reconfigure everyone. I've spent the night with five people squished into one of these three-man deals. They'll be okay. And I'm extra thankful because, unlike you, I'm *not* carrying a tent."

Wait a minute. Was he trying to reassure her?

Aaron gave her his lopsided smile, the one that made the dimple in his cheek pop out. He put a hand on her shoulder and squeezed gently before turning back to his pack.

Maybe he didn't hate her after all. Maybe the others wouldn't either.

Then she registered what he'd said. He had no tent. She did. One tent. Two people.

Oh God.

"Oh good," she squeaked, then cleared her throat. "What else do I have? Let's see." Alice laid each item on the ground as she extracted it from her pack. "Brooks had me carry an extra camp light, a bunch of cocoa packets, first aid kit, box of raisins, and a tarp. And for my own personal stash, I brought a couple of granola bars, an extra flashlight" – which she switched on – "my blow-up pillow, and some dark chocolate."

Aaron laughed. "Cocoa and dark chocolate. We can stay out here forever."

She shot a surprised look at him, but he didn't mean it the way she heard it. No way he wanted to stay forever with her. Hadn't he already made that perfectly clear?

"What about you?" Alice laid out the tarp and settled onto it, gratefully. She hated wet butt.

"I have dried soup, but no pot. A deck of cards," which he handed to her. The Queen of Hearts on the box eyed her suspiciously. "A camp shovel, three-pack of fire starters, matches, and a jar of mini hot dogs."

"We're officially camping in style," she said.

"One more thing."

Alice heard a click followed by radio static. He tuned the dial and the night was full of…

"Is that the death metal show at the local college station?" she asked.

"Sorry." Aaron messed with the dial some more. "Not much comes in out here." He sounded disappointed as he clicked off the portable radio. "We'll give it a little while. The DJ will change over soon."

Alice laughed. "Perfect. Weenies and death metal by firelight."

That got a chuckle out of him, and their eyes met again. His gaze held hers, then swept downward to her lips and back up again. Alice held her breath. The breeze caught a strand of her curly blond hair, and it tickled her face. Before she could brush it away, Aaron did it for her then looked down as if embarrassed.

The lightening of Aaron's mood gave Alice new courage. She reached to lay a hand on his arm, and his eyes snapped

back to hers. His skin was so warm it startled her, making her forget what she'd been about to say for a second. She pulled her hand back but forged on with her apology. "I'm so sorry, Aaron. This really sucks, and it's all my fault."

He sighed. "Hey, don't sweat it. Bears happen."

"But if you hadn't come to find me, you wouldn't be stuck in this mess. I know you're wishing anyone else had gotten roped into this."

"No," he said, eyes on his hands. He toyed with a twig.

"No?"

He spoke without meeting her eyes. "I volunteered to come find you. I wanted to make sure you were okay." His gaze darted to Alice's face then back down again as if he was unsure of her reaction.

What did *that* mean? Simply because she needed something to do, Alice took a sip of water. He'd barely noticed her in all their time in high school, and now he was leaving for college soon. She was nothing to him.

Alice nudged the tent. "Better get this set up."

"Fire first. Tent second. Food third." He clicked on a large metal flashlight and shoved it under his arm. "Let's go."

Aaron held out his hands to her, and Alice took hold of them. He hauled her up so easily she nearly fell into him, but he steadied her with a hand to her waist before stomping off in search of wood.

Alice grabbed her camp light from her pile of worldly goods and followed.

Aaron's laugh carried to her through the dark night. "This reminds me of that time at Morris Park Beach when we were tagging Sharp-tailed Sparrow nests. Remember?"

Alice spun, nearly dropping the branch in her hand, and eyed Aaron's shadowy outline. He remembered that? Their circles had overlapped briefly on and off throughout school, but she'd had little time for friends with all her family craziness. And when everything settled down, she hadn't seemed to want a social life, preferring her solo hikes in the quiet of the woods.

The trip to Morris Park Bird Sanctuary had been the only real time she'd ever spent with Aaron and one of the high points of her life. Not only had they raced around madly, tagging more nests than any other team, Alice got to spend ninety wonderful minutes alone in his company. The pinnacle had been the moment their hands touched as they tried to fold back a thick growth of marsh grass. Alice had thought her heart might stop.

Of course *she* remembered. But him? Whoa.

"We're good nesters," she said. "A good nesting team. I mean, we're a good team." Could she *be* any lamer?

"Hey!" Aaron said. "Here's a huge broken branch." He dropped the wood in his arms and tugged. "It's stuck."

"Here. Let me help."

After a couple heaves, the branch pulled free of the dirt and brush all at once. They stumbled back with the momentum, their feet and legs tangling together.

"Oh no," Alice shouted, and a moment later, they went down. Aaron hit the dirt first, and Alice sprawled on top of him. Because, really, this day wasn't embarrassing enough already.

"That's not how I imagined *that* going," Aaron said.

Alice cracked up laughing. "Really? I'd been hoping we could do that all day long."

"I can't move my leg," he said.

"That's because I'm lying on it," she said, laughing even harder. "I think you broke my rib with your elbow."

"Oh, Alice." He sounded mortified. "Are you okay?"

"Totally fine." She tried to shift to her knees, but their legs were still entangled and she only managed to squirm around a little. Then she froze.

She was lying on top of Aaron Malik, and they were face-to-face. Alice suddenly didn't have enough air in her lungs to laugh. She could hardly breathe.

"Hi," he said, his lips just inches from hers, yet she could barely read his expression in the dark, even from here.

"Hi," she whispered back. Never in her wildest fantasies would she have imagined being this close to Aaron. But now, she was all too aware of how every breath brought her that much closer.

"I guess we should have let sleeping logs lie, huh?" he said.

She snorted a laugh. Right in Aaron's face. But she couldn't help it. "You really didn't just say that."

"Hey, come on. That was slick."

"Yeah. Super slick." She giggled again.

"You just can't appreciate true comic genius," he said.

"Are we getting up or what?"

"Sure." Even in the dark, his lopsided grin was hard to miss. "Whenever you're ready to get off me, I'll get up."

"Oh God." Hooray for the veil of darkness. Hopefully her blushing wouldn't be too obvious. "Sorry."

She scrambled off and to her knees as quickly as she could. Aaron grabbed hold of her elbow. "Let me help you," he said.

"No, really. I got it." But he was already hauling her up, pulling so hard she stumbled into him. Their eyes locked. "Thanks," Alice said.

"No problem," he whispered.

Her hands were pressed into his chest, and she quickly moved them. "The wood," she stuttered.

"Right. Wood." Aaron broke away from her, clearing his throat.

"Well," Alice muttered, "*that* happened."

They finished their hunt, and once they had amassed a decent pile, they set to building the fire. Aaron dug out a pit with the camp shovel, and Alice laid out the first layer of twigs and branches. "I bet I can get this going with no fire starter," she said.

"Go for it," he challenged.

She just happened to be the best fire maker in her family, even better than her dad. Alice smiled smugly as she laid out the wood just so. Meanwhile, Aaron got started on the tent, training the beams from their lights so he could see what he was doing. They worked quietly for some minutes, but it was a comfortable silence, her nervousness from earlier forgotten now that she had a task to do. Soon, the fire was burning away and the tent was all set up.

Now what?

They sat awkwardly next to each other on a tarp-draped log. Alice was a jangle of nerves again. Lovely. It didn't help that Aaron's shoulder kept brushing against hers as he poked and prodded the fire.

"Hey, don't mess it up," she said. "That's a finely crafted pyramid."

"Impressive." He relinquished his stick. "How about food?" He handed her the jar of hot dogs.

Little gray masses floated in unappetizing liquid. Alice made a *bleh* face.

"They're good." Aaron prompted. "What do you think they use to make pigs-in-a-blanket?" He took the jar, twisted the lid off with a pop, and impaled a hot dog at the end of a stick. "Here."

"I don't think I'm a weenie girl," she said, and he burst out laughing. She smacked him on the arm. "Hey."

"Sorry," he said, still laughing. "You're right. You're *not* a weenie girl."

"Ha. Ha. Ha." She put her blanket-less pig over the fire and watched as the flames toasted it to a more appealing golden-brown. It smelled way better than it looked.

"See, told you," he said when she grabbed another from the jar.

Aaron tried the radio again, and this time he got the college station's classical hour. "We can chill to this. It's boring, but soothing."

"I kinda like classical."

They ended the meal with a couple of granola bars from her pack. Aaron crumpled his wrapper and stowed it away in

his bag, then slid off the log. He reclined against it, stretching his long legs toward the fire. He put his hands behind his head and stared up at the stars beginning to light up the sky. After pulling on a sweatshirt against the cold night settling down on them, Alice inched closer to the fire – closer to Aaron – and lay down too.

"Wow," she whispered. "It's so clear out here. We've got a fire, a starlit sky. Now all we need is a story."

"Go ahead," he said.

But all the campfire stories she knew reminded her of her dad. "I can't think of one right now."

"Then I'll tell one. Let's see. There's the one about the great king Vira-Bhuja. He got all paranoid and locked away his favorite wife, Guna-Vara."

"What's that?" she asked.

Aaron shifted, and his knee came to rest against her leg. She tried not to let him feel her shiver.

"An old Hindu fairy tale."

"Are you Hindu?" Alice whispered, trying to figure out if she was supposed to move her leg away or not. But Aaron seemed okay with the situation. Alice was more than okay with it. Way more.

He nodded. "My mom used to tell me that story."

"So, what happened to Guna-Vara?"

"The prince returned from exile and cleared his mother's name. Mostly, though, because he met the wise and beautiful daughter of an evil magician. She saved the prince, the queen, everyone."

Hearing Aaron's story made Alice think of her own days listening to fairy tales, except it had been her father, not her mother, who'd told them. He'd taught her how to take care of herself and how to make a campfire. Alice could picture it like it was yesterday. His strong hands arranging the wood, the look of concentration on his beard-stubbled face. The smile he'd get when the spark blazed to life. He'd put his arm around her, and she'd feel loved. So loved.

Alice smiled up at the shining sky even as the grief washed over her. Why did the good memories have to bring pain? Like some twisted freebie. No wonder Alice's mother refused to talk about him, choosing to bury herself in work the way an ostrich would bury its head in the sand. That was how her mother coped with all of life's difficulties, which had been fine as long as her dad was around.

Not so much now.

But that didn't matter anymore. Alice was seventeen, would go to college soon. It was time to get used to taking care of herself – she *was* taking care of herself. She felt a moment's pride at how well she was handling all of this. Her dad would be proud.

"I still can't believe we're stuck out here," she said.

"Well, we did sign on for a camping trip, didn't we? It's just a little different than we planned."

"Yeah, and way scarier."

"Don't worry, Alice. We'll be fine. Trust me."

Maybe it was the music. Maybe the stars. Or simply his voice in the night. Whatever it was, for the first time in a long

time, out here tonight with only this stranger, Alice didn't feel alone.

But it wouldn't last. He'd just graduated after all, and summer was just a few short weeks long.

"I hear you got into Northland," she said. "You must be so psyched."

"I can't wait."

"That's one of the best environmental undergrad programs in the country."

"Are you applying there?" he asked. "That day at Morris Beach, you said you wanted to study ecological science, right?"

Wow. He totally remembered.

"Definitely. I hope I get in."

"Doing Wilderland will look really good on your apps."

"I guess I'm lucky Mrs. Kasbrack thought to tell me about it then."

He cleared his throat and shifted. She studied him for a moment, but he kept his eyes averted from hers. "There are a couple other things you can check out, some local internships, volunteering opportunities. I'll give you some info when we get home."

"Awesome."

Did that mean he wanted to see her outside of Wilderland?

"The college application process is really freaky," she said. "So many forms to fill out. All those essays."

"Yeah. At least they're online. I can't even imagine paper applications."

She laughed. "I know."

"Do you think we should waste some of our water on that cocoa?" he asked.

"Probably not, but it sounds good."

"How about we share one?"

He mixed a packet of the powder with water in his tin mess cup, then held it over the fire. A few moments later, he said, "Ouch. Damned thing's getting hot." He set it down and sucked on his fingers.

"That's what happens when you hold metal over fire, dumbass. Here. Let me." She dug in her pack and pulled out a pair of gloves. It got cold in the woods at night. She came prepared.

With gloved hands, Alice carefully hovered the cup above the flame, stirring occasionally with a spoon from her mess kit until the scent of simmering chocolate blended with the wood smoke on the air.

"Here, taste." She held out the cup.

Alice watched his lips as he blew on the cocoa. He took a tentative sip and smiled. "Definitely worth wasting the water."

They shared the mug, back and forth, watching the fire and talking about everything and nothing at all. A haunting violin melody filled the air. Between the music, chilly night, and hot fire, Alice shivered.

Aaron scooted closer. "Here." He put an arm around her and drew her against him.

She nearly dropped the cup in her surprise. He was *cuddling* with her.

She needed to say something. Anything.

"Why do you have a white rabbit on your backpack?"

He laughed. "That. The hare is a moon sign in the ancient Vedic religion. He jumps the highest and runs the fastest, which gives him power over other signs. My dad gave it to me to remind me of the hare when I'm out in the wild. To keep me on my toes."

Tonight's moon was full. Alice tried to imagine it as a rabbit running. "It's beautiful."

"What?"

"The moon. The violin. Everything."

"Yeah," he said, his voice closer now.

She turned to look at him, and he was staring at her. Her breath caught in her throat. So did his.

He was going to kiss her.

Alice stared back, yet she needed to look away, to hide, but she couldn't move. And part of her didn't want to anyway. A tickling thrill sparked, grew, ignited; it raced her toward whatever was about to happen.

But just then the slow, sleepy violin tune changed to a lively, jaunty rhythm, and she jumped again. This time, she did spill the cocoa, only a little, but it ran down her hand toward her sweatshirt sleeve. Without thinking, she licked it, and only then noticed Aaron still watching her. Intently.

Her cheeks burned, and she looked down at the cup. You better take this," she said. "Before I douse us both." She handed him the cocoa and moved away, going for her pack and her cosmetics case. "I'm going to brush my teeth." Once done, she brought her sleep sweats into the tent to change.

Tents were definitely not made for standing. Crouching, she pulled her jeans off and nearly fell over, but managed to catch herself before she could go down and take the whole tent with her.

She was *way* too aware of Aaron out there, separated by a flimsy layer of plastic, while she shuffled around in here.

Half-naked.

Her figure probably silhouetted against the tent by her camp light.

Was he watching her? Despite the cold air prickling against her exposed skin, Alice was suddenly hot. She squinted, trying to see through the tent material, but the only thing visible was the faint glow of the fire.

She pulled on her remaining clothes as quickly as she could. Boy, it was tight in here. Were they really going to sleep in this tent? The two of them…together? Alone all night?

She emerged a minute later to find him staring into the dying fire.

"I was going to throw some more wood on," he said. "But we'd only have to put it out before bed."

That word echoed in her brain: *bed.*

"Yeah." She rejoined him on the tarp, but then Aaron rose to take care of his own needs. When he was done, he dragged their sleeping bags into the tent.

Alice lingered on the tarp near the last remnants of their fire, but she couldn't stay out here forever. And it was getting really cold now. He emerged from the tent and, without

saying a word, sprinkled some of the dirt he'd dug out of the fire pit over the dying coals.

That was it then. The fire was officially out. Nothing left to do but go to bed. In the tent. Alone with Aaron Malik. All. Night. Long.

He held the flap open for her. Alice swallowed, and her throat clicked again. Grabbing a bottle of water, she climbed in. He'd laid their sleeping bags out, side by side. Close. So close. But then again, he *did* say he'd slept five in a tent like this.

She snuggled down, resting her head on her blowup pillow. She'd never sleep. No way, no how.

"Do you snore?" she asked, voice barely above a whisper.

"Nope. At least, I've never heard it."

"Very funny. Well, I hope not."

"What about you? You snore?"

"Me? Never."

He laughed softly. "Do you think your parents will be mad when they find out you spent the night alone in a tent with a guy you hardly know?"

She was silent for a long time. How to answer? The truth was, her mother had probably forgotten she was even on this little outing. "Well, it's just me and my mom now. My dad – " And here's where it got hard.

When would it stop hurting so much? All the counselors and the grief books said it took time. That the pain would dull and eventually go away. But it had been over two years

since he'd gotten sick and nearly a year since he'd died. And it was almost as fresh as day one.

"You okay?" Aaron said.

"Yeah. Sorry. Spaced out there for a sec. My dad had cancer."

"Wow. I didn't know. That really sucks."

"Yeah."

He didn't say anything else, didn't try to comfort her or ply her with stupid, corny clichés, and she was grateful.

"What about you?" she said. "Will your parents be mad for sleeping out here with a girl?"

His sleeping bag rustled as he shook his head.

"Really? Why not?"

"Because they raised a proper Hindu boy. They know I'm a gentleman."

Some restless little flitting thing inside her settled down at those words. Only then did Alice realize she'd been frightened. She really *didn't* know him well. It was probably dumb to assume he was trustworthy. But for some reason, she believed his words.

And yet, a part of her was disappointed too, that he wasn't going to try anything with her.

"That must be nice," Alice said. "To be so close to your religion. We're Catholic but only go to church on holidays. Maybe you can tell me about Hinduism sometime."

"Sure," he said, voice gone sleepy.

"And in exchange, I'll teach you how to build a kick-ass fire."

"Deal," he said with a yawn.

Alice woke with a start, completely disoriented as to where she was. She felt an arm wrapped around her – heavy, warm, almost protective – and a body pressed against hers.

Aaron.

As the memories of their situation came back, she became aware of his sleep-breath gently tickling her neck. He stirred slightly, snuggling closer.

The layers of sleeping bag separating them felt both too thin and too thick.

She stiffened, not knowing what to do. But her eyes were so heavy, and he was so warm. One of Aaron's hands, resting against her, moved with her every breath. Not really meaning to, she covered it with her own hand, pulling it more firmly to her. Then Alice let her eyelids close until sleep took her again.

When she woke, Aaron was still there. She'd rolled over in the night, and he was watching her.

He smiled when she opened her eyes. "Morning. Sleep okay?"

"Like the dead. You?"

"Same."

She sat up. "My hair must be a mess." She felt her head, and indeed, her blond curls were sticking up at all angles. "What time is it?"

Aaron's jeans were in a pile next to his sleeping bag. He pulled a chain watch out of his pocket and snapped it open. "A little after six. And your hair looks fine, but your breath is awful."

"Hey." She hit him with her pillow. It had deflated in the night, so all it did was brush limply off his arm.

"Oh, you're dangerous. I'd better watch out."

"Like your breath is any better."

Alice scrambled from her sleeping bag, planning to go right for her toothbrush, but Aaron grabbed her arm, and she plopped onto the warm pile of down.

"I'm just kidding," he said. "You're fine."

"I seriously doubt that." Just to be safe, she held her breath. "We'd better get going. Find the group."

"Yeah." But instead of untangling himself from his own sleeping bag, Aaron wrapped his arms around her and pulled her back down. He snuggled up against her back, and she felt that warm protective weight from last night.

"Isn't this nicer?" he asked. "It always takes me forever to get out of bed."

"I think I'm okay with that," she whispered.

All she wanted to do was roll over and wrap her arms around him, too. But she couldn't move.

He pulled her even closer. "Alice."

"Hmm?" She didn't trust herself to say anything more because he was nuzzling his nose in her hair.

"I have a secret to confess."

"Yeah?" she whispered.

"Mrs. Kasbrack."

"Wait, what? My guidance counselor?"

"Uh-huh. I kind of told her about Wilderland. That you might be interested."

"You did?"

She felt his nod.

"After Morris Beach. After meeting you."

"Wait a minute. Wait a minute." Alice rolled over and propped herself up on her elbow so she could look him in the face. "You did what?"

"Are you mad?"

"Mad? Why would I be mad? But why'd you do it?"

"I used to see you sometimes. With your camera. You'd get this look on your face when you knew what you wanted to shoot. The same look you had when you were working on the fire last night."

And she thought he'd been totally focused on the tent.

"You'd kind of square your shoulders and straighten your back. And then you'd breathe. It was like yoga, how naturally your finger snapped the pic in time with your exhale."

His words burned inside her with a glow too big for her body to contain. Unlike anyone else in her life, Aaron had *seen* her, *known* her. She felt more naked, more exposed, than last night half-dressed in the tent.

And she'd been completely, utterly clueless.

"But then," he said, "your pics stopped showing up in the school paper. What happened?"

"After my dad…" She shrugged.

He nodded, and Alice knew he got it. She didn't need to elaborate, didn't need to talk about how hard it got to simply manage the essentials let alone try to hold down an extracurricular on the school paper.

"I wanted to see you again after Morris Beach, but I didn't know how to ask. And since you always kept to yourself, always went home right after school…"

Aaron Malik, like his Vedic hare: the guy who jumped higher and ran faster than all the rest; who all the girls whispered about in class; the star lacrosse player; the head of the Ecology Club and the Green Movement at school. Just thinking about him made her feel about an inch tall, invisible.

That Aaron Malik had wanted to ask her out. And it had taken getting stranded in the woods for it to happen. Why? Because she'd been totally spaced, preoccupied with herself and her problems. Wishing for him, yet hiding away all the same.

"You're not mad?" he asked.

"Of course I'm not mad."

"So, what do you say?"

Her brain fluttered as though filled with flapping butterflies. Could this be real? Was she still sleeping? No. In a dream her hair would look good.

She felt a stupid smile spread across her face, but who cared how dumb she looked. Aaron Malik just asked her out.

"I guess so," she said. "After all, we *did* sleep together…"

They ate a breakfast of dark chocolate and raisins, and shared her last granola bar. Then Aaron finished the two remaining weenies right out of the jar.

"Eew," Alice said. "Cold?"

"Sorry, but they were saying *eat me*."

They broke camp after breakfast, and Alice followed Aaron through the brush, watching his white rabbit bob and sway until they found the path again. They stepped out of the shade of the trees into the dappled sunlight of a golden August morning.

Alice turned her face up to the sky, eyes closed, glorying in the feel of the sun and the brush of the breeze across her skin. She breathed deeply, glad she was here. With him. She'd hidden away with her misery for far too long, but no more.

Without really knowing why, she pulled out her camera and snapped off a shot of Aaron's rabbit. A reminder to never waste time again.

"Aaron." He turned, an eyebrow raised. "Getting stranded could've really sucked. But it didn't. Because I was with you."

Alice stretched up on her tiptoes and pressed her lips gently to his cheek. She caught the lingering aromas of wood smoke from his hair and the ghost of cologne from his warm skin. Aaron inhaled in surprise then turned his head so his lips brushed hers. Just the slightest touch at first, like he wasn't sure.

But she was.

Alice put a hand on Aaron's shoulder, and that was all he needed. His arms went around her. One hand stopped to rest

on the small of her back. Fingers tangled in her hair, pulling at the strands like a shivery weight. She pressed into his chest, so solid, so real. He took over the kiss, his lips both soft and firm. She opened her mouth to him, to his taste, and then Alice was falling, falling…

She pulled away with a shaky breath and rested her forehead against his collarbone where she'd bumped it the day before.

"When we get back later," Aaron said into her hair, "maybe I can come over and help you with your Northland application."

She smiled up at him, and he kissed the tip of her nose before taking her hand.

Aaron led Alice down the trail. Where it narrowed, she followed and watched his white rabbit, letting it guide her back to camp.

Back to life.

Jessica Bayliss's love for reading goes all the way back to the sixth grade book bin, and it's never faded. She writes across genres and age groups, but Jessica's dearest dream is to dazzle the hearts of young readers.

THE AVIARY

CRYSTAL SCHUBERT

EVEN A CASTLE CAN BE A CAGE.

FOR JACK AND JIM.

Some days I avoid the aviary completely. It's hard to watch my winged friends wilt to bone and feather. To see them dead among the molding rug of leaves, disintegrating back into earth. Father hasn't sent anyone beyond the castle walls for nearly a year, and my birdies have all grown ill from thin scraps of cast-off meat.

I buried the first few, delicately wrapping them in cotton from an old dressing gown. Their graves were dutifully tended, and I cried for each bird in turn. Pearl gray and sky blue and pitch black, all reconvening in the Great Beyond. I long for the din of squawks and chirps and titters. I long for the novelty of death.

Last night a parakeet died, leaving its partner in mourning. I left his body on the aviary floor, but I realized there are only three birds left. Father's vacant stare and unpredictable outbursts have kept me quiet, and the cost of my silence has mounted.

I wait until breakfast. Meals are when Father is most pliant. "I've been thinking," I say. "Is there not better food to send to the aviary?"

Clarey and Pollock glance at each other. Min stares at his plate. I don't know why we still use these large plates when portions are so meager.

"There isn't any food." Father finishes his carrot.

I finger a tear in my brocade gown, because I can't look in his eyes. Not much fatherly warmth is left in them. "My birds are dying. Can't we at least let them go?"

His mouth twitches, and for a moment, I think he might say yes. He stands, his voice throaty and calm. "Would they

fare better amidst the plague-worn counties? They don't know how to forage or avoid predators. They'd never survive in the wild, Alice."

"But Father – "

"You have my answer." He turns his back on me to leave.

Clarey and Pollock slouch, as though we've just avoided conflict, but Min's muscles tense. He knows I'm not ready to give up. "Can't we just – ?"

"No." Father spins back around and charges toward me. My back flattens against the chair, and fire spreads through my chest. Min plugs his ears. This was a bad idea. Bad, bad idea. "We can't *just* anything. Shall I tell your mother about this incessant chatter and *whining?*"

"I'm sorry, Father." The response is automatic. Mother is gone, of course, but Father keeps a running list of our transgressions for when we see her in the Great Beyond. His breath smells rotten, like he's hiding bird carcasses in his stomach. But he can't be; he's all bone with nowhere to keep them.

His arms and legs quiver, a storm of limbs. I try not to flinch. So far he's only hit the servants, but he becomes less predictable by the day. He turns to the portrait of Mother above the fireplace. "Forgive me, Evie," he huffs. "I can't handle them like you could." When he storms out of the dining hall, the wooden door slams behind him.

Min frowns and Clarey squints at me, her dark eyes propped up by black under-eye circles. "You should've let it go."

Pollock's fork clatters onto the empty plate in front of him. "No one cares about you and your stupid birds."

"No one cares about any of us," I snap, and Min's frown deepens. Tears shine in his eyes, and I immediately regret my uncharitable spirit. "Except you, Min. Everyone cares about you."

But all three of them are done eating, and so am I, and there's no time to make things right as everyone disperses. They'll forgive me by dinnertime.

Alone, my footsteps are light on the threadbare castle rugs. I head to the garden, diverting briefly to my rooms to gather my cloak.

Mother could've defused Father, but I am not Mother. She would've said something wise. Her magic was in words, ivy twining around Father's arguments until the vines slowly overtook him. He was happy to be overtaken. It had to be magic, the way she soothed Father's nerves and still managed to nurture four children. But without her, no one can topple Father's resolve. He is dusty and angry, his heart hidden away like the wine casks in our cellar. He clutches us so tightly we might shatter. Keeping us safe until we can all be with Mother again.

I trail my fingers along the rough hedges. Clouds cloak the castle turrets, reaching their foggy fingers down to brush the top of the glass aviary. Echoes of our chickens bounce between the dried-out shrubbery and barren plots. The overcast sky saps any warmth from the air, and even vibrant spring sun can't edge through.

I note the servant's position, harvesting carrots in the small plot I built. Not much of our soil is rich enough to support food, but I've been rotating the crop across a few different sections of garden. Min is already on duty, holding a woven basket, his thin arms shaking under the weight. Even from here, I can tell he wants to drop the basket, but he will not. I would set the basket down, take a break, but sweet Min can deny himself every comfort if he believes someone else will benefit.

They are engaged in the harvest, and I slip through a hole in the hedge, branches scraping across my gown and snagging on my cloak, until I'm in Mother's sanctuary. If anyone remembers this small, hidden garden is here, they've not said as much. I've not seen a soul here after Mother passed away. The fountain is green with algae, but this sanctuary has the only blossoming flowers that remain. Violets and Bleeding Hearts. They come each spring, and I think Mother is still here somewhere, willing them to sprout.

Ivy tangles around the dirty birch trellises. A thin floral scent lingers, barely detectable, but enough to dredge up the fragile memory of Mother's skirt folds. The overgrown greenery reminds me, despite stagnancy inside the castle, life marches on.

I pull my cloak tight around me, like an embrace, and sit on a stone bench to wait.

A few moments later, the tall outer hedges rustle and then a whisper: "Alice?"

"Diana?"

"*King Jasper, King Luca, Queen Wen in a trance…*"

I smile. It is Diana. I whisper back my half of the rhyme. *"Ate all of the banquet and split down their pants!"*

We stifle our giggles. It's immature, at our age, to delight in such drollery, but there's little amusement to be found elsewhere. My hand finds hers through the prickly hedge, and we link pinkies. Her skin is velvet against mine. The first time we held hands, when we were younger, I washed ten times. I thought I brought plague into the castle, and I was up all night, watching for fever or skin lesions or ragged coughing. But now I trust Diana.

Anyway, we've never spoken of plague. She doesn't ask why I'm behind these walls, and I don't ask why she comes to visit me. I know when she first found the hedge and heard me crying in Mother's sanctuary, she envied me for living in a fairy tale. I envied her adventures. We wove our experiences together and built beautiful stories through the hedge. Faraway lands and brave knights and lost girls.

"I thought of you yesterday," she tells me. "I swam at Cherry Lake and anchored myself behind the waterfalls. The mist sprayed my face. I remembered what you said about missing the rain."

"Father doesn't like us to get cold and wet. After Mother, he worries," I say absently as I try to imagine Diana in the lake. It's been so long since I've seen waterfalls, but I can still picture them – rushing water, sliding around rocks and flinging itself off cliffs. It's Diana I can't picture. Is her hair silken draping over her shoulder? Would her hips curve beneath my hands? Are her eyes as warm as her skin?

Her voice is doleful and delicate, like the minor keys of my piano. "I wished you were there beside me."

My heart skips, and I'm thankful she can't see the flush creep across my cheeks. "Finish telling the story from last week. The one about King Jasper and the bird."

And as she does, my sorrows unfurl and slip from my body. Thoughts of dwindling food supplies and plague and dying birds can't reach me inside the story. I find my way into her words and live there.

Diana never comes two days in a row. Her family shares a single horse among nine people. On the days she skips, my lungs take a dramatic pause. Air is thinner. Our tapestries more faded and my hunger more pronounced.

I check the hens' nests for the twelfth time this week. Still empty. My stomach bubbles. Without eggs, without chickens – can we subsist on only carrots and cabbage? The next step is scouring nearby villages for food left behind, but can we be sure it's safe to eat? Would Father even let anyone leave the walls?

As the oldest, it feels my duty to fill in the gaps between Father's resolve and our familial well-being. But then Father will do something stupid, like kill our last rooster, insisting it would taste worse the longer it lived. Now we've no way to breed our remaining chickens, and the ones we have aren't laying.

My body cannibalizes itself; the deep pain gnaws my insides. I need my flock. Their twittering helps turn the gears in my brain.

When I walk through the glass aviary doors, familiar musty air greets me. My yellow parakeet alights on a branch beside me, desperate for company now that his friends have passed.

After a few minutes, I find my two cockatoos conspiring in the upper corner.

But something is amiss. All three birds are accounted for and still alive, and I can't figure out why I feel something is wrong until I see it – a brilliant blue macaw. Vibrantly colored among the brown and gray.

I creep toward the strange bird, careful not to spook it.

Even as I reach out my hand, the bird is still as a statue. I stroke a feather, and he presses against my fingers. "This is no place for such a beautiful bird. Do you belong to one of our neighbors? Have you lost your family to plague?"

The thought makes me wince, but I can't move away. Plague or no plague, the blue macaw draws me in. His eyes are icy blue, dancing with life. I touch his head, then his beak. He's docile. Submissive. And then he's not.

Squawk. Squawk.

I stumble backward, and the macaw spreads its wings, flapping wildly. Feathers fall away, scattering along the aviary floor, revealing tan skin underneath. Wings stretch and thin until they resemble arms. That can't be right.

His talons lengthen and become toes; thin bird legs puff up until they're meaty, and it's really happening. The macaw is becoming human.

It only takes a minute, and then instead of a bird, a young girl stands before me. Golden curls cascade down her front, hanging past her waist. The macaw's frosted blue eyes are hers, and I back up and up until I am against a dead tree trunk.

Her plain blue dress is faded, stained, but it doesn't matter. She is exquisite. Rounded cheeks and long, thin frame. Rosebud lips. I can't stop staring at her lips.

"Alice," she says. I'd recognize that minor-key voice anywhere. But it can't be. How?

My whole body shivers and darkness creeps in at the edge of my vision.

"You don't recognize me?" Tucked into her leather belt is the small stuffed rabbit that Mother sewed for me out of scrap cloth. An offering of friendship passed through the hedge when we were children, when I took Mother's gifts for granted. It's still white. Clean. Taken care of. Black button eyes peek out at me.

She steps forward and I try to step back again, but there's nowhere to go. I trip over the trunk's roots and tumble to the ground, my hands jabbed by fallen branches. She reaches out to help me, but I rear back.

Plague. Plague. *Everyone outside is infected*, Father said. Not Diana. I never believed it about Diana, and this girl sounds like Diana, but how hard is it to imitate a voice? She has my rabbit. I'm afraid to let myself believe.

I pull myself up to stand. "King Jasper, King Luca, Queen Wen in a trance…"

The girl stops. "I thought you'd know me. I knew you right away."

"Are you infected?"

"Infected?"

"Plague." I examine her flawless skin and the whites of her eyes.

She cocks her head, compassion drawn on her features. "Is that why you never leave? Plague hasn't been seen in the High Counties for nearly five years."

"You're lying." I straighten my back. "I'm calling the guard."

She sighs. "Ate all of the banquet and split down their pants."

"What did you say?"

Neither of us laugh this time.

"Ate. All. Of. The. Banquet – "

"I heard," I say. "But it can't be you."

A smile tugs at her red lips. "Why not?"

"Diana is not a bird."

"I saved money. Bought avian elixir from the mage. I came here to rescue you and take you home with me."

"Rescue me?" I laugh.

"You're locked in this castle. Even you said you missed the outside world."

"I'd rather be safe inside these walls with my family than risk dying."

She shakes her head. "I told you. Plague is long gone."

"Father would've told us." Yes, he was wrecked with grief after Mother's death, but with the food shortage

looming, all of our animals dying around us – he talks of keeping us safe until we can be with Mother, but he wouldn't keep us barricaded in the castle without reason. Would he?

"I've brought elixir for you, too. We can fly away together. Swim at Cherry Lake. Feel rain on our cheeks." As if on cue, her cheeks pink.

"What about Min? Clarey and Pollock? Father?"

Diana looks at the mottled floor of decomposing leaves. "This isn't about them. This is about *us*."

Her spearmint scent is intoxicating; I'm dizzy.

"Us?" I echo. It's the first hint she's ever given that *us* might mean something bigger. That she might be staring too long at my lips, too. In my fantasy world there is an us and a happily ever after, but I never imagined there could be an us in the harsh light of day.

She glances up through long lashes. "I'm-I-don't know how to – "

I step forward and touch her skin as cautiously as I approached the macaw. She's real. Her skin is the same velvet I've dreamt about.

She comes closer and our faces align. My knees buckle. I can't look away.

Her breath on my cheek is ragged and hot.

I can't breathe. I stop trying.

"I-I think – " she stutters again.

I close the space between us and touch my lips to hers. My eyes open, gauging her reaction. Her mouth is soft and yields to mine. I shut my eyes, and blood runs thick and

jittery through my veins. I don't want to stop, but I don't want Min or one of the others to find us here.

"Come with me." I pull her out of the aviary, her elegant long arm a strand of ribbon connecting us. *Us.*

We stand behind the garden shed, and I peer out. No servants. No siblings. We run, breath puffing out in tiny clouds, heading toward the hidden sanctuary. Diana giggles as I drag her behind me, and I want so badly for her to clamp her beautiful mouth before we're caught.

And then, Clarey's deep-throated voice booms across the garden. "Alice. Father's waiting on the eggs, but – "

The three of us stop. Wind whistles through dried-out branches.

"Clarey – "

"What's going on? Who are you?" Clarey's hard, dark eyes eat away at Diana's smile until it shrinks on her face. Clarey cuts her eyes at me next. "What have you done?"

"It's not what you think," I explain. "Diana isn't infected. The Plague is gone." Neither Clarey nor Pollock inherited Mother's empathy, so I know this cannot end well.

Her muscles tense. "Everyone is infected."

Diana drops my hand and leaves a cold spot behind. "I'm not – "

"*Everyone* is infected." Clarey looks from me to Diana and back again. "You've damned us all." Then she runs fast toward the castle door.

"She'll tell Father." The cloistered garden air is not enough to fill my lungs. It's stale and oppressive, musty from

years of confinement, and in this moment I can no longer breathe it. It's spoiled like old meat.

Diana coos in my ear: "Inhale. Exhale. It's going to be okay."

I do as she says. It's not helping. "You don't understand. He'll lock you up. Quarantined."

"I'm a bird." She smiles. Those red lips. Those crinkled eyes. "I have more elixir. I can fly."

I look at the aviary. "This is a dangerous place for birds." She doesn't know Father. I haven't told her about how his eyes have gone dead. How he still talks to Mother. How none of us can reason with him or predict his reactions anymore.

"Come with me, then."

"I can't." What will they do when the food runs out? I'm the green thumb. The only one who plans for our future needs. Who will take care of them?

For the first time, Diana's face betrays a hint of annoyance. "You want to stay here? Caged? This is not a life. We can have a life together."

"We'll meet by the hedges. It can be enough." After tasting her kiss, I know I can sustain myself for months, powered only by the promise of more.

"We can't do this through the hedges." She entwines me in her ribbon arms, her rosebud lips on mine, and the dead garden drops so far away I think I've already transformed into a bird and I'll come crashing down at any time.

She pulls two small green bottles from the leather satchel on her belt. She hasn't mentioned my rabbit, but he's still there. Safe against the curve of her hip. "All it takes is one

brief moment of courage," she says, "and you can change your life forever."

My thoughts turn to Min, but even if his arms shake, he'll hold himself together. I picture rain and swimming and open air. Snow and grass and the smell of pastured sheep. I miss being surrounded in things that are sparkling with life. And I want to keep feeling that soaring feeling encased in Diana's kisses. I want her arms. Her hips. Her lips.

If Diana is right, that plague has disappeared from the High Counties, I could be happy on the outside. I'd be one less mouth for Father to feed.

Linking my pinky with Diana's, I take one of her bottles and gulp it down before thinking any more.

Within seconds, my arms are scaled with red feathers.

Min's small face appears in the castle doorway, his mouth dropped open. I wish I knew what he was thinking. *How? or impossible or please stay.*

My limbs shrink, my toes become sharp talons, and my dark hair molts onto the garden ground.

I can't stop it now, even if I wanted to.

The castle drops away, my family turning into ants below. Flying is easier than I expected. My strong wings do all the work. It's best this way, because if I had to really think about it, I might drop from the sky, heart too heavy to fly.

I push forward to catch up with the brilliant blue macaw. Diana. She leads me over lush green forest, and I dip down into the shady branches, letting crisp green leaves brush my wings. The fresh organic smell sings to me, siren songs of the world I've missed.

When I pop back out, we are cresting Dryer's Hill, the old farmhouse not abandoned but thriving with cows and sheep munching sweet grass side by side. Father told us there wasn't a living soul within fifty miles. Did he just not know?

Once over the hill, more farms stretch out in a patchwork of crops. Life everywhere.

He couldn't have known.

Finally, Diana angles down into a patch of gray woods and we land in front of a ramshackle house freckled with peeling paint. The walls list precariously to the right, as though seeking out sunlight from the dark forest floor.

Diana transforms back with a squawk, leaving a bed of blue feathers at her feet. "Imagine arms and legs and all the experiences that are uniquely human. That's how you turn back."

I picture my wings becoming arms, but it doesn't work.

"It might take a second." Her smile is beatific.

My talons stay talons, despite memories of feet. I think of my family and the stone castle walls, feeling trapped. Then I think of Diana. Our conversations through the hedge, making up our own fairy tales to drown out the sorrows of our lives. Her velvet touch. My hand on the small of her back. Wanting to kiss her neck and whisper into her ear. Red lips.

I'm still thinking of her when I feel taller and realize that I, too, am standing on a bed of feathers.

"What did you think of?" she asks.

My face is on fire. "Arms and legs. Running. Dancing."

Diana's skin glows in the bare light that reaches us through the canopy. "I thought of you."

Now, I wish I'd told the truth.

She directs me inside the leaning house. "It's not a castle, but it's everything we have."

We walk into a small room with ceilings low enough to touch. Tattered red curtains frame slanted windows. An older woman sits by the fire, sewing a patch on a small pair of pants, and several children sit at the long table, playing cards. Toasted logs crackle in a fireplace, and it *feels* like a home. Behind the table, an intricate tapestry shows a pastoral scene with birds in flight above golden wheat fields. Two more kids rip into the room, chasing each other and laughing.

Diana introduces me to her family, and every one of them gives hugs to rival Min's.

"Is this the girl?" her mother asks.

Diana nods, flushing red down to her neck.

"You've chosen well."

Now I'm flushed, too. The children giggle. They're always giggling.

As night slides down over the hovel, shadows creep over her beautiful face and we talk like through the hedges. Hopes. Dreams. Fairy tales. The rooms darken and Diana's mother lights candles.

"We can live here," Diana says, golden light flickering over her features.

I nod and smile, my eyes misting. I could really live here.

With my life on hold, in a house of constant mourning, I'd forgotten how varied the shades of color could be. There's the deep green of a turtle's rough skin and the yellow-green of a sunlit valley. The pale blue of open sky and the clear, shimmering blue of clean water. Diana and I tour the countryside like we've never seen leaves or bugs or flowers.

We while away hours swimming, hiking up mountains, and finding tufts of grass to make our beds. Then memorizing the hushed trickle of a creek as we ghost our fingers across each other's skin, from armpit to hip to thigh to calf. Dappled light pokes through the branches and plays across her creamy tan skin.

I can touch her. There's no more fantasy or wondering. What does the inside of her belly button look like? I can look and find out. It's a swirl of folded skin, tucked daintily in the middle of her stomach. Her back? A constellation birthmark. A long, beaded spine that bends with swanlike grace.

I almost forget Min. Clarey and Pollock. Father. Almost. Thoughts of them shiver in my periphery, mirages in the distance until Diana pulls me back in and drowns me in kisses. Until her ribbon-arms tug me to a mountain or a valley or our favorite: Cherry Lake.

The lake is a blob of water with uneven edges that cut deep into the forest and curve back anxiously, like a baby bird testing the strength of its wings. Above, a quiet bridge looks down on the biggest part of the lake. The waterfall, falling as if from the road itself, mutes everything outside of us. *Us.*

We're at Cherry Lake when we hear them, even over the thunderous waterfall. Horses on the bridge. Gruff men's voices shouting.

"Does he really think we'll find his daughter? They were birds. They flew."

"They could be anywhere."

"Why did you promise him anything?"

"Did you see the sacks of gold?"

Father. He's sent men out in search of us. Not his own men. He doesn't have many left. I wonder how he found these men. Did he allow them into the castle? Did he leave?

We stay hidden beneath the waterfall as the men pass by on the road above and thoughts chip away at some truth inside my brain. Birds cheep from the trees surrounding us, and my thoughts streamline and fall into place. He spoke with these men. Father knows. The plague is gone and Father knows.

When we walk back to the hovel, we don't take the road but crouch and hide in the shadows. Both of us quiet, though I'm bursting with questions:

When did he know?

Why would he keep this from us?

How could he?

Father was not fencing out the world, but fencing in his family. Starving us. Until we could be with Mother. The realization shatters me. He was killing us.

Diana pauses as we round a tree and the hovel comes into view. She turns to me and tucks a strand of hair behind my ear. "I think it's safe to talk now. If you want to."

"Father knew about everything. He wasn't our protector; he was our warden."

She frowns. "What do you want to do?"

"Min, Clarey, Pollock. I have to go back for them."

I borrow a sturdier gown from Diana's closet, and it fits me like she does – perfectly. I tie one of her belts around my waist.

Diana tucks Mother's little white rabbit into the belt. "For courage." She links her pinky with mine. Her little finger is a counterweight, keeping my mind firmly set on the task ahead. I lean in and kiss her. Her mouth still tastes like freedom, even as we head back toward my former cage.

Our boots scuff the dirt road, fogging our feet with dust. All the hiking has strengthened my legs, and we come upon the Dryer's Hill farm long before I thought we might. The road snakes past the farm and into the forest. The smell is still green and pure, all the freshness rushes into my brain.

We plod along quietly, and less than a mile later, the woods part and the castle gates tower above us.

No servant stands guard. Unusual. The few remaining must've formed part of the search party. The outer hedge is impossibly tall and thick – the middle fortified with narrowly-spaced iron bars. Precautions against the onslaught of plague. I once felt so safe inside the confines of our garden. Father showed me all the ways we were protected from outsiders. It's eerie to know the truth. I finger the stuffed rabbit in my belt. We've been little rabbits since Mother's death, caught in Father's snare, and thanking him for our shackles.

The others need to know.

Just then, Pollock strolls by in his armed guard uniform. Father always let him patrol when guards were needed elsewhere.

"Lock!" I wave my arm through the wrought iron gate. "It's me, Alice!"

Pollock isn't close to the gate, but he backs away all the same. He glances behind me, at Diana, and his eyes widen. "Get out of here," he hisses.

"I have news!" I call out. "The plague is over."

He shakes his head, dark curls bouncing. "I'm warning you, Alice. Leave!"

My own brother, turning me away. But it's too late. Father's voice booms from across the courtyard as he storms into the gateway. "Open the gates!"

I barely have time to register Pollock's betrayal and distrust before I'm rushed into the courtyard, Diana at my side.

Father embraces me. His heavy black mourning cloak falls off his bony shoulders and nearly pulls me under, too. He sighs. "Alice. My Alice."

I pull back. Question myself. Maybe he really didn't know. So, I tell him, "Father, it's gone."

His hand is heavy on my arm. "What's gone, Little Dove?"

"Plague."

He shakes his head and looks at Diana. His eyes narrow. "She'd have you believe that, wouldn't she?"

"I saw it with my own – "

"Vile temptress," Father spits the words as he motions to two guards behind him. "Take her to the north turret."

"You can't." Locked away from the rest of the castle. Windows barred. No escape. I grip Diana's hand. "Stop."

"Alice." Her eyes are full of questions. Confusion. Fear.

My heart feels rubbed raw, every beat blisters in my chest. I try to hang on to her ribbon-arms, but the guards wrench her from my grasp. "Diana." Before I can chase her, two other guards flank me, their sturdy hands cinching my wrists together. "Father, what – ?"

"I can't risk it, Little Dove." He won't look at me. "You could be infected."

Pollock stares on, helpless. Tears in his eyes. He'd been trying to warn me. The guards drag me between them. "I'm not. I'm not infected."

"We shall know in time."

Food is scarce in the south turret. I only hope Diana is being fed at all. Being away from her is like missing a limb.

I get bird food. Scraps of near-rotten meat, carrots, and cabbage. One of the guards apologizes to me. Says it's all he's allowed to give. Father doesn't want to waste proper food if I'm to die anyway.

It's been several days, and so far, only Min has come to see me. He slipped fresh boiled chicken and carrots beneath the door. I inhale them greedily.

When I'm done, I see that his shadow is still there outside the door. "Min."

"Alice."

"You have to know I'd never bring plague into our home. I'd never risk the family."

"I know," he whispers.

"Father is letting you die. Letting *us* die." A knot in my throat strangles my voice. "To be with Mother."

Min doesn't respond. His body shuffles around outside the door.

"So it's not – there's no one infected at all? Out there?" His voice shakes, confronting the giant crevasse between the world we thought we knew and the one that really exists.

"It all looked the same. It looked better than the same."

I hear his body slump against the door. "Tell me about it."

I tell him about the river we found, rocks worn smooth from water. The acrobatic fish tossing themselves into the air. I paint a picture for him with as many colors as I can name.

"I'm afraid." His voice is tiny. "Will Father really let us die?"

"You should go. Take Pollock and Clarey. You all should have a life."

Min doesn't respond, and I know it's because he can't. He can't respond because he can't leave. He won't leave me.

"Can you bring any food to Diana? Do you know where she's being held?"

"In the north turret. I brought her my breakfast this morning. The guards aren't allowed to bring her anything."

My eyes melt into tears, thinking of his dinner I just polished off. "But what will you eat, Min?"

Nothing. That is what he'll eat. We both know.

"We all missed you," he says.

I poke a finger under the door to touch his hand. "I missed you, too."

The next night, he brings Clarey and Pollock, and they each pass slivers of cabbage under the door in exchange for my stories. I regale them with descriptions of the waterfall at Cherry Lake, careful not to dwell on my swimming partner for fear of bursting into tears.

I painstakingly describe the meal Diana's mother cooked us over the fire. Fresh fish. Salty and light. Fish was one of Mother's favorites.

They weren't sure whether to believe me, but when Clarey asked Father about the rumors — that the plague was gone — he struck her across the face. And then they knew.

"Tomorrow is chicken pie. I'll bring you my slice," Min says.

I want to refuse, but I am weak from hunger.

The next evening he comes alone and makes good on his promise. Chicken pie. His shoes click away as fast as they approached.

I bite into the pie, and my teeth quiver on something hard and metal. I dig it out – a key.

The key is loud in the lock. Clanging, metal on metal. At night, no one is around to hear it. I creep down and down the spiral stairs until I come out near Min's rooms, and he slips out to meet me. I don't even have to knock. He must've been waiting.

We pass Clarey's room. Min taps once on the bottom of her door, and she quietly comes out to joins us. Then Pollock. They fall in line behind me, a string of somber ducklings. We waddle toward the north turret, and there on the bottom step, clutching a key of her own, is Diana. My Diana.

I run to her, my tattered borrowed skirts dragging across the stone floor. She holds out her arms, and I don't slow down. I crash into her. Somewhere beneath the grime is spearmint, subtle and sweet. My body is complete again.

With five of us, it's nearly impossible to keep quiet. We try and fail, feet skittering and clothes rustling. Small whispers bruise the silence.

"Are we really leaving?"

"We have to."

"What about Father?"

We pass his room last before heading downstairs to the parlor. When he hears us approach, his skeleton body darkens the doorway.

I stand in front of everyone, stretching out my arms to protect them. "We're leaving."

"You're staying," he rasps.

"It's over," I say. "Mother wouldn't want this."

"I'm to protect you." He steps forward. "I promised."

From behind me, Clarey clears her throat, her voice thick. "You're killing us."

Pollock pushes forward. "We can't live like this. We miss Mother, but she's gone and we're not."

"I don't want to go with her," Min whispers. "Not yet."

Father stares at us. Eyes branching from one to the next, twitching. Filling with more emotion than I've seen since Mother's funeral. "Go." He falls against the wall then shoves back into his room.

I reach for the door. "Father – "

"*Leave.*"

And there's nothing left to say. The five of us race downstairs, no longer playing at silence.

"Wait." Diana shouts and diverts our path toward the aviary. She props open the door with a fallen branch. We don't wait for the birds, who are so accustomed to their cages they might never leave. Instead, we run – Clarey and Pollock ahead of us, Min behind – until we're through the gate.

That night, we all sleep huddled in blankets on the grass in front of the hovel.

Under the stars.

 Crystal Schubert lives in Richmond, Virginia with her husband, son, and cat. She graduated from Virginia Commonwealth University with a BA in English. She's a sucker for love stories.

BROKEN TETHERS

HOLLY ODELL

BY GETTING LOST, YOU MIGHT JUST FIND YOURSELF.

TO MY SON, CALEB.

Black crows punctuated the damp April morning with bleak conversation. Long-neglected hedges and comically unkempt shrubbery guarded the perimeter of a vast, overgrown property. A young woman fought her way through the snarled branches and emerged from a particularly slovenly-looking clump of bushes. Her appearance suggested she had already endured a gauntlet of physical indignities, of which this was the culmination.

"Come on, Alice." She perked up. "Urban exploration is a dirty business. I should've thought about how messy this was actually going to be, though." Next time she'd bring a towel, and…she looked down at her clothes…maybe a plastic jumpsuit, on second thought. Wiping her muddy hands down the front of her jacket, she shifted attention to the object of her efforts.

At last she had a clear view of the mansion. Alice gasped. Abandoned for decades, it had slumped into an exquisite state of disrepair. "What a spectacular wreck."

Things of beauty succumbing to the ravages of time and nature sent her heart leaping into her throat. Was it the catharsis of tragedy, the ache of nostalgia for a bygone age that thrilled her so much? Or the fact that she wasn't supposed to be here? D, all of the above.

She forgave herself a mischievous chuckle at the thought of her phone ringing in the medicine cabinet where she "accidentally" left it. Why was the concept of voluntary solitude so difficult for some people to grasp? Certain places practically clobbered you over the head, demanding to be designated as tether-free zones. Nothing can rip the

cheesecloth from the lens of a Tolkien-esque excursion faster than a techno ringtone or someone handing you their soda so they can pee in the bushes while badgering you about how late it's getting. A badass adventuress can only tolerate so much pestering; she was entitled to a little harmless payback.

Her eyes roamed across the decaying exterior as she strode through the long grass to the top of the hill. After rummaging for a moment she produced a small digital camera from her pocket and took a picture of thick, tangled vines embracing the chimney, which lurched as if recoiling from the side of the house. She relished a delicious gothic shiver before resuming her assessment of the formidable structure.

The front door was boarded up and the porch was an obvious deathtrap, so she began checking windows. "Ah, I think we've found a winner." She pushed up with all her strength. "Half-open will have to be good enough," she muttered. Judging by the condition of the wood and surrounding vines, this had been a popular entrance for previous visitors. "Wait, my leg – whoa!" She pitched through headfirst and tumbled to the floor. Narrowing her eyes at the windowsill, she brushed herself off and surveyed the room.

"Well, nice fireplace. Hideous wallpaper, though." What had they been drinking when they picked it out? She wrinkled her nose.

Alice peeked into the main hallway, where a moldy aroma promptly greeted her nostrils. A grand staircase sagged in a manner that did not inspire confidence. She grimaced in disappointment. Upstairs was probably out of the question.

The flash from her camera made the dusty chandelier sparkle, likely for the first time in ages. Where to go next? A door on the other side of the hall was half-open. It issued a shrill creak as she pushed it farther and peered in. She widened her eyes and let out an awestruck whistle.

It was a chaotic sight. What had clearly been a library looked as if it had been turned upside down, shaken vigorously, then placed right side up again. A large chasm in the center of the floor gaped open like a yawning mouth, and splintered floorboards protruded jaggedly from the sides like a set of decimated, wooden dentures. A corresponding hole moaned from the ceiling above it. Moving closer, Alice saw weak shafts of light stream down from somewhere above. Thunder rumbled. Rain gently spattered the windows and dripped down through the hole in the ceiling.

The floor must've rotted and some heavy piece of furniture must've crashed through. Twice. "Wish I'd seen that."

The room had been thoroughly ransacked. Very few books remained on the shelves; the majority teetered in haphazard piles and towers on the floor, pages ripped out, shredded, and tossed around, giving the general appearance that a confetti cannon had gone off. An overturned desk with broken drawers, a large battered globe (likely kicked around like a soccer ball), pictures torn off the wall, window panes shattered, and the finishing touch: "REEDING IS STOOPID" spray-painted on the wall in bright red.

"Someone should've consulted a dictionary instead of ripping it up," she quipped, drinking in the visual assault. As

she photographed the damage, her emotions played tug-of-war. Thick spider webs clung to the ceiling and empty shelves. The cavernous hole gnashed its spiky jaws; the weak floorboards creaked and crunched with shards of glass. Not a place to be loitering longer than was necessary. Yet a stubborn desire to stay tugged at her like a persistent child.

As Alice turned to leave, something shiny caught her eye. At the bottom of a random pile of books, large gold letters leapt out at her: *Buddy Rabbit Takes A Nap*.

"I know that book." Her pulse quickened as she crept over and pulled it from the stack. "I had one just like it. Grandma read it to me all the time."

She sat cross-legged in the corner and studied it lovingly. A large, old children's book with a bright blue cover and thick board pages, and a stuffed Buddy Rabbit doll was anchored to the center of the final page. Each previous page had a Buddy-shaped cutout in the center so the doll was flush with the cover when it closed.

"Buddy's in such good shape considering how trashed it is in here." She brushed dust from his fur and opened the book.

Buddy Rabbit takes a nap,
Warm and cozy on your lap.
Stroke his fur, so soft and white,
Alice dutifully complied.

Join him as his dreams take flight.

She turned the page.

Buddy dreams about some bears,
Dancing gaily on the stairs.

She pushed a small lever up and down, and the little cardboard bear figures pranced on the staircase.

The next page showed the stuffed rabbit flanked by a pair of lovely silver wings.

Buddy dreams that he can fly!
Watch the stars go shooting by.

She pulled the lever back and forth gently and smiled as the stars glided across the page in their tracks. She skipped ahead to the final page, her favorite.

It's time for Buddy's nap to end.
Won't you wake him, faithful friend?
Just press his nose and you will see,
He's wide awake as he can be!

Alice pushed on his pink nose, and Buddy's eyes popped open cheerfully. "I must've done this a hundred times before." His little face looked so sweet and familiar, with eyes just as blue and twinkling as she remembered.

She stood up and leafed through the pages. "Buddy dreams about swimming, Buddy dreams about flowers, Buddy dreams of carrots, Buddy dreams about…SPIDERS!"

Two black spiders crawled across the page toward her hand. Reflexively, she flung the book away from herself and watched as it skidded and came to a stop uncomfortably close to the edge of the chasm. "Of course." As if she needed another reason to dislike spiders.

She struggled with herself for a moment, then sighed heavily. She patted the camera in her coat pocket, zipped it firmly, and approached the book as one would a bone lying next to a slumbering attack dog.

"This is probably the wrong decision." She got on her knees and strained forward to grab it. She then heard an ominous crack. "Yep." The floorboards gave way beneath her, and she plunged into darkness.

Alice opened her eyes then closed them again. It was equally dark both ways. Sprawled on her back, she searched around with her hands and guessed she had landed in a pile of soggy paper. Rolling over, she crawled through the squishy mess.

"I bet the vandals threw all this down here." The hill of mush sloped downward, and after a moment cold water splashed beneath her hands and knees. Her eyes began to adjust; a wide, shallow stream flowed away from the pulpy mound. She stood up and took physical inventory. No pain, no scratches, gashes, or splinters. After that plummet, it was difficult to believe.

"I'm either dreaming or incredibly lucky." She followed the trail of water, murky and speckled with shreds of paper.

After a few minutes she stopped and furrowed her brow. It didn't make sense. "I should've hit a wall by now. No basement is this big." A rectangular patch up ahead began to stand out from the surrounding darkness, like the hazy outline of a doorway. Alice approached it, reached forward, and her hand vanished. Startled, she drew it back. It felt normal and seemed unharmed. Did that actually just happen? Her growing curiosity soon eclipsed apprehension. She leaned forward, and her senses were overwhelmed by blue sky, lush green, warm sun on her face. She pulled her head back, and it was dark again. Forward. Back. Her dreams were never this vivid or convincing.

Could this truly be happening? Inter-dimensional portals didn't just inexplicably appear in random basements, did they? Her senses hadn't lied to her before, and the excitement that gripped her at the prospect of it being real made her hope it was.

A rush of spirited determination quickened her pulse. "I won't find out standing here, will I?"

Alice passed through into a perfectly manicured garden surrounding a massive country estate. She blinked a few times as the sun dazzled her eyes. Two men relaxed at a table on the lawn, drinking lemonade. One was wearing a fedora and had a five o'clock shadow. A trench coat was hanging off the back of his chair. The other one appeared to be a hulking Roman centurion. As she stood brazenly gawking, Mr. Fedora spotted her and waved her over.

"Don't worry about him, honey. He's an okay guy. You don't speak Latin, do you?" She shook her head as he leapt

up and pulled a chair back from the table. Alice sat down. The man thrust out his hand, and she shook it firmly.

"The name's Dirk Flanagan, and you look like a dame who doesn't know where she is or how she got there. Am I right?" He lit a cigarette with cinematic flair.

"That about sums it up." She shrugged and gave him a bewildered smile. "I don't know anything about anything at the moment. Where am I?"

"I know how you feel. I was just as confused at first. One minute I'm wrapping up the case of the Sunset Boulevard Slasher. I walk out of my office and suddenly I'm stepping into the dining room of the big house up there. I sure spoiled their dinner." He burst out in a throaty chuckle.

"Are there more people around here in the house?"

"Let me tell you something, sweetheart. That house was filled with nothing but bone-headed layabouts. It was this crowd of young, upper class do-nothings, with Limey accents, too much dough, duds thirty years out of style, and not a full working brain between them. They were saying things like *jolly good*. And *right ho*. I didn't like it. Didn't like it at all." He squinted into the distance.

"They were just offering me a *spot of tea* all nervous-like when this guy here suddenly shows up at the window." Dirk threw a thumb toward the centurion, who was yawning and twirling a flower between his fingers.

"You should've seen them. They jumped up all screaming and running around like headless chickens. They took off in twenty different directions, and they haven't been

back since." He chuckled again. "The only one who didn't clear off was Pemberton. Aw, great, here he is with the food."

A tall, well-dressed man glided across the lawn toward them and placed a tray of cakes and sandwiches silently on the table. "Will there be anything else, sir?"

"Hey, you want something to drink, honey?" Dirk offered.

"No, no, I'm all set, thank you." Alice grinned broadly, suppressing the urge to laugh.

"Nah, thanks, Pemberton. That'll do it for now."

"Very good, sir. Dinner will be at seven."

Pemberton leaned over and whispered something in Latin to the centurion, who burst out laughing and fell out of his chair, holding his sides. Then the butler glided back up the lawn.

"Damn, I wish I knew what those two talked about." Dirk drained his glass of lemonade, threw his fedora on the table, leaned back in his chair, and heaved a contented sigh.

"Those spoiled numbskulls didn't really appreciate this place. At first I didn't know what to do with myself. There's no crime here, no grisly murders, nobody calling me up, nobody chasing me. There are scrambled eggs and kippers waiting on the sideboard every morning. Drinks on the lawn. Nobody bothers me. I've earned this. I'll bet my big warrior friend here has earned it, too." The centurion had picked himself off the ground and was poking Dirk on the shoulder and pointing down the lawn.

"Yeah, okay, why not? Hey there, doll, how do you feel about lawn bowling? You wanna join us before dinner?"

Alice smiled at them, "No, thanks. You guys go ahead. Have a good time."

She watched them amble away together. "This is insane, totally insane." She laughed as she pulled out her camera and snuck a picture of the two friends before they disappeared from view.

Alice started up the lawn in the opposite direction. "It's so beautiful here. I've never seen flowers that perfect." *Click.* She stopped short as an armadillo trundled past her. *Click.*

After vaulting over a small stone wall at the property's edge, the sky turned white like a blank page, and it became eerily quiet. She found herself in a small clearing surrounded by trees of every type. Leaves appeared to be rustling here and there. She could detect dozens of small, darting movements, but there was absolute silence.

A small bird flew down and hopped toward her. Alice squinted, shook her head, and squinted harder. It wasn't so much a bird as a very detailed illustration of a bird, and there appeared to be some small cursive text hovering just over its back.

She leaned down and read, "Brown-headed Nuthatch." Another bird sailed past her in slow motion. "Red-winged Starling," she read, her eyebrow arching incredulously.

"This is nuts. Anybody want to tweet or warble or something? You guys are a little creepy."

Several more birds hopped into the clearing, all facing her and blinking in unison. *Click.* One flew onto her shoulder. "Whoa, back off." She squinted. "White-crowned Sparrow,

298

don't crowd me, please." It flitted to the ground. She sighed then chuckled.

"You're all very sweet, but this silence is getting to me. Can't somebody make a little noise?" Suddenly a thundering shout cut through the stillness.

"Ah! My Salvation!"

Alice jumped, and the birds dispersed in a flurry of hushed wings. A tall man loped toward her with great purpose in his blazing eyes. In spite of there being no breeze whatsoever, his dark hair floated behind him and his frilled sleeves were like a ship's sails billowing at his sides.

"So long since I have heard another human voice. So very long. And what a voice it is, the voice of an Angel, of a Goddess!" He grabbed Alice's hand and pressed it to his lips with melodramatic passion.

"Hey, whoa, excuse me, but what are you doing?" She yanked her hand free. "Who do you think you are, anyway? Get a grip...on yourself, not my hand."

"I do not think. I *know* who I am, my dear lady." He said. "I am a man in love, a man bewitched by your loveliness, languishing here in solitude for what has seemed an eternity; a man who has prayed to the stars each night" – he clasped his chest with one hand and gestured heavenward with the other – "for relief from my sorrow and distress. And they have sent you, my darling, my love."

Alice backed away. "Yeah, I don't think we're talking about *love* here. I think this is more like a 'ham sandwich looking like a feast to a starving man' type situation. Try to think rationally for a minute, okay?"

299

"How am I to think rationally, my angel, when my heart burns with such a flaming desire?" He stretched out his arm toward her, and two tiny birds sailed down and perched on his sleeve.

"And these birds. How am I to think rationally with all these cursed birds everywhere? One moment the fair Lady Caroline is about to declare her undying love for me. I rush to her side, and suddenly I'm in a tree covered in birds." He shook them off with a contemptuous snort.

"You cannot imagine the torment I have endured here alone with these detestable creatures."

"I don't care," offered Alice.

"They blight my existence. They haunt my every dream."

"Good for them," Alice gave a thumbs-up to the small flock of birds approaching his boots.

"Oh, the agony, the suffering. Won't you comfort me, my dear sweet love? I know your kiss can erase the painful memories I've collected in this silent chamber of loneliness."

"This is the most nauseating drivel I've ever heard." He rushed forward and grabbed Alice around the waist. She smacked him in the forehead with her camera.

"Why do you not melt in my embrace?"

"Are you serious? Why? You're a poorly written, stereotypical lothario from a trashy, bargain bin paperback. And that's just for starters." She struggled to free herself.

"Well, yes." He paused and considered. "I suppose I am. But why should it be an obstacle to our happiness? Don't fight the passion that sweeps over you, enchanting creature."

"Okay, screw this. You're really not giving me a choice here." Alice raised her knee with speed and deadly accuracy. "I don't have any more patience for this garbage." He crumpled to the ground as she took off into the forest.

"Sorry about killing your mojo," she called to him over her shoulder, "but it's your own fault." She looked back; a bird landed on his head as he moaned and rolled around in the grass.

"Absolutely ridiculous." She proceeded through the woods. "I hope he eventually escapes to a place where he can learn some subtlety and better pick-up lines."

Faint shouting and galloping up ahead grew louder by the moment. She concealed herself behind a bush; five seconds later a stern-looking yet terrified school master blazed down the path screaming, pursued by a determined unicorn with a triumphant young boy on its back. Once they were out of sight, she emerged from hiding and gazed after them with reverent admiration. "That was just awesome."

As she continued forward, the trees thinned out and the sky shifted to a pale, early morning blue. A delicate mist hovered over the fresh grass. Hooting, laughing, and clanking drifted up from behind a ridge. She peeked over into an expansive valley below.

The terrain reminded her of a pockmarked battlefield, with traces of trenches and explosions, but it seemed to have been converted into a kind of fairground. People from every culture and era strolled, played games, picnicked together in the gentle sunlight.

A massive red-bearded Viking and a prim governess lounged in the grass, holding hands and exchanging shy glances. An old hunchbacked woman in a tattered cloak roared with delight as four Benedictine monks raced her around the field in a sedan chair. A raven-haired young girl in a blue dress patrolled the grounds on the back of a Bengal tiger, stroking its fur while chatting with the frog perched on her shoulder.

In the center of the field a group of men lounged in a large circle, wearing military uniforms of every country, description, and time period. They drank, ate, threw their arms around each other's shoulders, and sang in lusty voices as they clinked glasses together. Her eyes welled up. She thought of lions lying down with lambs. If someone was literally beating a sword into a plowshare somewhere down there, she wouldn't have been surprised.

Wiping her tears, she took picture after picture, finally stopping when she realized she'd never be able to capture it all, the quantity of kindnesses far exceeded her camera's capacity. "I'd better get out of here before I start bawling."

Alice returned to the path, sniffing and red-eyed. She needed to stop and rest her head. Steadying herself against a tree, she closed her eyes. It was only for a minute, but when she looked up again it was almost twilight, and she stood at the edge of a small hamlet. It appeared deserted – only candles flickering in some of the windows indicated otherwise.

"Plain, rough houses…a seventeenth-century settlement, maybe?" *Click, click.* The camera's flash accentuated the

lengthening shadows. "Not a single person outside?" She frowned.

"I wonder if I should knock on someone's door. It's getting dark." She studied the cluster of houses thoughtfully. For the first time, she felt a twinge of uneasiness. "No, this place feels wrong. I should go."

With no warning a muscular hand gripped her shoulder from behind and wrenched her around with such force she nearly lost her balance. A man with fierce, steely eyes glowered at her, his face contorting in disgust.

"What is this sorcery?" he hissed, snatching the camera from her hand and smashing it to the ground. "Casting your spells against us in the shadows?"

"Spells?" Alice grappled with confusion and anger as she cradled her throbbing shoulder. "What are you talking about?" She stared down at her camera in shock.

"Who do you speak to alone in the woods?" he challenged.

"I was just talking to myself. It's a silly habit. I wasn't – "

"Don't waste your breath with lies. And the light you conjured with your talisman, what of that? Spare me another dose of your transparent deceit." He seized her by the wrist and dragged her forward.

"Let me go. Please let me just – "

"Hold your tongue, witch."

The word startled her like a slap to the face. He was deathly serious. How could she possibly convince him to reconsider his paranoid interpretation of her actions? Her

mind raced in useless circles as he pulled her toward a dark cabin at the edge of town.

"When will you unholy intruders learn that your dark practices will not be tolerated here?" They had almost reached the cabin when he stopped short, grabbed her by the neck, and forced her to look down. There was still enough light to make out a row of shallow graves.

A sudden burst of nausea punched her in the throat. Fear surged through her body like electricity. She tried to break away from his grip as he hauled her inside, but it was useless. He threw her to the floor with ease. She shivered in the corner as he lit a candle.

"Please let me go. Don't do this," her voice shook, and she could feel her pulse whirring in her eardrums. "I haven't done anything wrong."

"What a brazen liar. We know well how to deal with your kind, woman." He grabbed Alice by her hair, dragged her across the room, and slammed her onto a massive wooden table as she clawed and struggled to free herself.

"Stop this! Will you please listen?" Alice wailed as he secured her wrists and ankles in heavy manacles.

"Silence." He strode to the door. "You will have time enough for your screaming when I return with the Council of Elders," he sneered, his eyes gleaming with sadistic pleasure. The door slammed with a hinge-rattling clap, and then all was still.

Alice hyperventilated as she strained against the shackles. Calling for help seemed pointless. Anyone with an ounce of sympathy probably didn't last very long here.

"What can I do?" She tried to calm herself, but she could feel a drumbeat of terror pulsing in her throat, ready to burst out. She pulled up with her arms as fiercely as she could. It was hopeless.

"I'm completely stuck." She choked and sobbed in despair.

A basket in the corner of the room shifted. She could hear faint rustling, then a tiny, sweet voice. "I know just how you feel."

Alice looked over at a pair of shiny eyes peeking out from the basket. "Buddy? Is that you?"

He hopped out into the open. Clumps of cardboard stuck to the side of his body.

"How did you get out of your book? How are you here?" She tried blinking away the tears so she could see him better.

"My book landed in the water. All of a sudden I could move, and after a while I didn't feel stuck down as tightly, so I pushed very hard with my paws until I broke free. I hope you don't mind that I followed you." He looked up at her with a shy smile.

"Mind? Oh, Buddy, I'm so glad to see you." Alice fought back tears. "I don't know how much time I have. I'm so afraid, but seeing you makes me happy. I'm sorry I threw you across the room and got us both stuck down here. I'm sorry for everything." She started sobbing again.

"Please, no, don't be sorry," Buddy reassured her. "I love it down here. Well, *this* place isn't very nice at all, but most of it is wonderful. I can hop around quietly and nobody seems to notice me. I won't have any trouble, and being free from

that book is the best feeling in the world. I've never been so cheerful; I can scamper, and I can shake my own tail. Look!"

He turned around and wiggled his furry backside at Alice. She laughed, then burst into tears again.

"At least one of us is free. Maybe you should get away from here. Those guys could come back any minute."

Buddy shook his little head from side to side.

"Just because I was careless, there's no reason for you to end up in a stew pot out of a sense of loyalty." Alice's voice shook. "Please go hide."

"I won't go, not when I can help you." His eyes widened with excitement as he hopped in circles.

"There's nothing you can possibly do." Her voice was sad and gentle. "You're the tiniest rabbit I've ever seen. I don't think these guys are susceptible to being cute-ed to death."

Buddy backed up, then scampered forward, hopped as powerfully as he could, and landed next to her on the table. He rubbed his furry little head against Alice's tear-streaked face.

"Oh, Buddy, thank you. You're so sweet, but you'd better go. Can't you hear them?" The shouts and murmurs grew louder by the moment.

"Please don't worry," Buddy lilted, his voice musical and soothing. "I'm very glad that I finally get to return the favor. Just close your eyes, okay?"

"Really – " Alice whispered. The tangle of low voices growled just outside the door.

"Stay still now, faithful friend." Buddy put his small front paws on her nose, eyes twinkling, and pushed as hard as he could.

Alice's eyes fluttered open. The side of her head throbbed. She lay sprawled on her stomach in the clammy embrace of a waterlogged Victorian sofa. As she tentatively shifted her weight a searing pain shot through her hip. Rolling over, she placed her hand over it and heard a crunching noise. The camera.

How long had she been lying here getting rained on? Her hair and clothing were drenched, and her teeth chattered. Dragging herself to a sitting position she lowered her legs and found herself shin-deep in dark, stagnant water. Shattered floorboards fanned out in an array of startling angles all around her.

Wading through the murky soup, she scanned for any sign of Buddy's book floating or poking from beneath the surface. She knew it was pointless; the weak afternoon light filtering down from the hole was enough to get her to that door on the back wall, but even a floodlight couldn't penetrate this Brew of Satan she was sloshing around in.

What an epic failure. No pictures, no book, limping and shivering. Some badass, rescued from certain death by a bunny. It had all gone so wrong.

Then she looked over at the sofa. It was unbelievable luck to have landed how she did. What if she'd shattered her leg or broken her back? No phone, screaming herself hoarse in futility? She could have hit her head on the floor and drowned, or been impaled on one of those enormous, menacing toothpicks. Discovered weeks or months later by another trespasser. Alice shuddered.

Enough was enough. There might be lots of places out there that were tether-free zones, but this wasn't one of them. She headed for the basement door, then glanced behind her at the water one last time.

She wouldn't worry about Buddy; everywhere was a tether-free zone for him now. Alice smiled at the thought of his little, emancipated cottontail, and rubbed her nose, which was still quite sore.

The basement door yielded without a struggle, and the hatchway at the top of the stairs only required a gentle push to surrender its structural integrity.

Alice limped back down the hill to the tangled hedges, feeling humbled. She was never going to leave her phone behind again. She'd learned her lesson, and by this time they'd probably learned theirs, too. A twinge of guilt for downloading that dog whistle ringtone quickened her pace. She really had to get back and turn it off. If they'd been trying to reach her all day, there wasn't going to be any ibuprofen left for her.

Holly Odell grew up in East Longmeadow, MA and has split most of her adult life between working as a pipe organ voicer/fanatic/evangelist, and trying to make people laugh with her writing skills. She and her son currently live in Manchester, CT.

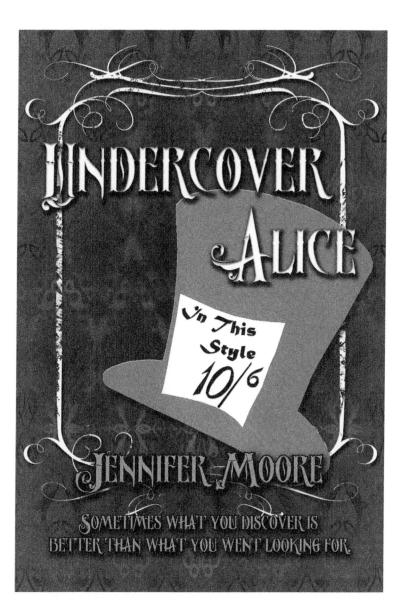

FOR LUCY AND DANIEL.

WELCOME TO WONDERLAND, says the glittery banner stretched across the entrance. THE HOME OF HAT COUTURE. Wow. This place looks even bigger and swankier in real life. And the short, scared-looking girl staring back at me from the mirrored windows seems even more terrified than the last time I looked. Maybe just one more equipment inspection to steady my nerves:

Swanky new camera phone?

Check.

Embarrassing lucky troll charm from an old cereal box?

Check.

Courage to actually see this thing through? Damn it, I knew I'd forgotten something. Maybe I should just turn round now and forget all about it. There must be a hundred other stories I could be reporting on instead, a hundred other ways to impress Jason.

Alice, if you can get us the inside scoop on the Maddy Hatter launch at Wonderland, it'll be the biggest story since the skinny-dipping scandal of 2012. Bigger maybe. After all, if there's one thing the students of Dodgson High like even more than naked Spanish teachers in the school pool, it's celebrity gossip. And gossip follows that woman round like a bad smell. Get me the lowdown on her new hat range and a picture of Dana Duchess and I'll be your slave for life.

Heart beating twice as fast at the merest thought of Jason Hopper?

Check.

Okay, deep breath. I can do this. I can. Just walk right in like I'm supposed to be there and see how far I get. I mean, what's the worst that can happen? No, don't answer that one.

"I'm sorry, Miss," says the tall white rabbit guarding the door. "We're not open to the public today. Private viewing only. I'm afraid you'll have to come back tomorrow."

"N-no, I'm not a customer," I stammer. Why would he even think that? The kind of people who shop at Wonderland are seriously rich, seriously beautiful, and, in the case of Dana Duchess, seriously famous. I wouldn't imagine they sell much to short schoolgirl reporters with oversized heads. Last time I bought a hat, I needed an extra-large men's. "The agency sent me. I'm supposed to be working the new Bunny Beret launch…you know Maddy Hatter's new range."

"Oh yes, I know all about her new range," he cuts in. "That's why she's got the entire staff dressed up in these ridiculous rabbit outfits. Do you have any idea how hot it is in one of these things?"

"Pretty toasty," I guess. If only I'd known that I could have hired myself a costume, too. Impersonating a rabbit shop assistant might've been a bit easier than blagging my way in as a bartender.

"Try boiling," he moans, rubbing his tail against the door handle. "Boiling hot and incredibly itchy. I'm starting to think this costume's got fleas."

Could I make a story out of that? WONDERLAND EXCLUSIVE: MADDY HATTER'S ITCHY INFESTATION. What about BUNNY BERET FLEA FIASCO?

"From the model agency, did you say?" asks the rabbit.

What? Do I *look* like I'm from a modeling agency? I guess it's hard to see properly with a furry white head stuck over your eyes.

"Er, yes, that's right," I manage. "In fact it's my first ever booking, so I'm a bit nervous. Not really sure what I'm supposed to be doing."

"Well, you're late," says the rabbit. "The others got here hours ago. You'd better get a move on. Straight through the double doors at the back of the store and right to the end of the corridor."

"Thank you," I call over my shoulder as I go, rushing off before he has a chance to realize his mistake and call security. I'm in. I've actually done it!

Inside the store it's a furry flurry of activity; giant rabbits scurrying around the makeshift catwalk with chairs and tables and crates of champagne, and another two up ladders, adjusting the spotlights. Hundreds of fluffy pom-pom cottontails hang down from the ceiling, and the walls are covered in glossy framed prints of what must be the new Bunny Berets. No one seems to have noticed the short-looking human in a sea of white rabbits. I creep over to the nearest picture for a closer look. It's pretty much like a normal beret, to be honest, only with a stuffed white rabbit perched on top. Nice. I can't really see it catching on amongst the Dodgson High in-crowd, but it's incredibly life-like. Or should that be death-like? In fact, if it wasn't for the fuss Maddy Hatter made about that other hat designer using proper fur in his advertising campaign, I'd swear that was one of Bugs Bunny's cousins.

"Not *there*, you fool. I meant there." A painfully thin woman with a face like a fox is barking out orders from behind the counter. "Don't carry it like that, you sniveling

imbecile. You'll scratch the paintwork. Someone fetch me another shot of Vitamin T and be quick about it." That, I'm guessing, is Maddy Hatter herself. "Come on, you dithering dolts. I won't settle for anything less than perfect. Do you understand? If there's so much as a single crease in that red carpet, heads are going to roll."

I duck back behind a mirrored hat rack and reach into my pocket for my phone. *Click*. Yes, that's a great shot. Caught her mid-yell. *Click*. And again. *Click*. Wow, she looks even angrier in that one. I should probably record some sound files to go with them. I can see the headlines already: HATEFUL HATTER BULLIES BLUNDERING BUNNIES.

"You, fat rabbit with the droopy whiskers, fetch my PA and have her call Dana Duchess's people," she shouts. "I want confirmation on the temperature of the Swiss mountain mineral water in the limo we sent. You, Wonky Ears, go check on the rent-a-crowd for the red carpet shots. Make sure they've studied the new script. It's '*Maddy Hatter, we worship you*,' not '*we love you*.' Got it? And someone take some more champagne and smoked salmon down to the pressroom, pronto. We want nothing less than glowing reviews from that lot, so keep them properly fed and watered. Everyone knows 'launch' is just 'a lunch' for fashion reporters who can't spell."

A pressroom did she say? That sounds like the perfect place for me. Maybe I can rustle myself up a fake press pass while I'm at it: Alice Liddell, High School Reporter Extraordinaire & Future Girlfriend of Jason Hopper. Yes, I like the sound of that.

Leaving the safety of my mirrored hiding place, I sneak round the edge of the store and through the doors at the back, into a long dark corridor. A single flickering strip light crackles and pings above my head as I peer through the gloom, trying to get my bearings. There's a row of unmarked doors off to my left and what looks like a big stockroom to the right. And all the way down there at the end? That must be where the real models are, with their long, skinny legs and perfectly-proportioned heads.

Hmm, on second thought, maybe this *isn't* the way to the pressroom. If Ms. Hatter's trying to impress the reporters, she'll have put them somewhere a little classier than this, I imagine. Somewhere a little less behind-the-scene-ish. Which means that any photos I get will be genuine exclusives. This could be my scoop! REAL WONDERLAND REVEALED: THE GLOOM BEHIND THE GLITZ.

I snap off a few pictures of grubby flooring and chipped paintwork, but to be honest, they're not much to shout about. Not compared with naked Spanish teachers doing the backstroke. No, I don't think Jason will be rushing to put these on the front page. Still, at least I'm out of the way back here, and I can lie low until the main event. Who knows? Maybe there'll be a spare rabbit costume I can borrow behind one of these doors. A nice small one, preferably with an extra-large man-sized head.

The first one's locked – no chance of a bunny disguise in there – and the second one turns out to be a broom closet. Might be a useful hiding place in a hurry, I guess, but otherwise utterly useless. No luck with the third door either –

that's the staff toilets – and the fourth one opens into an empty room. Nothing there save for a battered old desk and chair. No, wait a minute. It's not *completely* empty. There's a small stuffed rabbit sitting on the desk, staring back at me with sad yellow eyes. Must be a forgotten prop for the launch – heaven help the poor soul in charge of stuffed rabbits if old Fox-Features finds out – or maybe it's an escapee from one of her berets!

"You're late," says a squeaky voice as I turn to go.

I spin round in surprise, but there's no one there.

"You're late, you're late, you're late."

Okay, this is a bit weird. "Who said that?"

"Me," sniffs the rabbit. At least that's where the voice sounds like it's coming from. It must be one of those awful talking toys like my sister's Portia Puppykins. Man, I hate that yappy thing.

"Er…sorry," I find myself saying. "I think I must've gotten the wrong room." Hang on a minute. Why am I explaining myself to a battery-operated bunny?

"No, this is definitely the right room," says the rabbit. "Just the wrong time, that's all. Like I said, you're late. The others are all waiting for us downstairs."

"Others? Downstairs?" Repeating words at random seems to be the best I can manage all of a sudden.

"Yes. Hurry up and shut that door behind you," orders the rabbit. "We haven't got much time."

"Er…okay." This obviously isn't happening. I must have knocked my head on the top of the broom closet and not noticed. Yes, that's it. I knocked myself out cold and my

body's still slumped out there in the corridor while my subconscious carries on without it. Because that's pretty much the only explanation that makes any sense right now. Trust my brain to give me a bossy talking rabbit fantasy, though. Why couldn't I be dreaming about Jason Hopper instead? A nice cozy dream about my Maddy Hatter story getting taken up by the national press, while I get taken up by Jason's strong editorial arms.

The rabbit's having none of it, though.

"Good," he squeaks as the door clicks shut behind me. He sniffs the air thoughtfully, stretches out his back, and then leaps smoothly off the desk to land by my feet. "Now then, follow me, and no dawdling."

"Where are we going?" I ask, as the rabbit hops across the room toward a solid wall.

"You'll see. Press that button to your left and stand well back."

"Button? What button?" I scan the wall a second time, but there's nothing there except for the red fire alarm box.

The rabbit sighs. "We're wasting precious time. Can't you read? 'In case of emergency, break glass. PRESS HERE,' it says. And trust me, this is an emergency. Press the glass and let's get going."

Now I'm not stupid, I know what happens when you break the glass in one of those things. It's all screaming alarms and sprinklers systems and mass evacuations. That's not really the undercover reporter look I'm going for here. But then, I wasn't really counting on talking rabbits either and it *is* only a dream, after all. It has to be. Any minute now I'll

wake up back in my body, back out there in the corridor, with a broom closet sized lump on the top of my head.

Why not go along with it for now? There's something rather tempting about emergency fire buttons, don't you think? With those little arrows pointing into the middle shouting PRESS HERE. PRESS HERE. GO ON. YOU KNOW YOU WANT TO. WE WON'T TELL ANYONE IT WAS YOU. I mean, I'd never do it in *real* life, obviously, but it's not every day you crack your head and have a weird out-of-body dream experience.

I might as well make the most of it. And besides, I'd feel kind of mean saying no to a fluffy white rabbit. Especially one with such sharp front teeth.

I do it.

I press the button like he says and wait for the wailing to start.

Only it doesn't. No high-pitched alarm or water squirting down from the ceiling or the sound of screaming models rushing for the nearest fire exit. No, what happens next is much more exciting than that. An entire section of wall opens up, spinning round on itself like something out of a film, to reveal a secret passage. Yes, I kid you not, a real life, genuine secret passage, with spiral stairs and everything. Top marks, subconscious. I really didn't see *that* one coming.

The rabbit's already halfway down the stairs. I trot after him, the wall easing back into place behind us.

Round and round we go. Down and down, the rabbit muttering to himself the whole way. "It wasn't my fault. She

was late. And now *I'm* late. Oh my ears and whiskers, whatever will they say? I'm late, I'm late, I'm late."

"Are we nearly there?" I ask, trying to take his mind off his time-keeping issues. Not that I have the faintest clue where *there* is, but I'm guessing reaching the bottom will be my cue to wake up again, like when you dream you're falling and you land back in your bed with a start. I hope so, because after a promising start this is turning into a rather tedious hallucination. Just stairs and wall, on and on, round and round.

"No time for talking," snaps the rabbit, picking up speed. "We're late, we're late."

"Okay, yes, I get it. We're running slightly behind schedule. But if you don't mind me asking, how do you even know? I mean, how does a rabbit tell the time?" Ha, that sounds like the start of a joke. *I say, I say, I say. How does a rabbit tell the time? Why, my dear fellow, he swallows a dandelion clock, of course…*

The rabbit carries on as if he hasn't heard, disappearing from view round the final twist of staircase. Hooray! At last!

Here we are then. That's the last step well and truly stepped, and I don't seem to have woken up yet. Actually, I'm feeling surprisingly out of breath too, given that this is all in my imagination. You'd think I could have made myself some longer, fitter legs for the occasion, or snuck in a crafty pair of wings to make life easier. I could've dreamt myself an elevator, come to think of it.

Oh well.

Just as long as I get back to reality in time for the launch, and don't end up in the hospital with a concussion. That's not the story I'm after: KLUTZY CORRESPSONDENT CRASHES PARTY AND CRASHES OUT, though I suppose I could do some selfies in the ambulance to go with it.

"Come on, Alice," squeaks the rabbit as I follow him into another long, gloomy corridor. "We haven't got all day."

Wow, will you look at that? This place is exactly the same as the corridor upstairs: same row of doors, same flickering strip light above my head, same everything. Honestly, you'd think my brain could come up with something a *little* more original, wouldn't you? I mean, Mrs. Forrester gave me an A for my creative writing portfolio just last week.

Unless…yes, maybe *that's* it. Maybe they're identical for a reason. Perhaps if I hit my head on *this* broom closet door, I'll wake up back upstairs as if none of this had ever happened. It has to be worth a try. Second on the left, wasn't it? Look, someone's even left the door open, ready for me. My subconscious probably. Aren't I thoughtful?

The rabbit's one step ahead of me, his tail already bobbing through the open doorway into…no, not a broom closet after all but a…well, I don't know exactly. What would you call this place? It's big – surprisingly big – with cages running the entire length of the room. Cages stacked on cages stacked on yet more cages; row after endless row of them. And in every single one of those cages is another white rabbit, staring out at me with sad yellow eyes.

"You're late," they all squeak together. "You're late, you're late, you're late."

Okay, this is getting a bit much now. I think I'd like to wake up, please. Maybe if I pinch my arm really hard. That's what they always do in books, isn't it? Ow! Maybe it's the other one, then. Ow, ow, ow! So much for that. Now I've got a roomful of resentful rabbits *and* two sore arms.

"Are you sure she's the one?" comes a doubtful squeak. "She doesn't seem very bright to me. Why does she keep pinching herself?"

"I'm certain of it," says the first rabbit, or *my rabbit* as I'm starting to think of him. "Look at the size of her head. It's massive."

Hang on a minute. I didn't follow him down hundreds of stairs into some weird rabbit prison just to be insulted.

"Can she talk? It's no good if she can't say anything."

"Yes," says my rabbit. "Annoying questions, mainly, but she can definitely speak."

"Excuse me," I cut in. "I can answer for myself, thank you very much. And yes, for your information I do know how to talk. That's pretty much a given where I come from. Humans talking, rabbits less so." Which is why a secret underground warehouse filled with back-chatting bunnies would be an amazing scoop. INTREPID STUDENT REPORTER REVEALS RABBITS' SPEECH SECRET. If only this were real.

"Well, that's something," says the second rabbit. "Now then, human, what we need you to do is this. Are you listening carefully?"

"I'm Alice."

"Well, Malice," squeaks Number Two, "I need you to concentrate, because we haven't got long. The first job is to let us all out of our cages, obviously. The doors are computer controlled. It should be a simple case of hacking into the system and operating the release switch. Then you need to disguise yourself as a hat model and gatecrash that hideous woman's launch party so we can show the world what a murderous fraud she really is. I'll be playing the part of the dead rabbit, but the only beret we could get our paws on is from last season's extra-large men's range. That's where you and your oddly oversized head come in."

"What do you mean 'murderous fraud?' They're not *real* rabbits, you know, just clever models. Maddy Hatter's famously anti-fur. In fact, she's the honorary president of three different animal rights organizations." I've done my journalistic homework. I know what's what. She might be a horrible harridan of a woman who bullies her staff, but the self-proclaimed Mistress of Millinery is no critter killer.

"Huh!" scoffs Number Two. "Try telling that to my cousin Robert. He spent his entire life crammed into one these little prison cells, only to end up robo-stuffed and sprayed and stapled onto an early prototype. Stapled! Right through his poor dead feet."

"It's true," pipes up my rabbit. "This place is a one-woman killing shop. One day it's a plumping vitamin dose coming down the feeding tube, and the next it's a lethal shot of rabbit relaxant. Good-bye first three rows of cages; hello new batch of hats." A shiver ripples across his fur. "I used to

have nightmares about rabbit stew, but now it's the beret terrors every night."

"That's awful! Look, I'd love to help, really I would, only I'm more of a hack" (that's another word for a journalist, right?) "than a hack-*er*. I wouldn't know the first thing about breaking into a computer system."

Rabbit Number Two sighs. "Terrific. You'd think there'd be a bit more brain in a head that large, wouldn't you? Okay, you see that big computer screen there?"

"Yes."

"With the big flashing ENTER PASSWORD sign?"

"Yes."

"Good. *That's* where you need to enter the password."

Now I'm being patronized by a talking white fur-ball. This really isn't what I signed up for. "And what *is* the password?"

He sniffs. "How should I know? I'm a rabbit."

I sit down in front of the computer and count out the number of asterisks. ******* So I'm looking for a seven-letter word. M-H-A-T-T-E-R, maybe? It has to be worth a try.

Your password has not been recognized. Please try again.

Okay then, something else. R-A-B-B-I-T-S? No. F-O-R-T-U-N-E? No. H-A-T-K-I-N-G? This is getting me nowhere. E-V-I-L-C-O-W? Come on, brain, think. Perhaps it's nothing to do with Maddy Hatter. I mean, if this is my dream then maybe it's something *I'd* have chosen. W-A-K-E-U-P-!? All right then, how about I-L-O-V-E-J-H? Man, I hate having to think up passwords. Is it any wonder so many

people choose stupid ones like 1-2-3-4-5-6-7? Wow! That's it. I'm in.

From there on in it's plain sailing. There are only a handful of options available, the last one being OPERATE RELEASE MECHANISM. I select that box and double click on the mouse.

"She's done it," squeaks Number Two as the cages swing open. "We're free."

"Hooray for Malice!" chorus the other rabbits as they come hopping out of their cramped little boxes to stretch their legs. Soon the entire floor is awash with white fur, and I hardly dare move for fear of squashing someone.

"Now for the next part of the plan," calls Number Two. Or at least I'm guessing it's him. It might be Number Six Hundred and Fifty-Three for all I know. They all look the same. "Peter – our rabbit on the outside – has hidden the beret in the old broom closet upstairs. You need to fetch it out, put it on that massive head of yours, and then help me climb up on top. Then it's just a simple case of crashing the party, spilling the beans, and putting an end to Maddy Hatter's hateful hattery once and for all."

"Fine," I agree, though as brilliant plans go it sounds a bit rushed to me. "Whatever you say." It doesn't really matter because I know what else I'm going to find when I reach that broom closet. Me. And then I can wake up and carry out my own brilliant plan instead. As soon as I've had a chance to make one, that is.

Back up the stairs we go. Up and up and up and up. It seemed pretty endless on the way down but going the other

way? Wowzers. My heart's hammering so hard I'm worried I might not make it to the waking up bit. What happens if you keel over and die in your dream? Does that mean you're dead in real life, too?

"Hurry up," squeaks the rabbit, bounding on ahead of me. "We're late, we're late, we're late."

Finally. I'm so puffed now I can hardly think straight. The wall swings back round as if it's been waiting for us all this time, and I tumble through into the empty room. It's still empty. That's good. No dream security guards waiting to carry me off. Just a desk, a chair, and a door leading back into the corridor.

Looks like the coast is clear. There's no one around out here either. Not even me. Someone must have discovered my poor lifeless body and carted me off in an ambulance. The real me must be lying in a drug-induced coma in some hospital bed, dreaming strange drug-induced dreams about talking rabbits. Hmm, I wonder if Jason will come visit.

"Open it up then," orders the rabbit. "We need that beret."

I do as I'm told – who knew bunnies were so bossy? – and fish out a slightly dusty red beret. It's big and baggy and the perfect fit for my giant head.

"Right," says the rabbit. "Lift me up on top, and for goodness sake keep still. It's very hard playing dead when you're bouncing around all over the place."

His fur is soft and warm against my fingers, and if he wasn't such a sharp-toothed crosspatch, I'd be rather tempted to tickle his tummy. But I follow his orders and put him

down gently on top of the beret. He's surprisingly heavy for such a little guy. I guess Maddy takes all the weighty organs and things out before she stuffs and mounts them. It wouldn't do to give her exclusive celebrity clientele headaches, would it?

"You!" snaps a voice. I look up to find a human-sized rabbit glaring down at me. Is that the doorman from earlier in there or one of Maddy's other minions? Whoever it is, he sounds furious. "What are you still doing out here? The other models are already waiting backstage for their grand catwalk entrance. Get up there at once. And lose the cell for goodness sake. If I can see it sticking out, then so will the audience. You know the rules – no personal effects that might detract from the hat."

With that he snatches my phone out of my pocket and bungs it into the broom closet. I feel strangely naked without it. Well, naked *and* overdressed (in a balancing-a-rabbit-hat-on-my-head kind of way) all at the same time.

"Er, right, okay then." *Good-bye lovely new phone. Wait for me!* "Which way was it to the backstage area again?"

It's just as well I asked because I'd never have found it on my own. I slip into line behind the last model and try my best to look inconspicuous.

"Critics are already calling them millinery works of art…" comes the sound of Maddy Hatter's voice through the curtain. "So lifelike it's hard to believe Nature didn't craft them herself."

My hat lets out a snort of anger, and I have to cover it up with a cough.

330

"Shhh, be quiet back there," someone hisses, "or we'll miss our cue."

"And so, without further ado," says Maddy, "I give you Wonderland's latest creation: the Maddy Hatter Bunny Beret!" There's a tumultuous burst of applause and the sound of cameras flashing as the line of beret-bearing models moves toward the stage.

"Hurry up," orders my hat. "You don't want to get left behind."

I shuffle forward, waiting to be spotted and hauled out of line. Given that all the other girls are wearing matching white suits and six-inch heels, I must stand out like a sore thumb. Oh yes, and their berets are white, too. With properly dead rabbits stapled to the top, not a hot, heavy live one whispering helpful comments like, "This is it. Get ready for the big showdown. Watch out below. This could get messy!"

I'm close enough to see the stage now – I mean, catwalk. It's a dazzling blare of light and noise out there, and my legs are starting to feel decidedly wobbly at the thought of all those people just watching and waiting.

"You're on," hisses my hat, thumping his back paw down onto the top of my head to spur me into action. "Go, go, go."

"All right. I'm going." It feels like I've forgotten how to walk all of a sudden, but I force my legs forward. And now I'm through the curtain, blinking in the camera-flashing glare like a rabbit caught in the headlights.

"What is *that*?" snarls Maddy, pointing at my beret with a look of ill-concealed disgust. "It's not one of *mine*. That's for

sure. It's all red. It's all baggy. It's hideous!" I guess last season's extra-large men's berets are no longer flavor of the month.

"Go on then," I whisper, giving my hat a gentle prod. "I think you've got their attention now. Time for the big reveal."

"*I* can't do it," he hisses back. "I'm a rabbit. You lot don't even know we can talk, let alone give impassioned speeches to the media. They'll lock us up all over again for scientific experimentation, slice us up into little pieces to see how we work. *You've* got to do it."

Okay, now would also be a really good time to wake up. "Me? But I don't know what to say. I'm terrible at speaking in front of a crowd."

"Get her off! She's an imposter, a fraud," screeches Maddy as a TV camera zooms in for a close-up of my face. But my hurriedly applied mascara is the last thing on my mind when I spot the herd of rabbit-costumed heavies heading straight for me.

"No, wait!" I yell back. "*She's* the fraud. Those aren't beautifully crafted works of art on their heads. They're corpses!"

"Dead little bunny-wunnies?" gasps the stunning lady in the front row. I know that face. It's Dana Duchess! She whips off her complementary beret and begins weeping over her poor stapled rabbit.

"Yes, Dana," I cry, "dead little bunny-wunnies. Stiff, lifeless little rabbit-wabbits."

A collective gasp goes up from the audience. Now there are hundreds of cameras zooming in for a closer look at my clumpy mascara.

"Don't listen to her," Maddy shrieks. "Stuff and nonsense. Lies and poison."

"Yes, poison. Exactly," I say. "She feeds them up in her horrible underground warehouse, and then she poisons them. Slaughters them needlessly in the name of fashion." I'm starting to get into this now, though I could do with something catchier – something with a bit of headline punch. "It's rabbit death row down there!" That's better. "And Maddy Hatter is a beret bunny boiler!" Ooh yes, I like that last one. And so do the reporters.

A fresh wall of camera flashes hits me in the eyes, half blinding me, and I don't see the big, burly bunny bouncer until it's too late.

My hat-hopper's reactions are much quicker. He leaps into action, launching himself clean over the bouncer's head with a pitiful squeal.

"You see," I manage through a mouthful of furry arm. "A real rabbit. And there are hundreds more downstairs where he came from." Only that's where I'm wrong. They *were* downstairs, but not anymore. The single pitiful rabbit cry becomes an entire orchestra of high-pitched squealing as a river of white fluffiness rushes out onto the catwalk, knocking me clean off my feet. There's a dull thump inside my skull as I hit the deck and a single blinding moment of pain. And then nothing.

Well, I did it. I finally woke up. And it looks like I was right about the hospital bed. I wonder how long I've been out. Wow, long enough for Jason Hopper to have made it to my bedside with a huge bouquet of flowers.

"How are you feeling?" he asks as I do my best attempt at a smile.

"Oh, you know. A bit sore."

What's he grinning like that for? Like I've just cracked a joke?

"I'm not surprised." He laughs. "You went down with quite a thump."

How does he know? He wasn't even there. Has he been reading my medical notes?

"Quite the YouTube sensation actually. Seven million and fifty-six views at the last count. But they're all *likes*, because everyone thinks you're a hero."

What, viral YouTube footage of me knocking myself out on a broom closet? Terrific. So much for my undercover reporter routine.

"I'm sorry I didn't get your scoop," I mutter. "A few photos from before the event and some pictures of a corridor, that's all, I'm afraid." I feel down the sides of my hospital gown. "They're on my phone. Wherever that is."

"Don't worry, Alice, I think we've got plenty of material to go on." He holds up a copy of *The New York Times* with a color photo of me plastered across the front page. Me in my ridiculous rabbit hat. Only that can't be right because it was all a dream. Wasn't it? STUDENT REPORTER UNCOVERS UGLY TRUTH says the headline underneath.

He holds up another paper: BERET BUNNY BOILER BEHIND BARS.

"Obviously I'll be expecting an exclusive interview for the *Dodgson High Echo* once you're back on your feet," he says. And then he blushes and looks at the floor. "I was thinking we could do it over dinner, maybe?"

"You and me?" I stammer. "Dinner? Together?"

"Only if you want to, of course. And then perhaps a few photos of you and one of the rescued rabbits another time?"

I want to, I want to, I want to, I'm screaming inside.

"Okay then," I say, playing it cool while my stomach leaps around like a demented rabbit. "Dinner might be nice." *If this is just another dream,* I'm thinking, as he smiles that killer smile and hands me the flowers, *then please, please, don't wake me up. Not ever.*

Jennifer Moore is a freelance writer and children's author from Devon, England. She has two chapter books published with Knowonder (writing as Jaye Seymour) and is a former winner of the Commonwealth Short Story Prize. Her publications include *Mslexia, The First Line and Futuredaze: An Anthology of YA Science Fiction.*

Follow
the
Steam
Rabbit

Liam Hogan

Happy ending not guaranteed...

FOR MY THREE NIECES,
KAIT AND LOIS AND NEVE.

Alice peered over the top of her book as the rabbit – white, about three feet tall, and standing erect on its hind legs – went rushing by. It stopped a little way ahead of her, pulled a pocket watch on a chain from its oversized waistcoat, and hopped in alarm. After announcing in a metallic, clanking voice just how late it was, it rushed off in a cloud of steam, with only a sly backwards glance of a pinkly glowing lens to show that it was even aware she existed.

She sighed, made a mental note of her page number, 345, easy enough to remember being half as large as the sum of its proper divisors, and put the book down on the root of the tree that shaded her reading spot, before setting off in pursuit.

It was obviously one of Uncle Charles's inventions: a steam-powered, oversized mechanical rabbit indeed. But without a closer look, she couldn't tell if it was malfunctioning or merely following its creator's increasingly bizarre instructions.

When she had been younger and not much taller than that fur-covered automaton, she'd delighted in her uncle's flights of fancy and in the marvelous inventions that came out of his underground workshop. Indeed, it was this inspiration that had turned her inquisitive young mind to the pursuit of science and to mechanical textbooks such as the one she had just abandoned on the riverbank.

But her uncle's genius never seemed to go anywhere; he might as well have been a mere toymaker. That would have suited his childish delight in getting each new clockwork or

steam-powered device to work. Such a waste. For Professor Charles Dodgson, engineering was merely an enjoyable diversion, a way of entertaining his mind while not engaged on the latest arcane mathematical challenge. Whereas it seemed to Alice that his dusty dry mathematics ought to be relegated to his moments of leisure and he should give himself over fully to his inventions, he seemed blind to his own genius, to the concept that his mechanical marvels could in a very real way free mankind from its arduous toil, from the dangerous and menial burden of manual work.

Alice would not make the same mistake. There had been great strides forward even in her short lifetime. Airships sailed over London, ever-faster locomotives sped up and down the country, and steam-powered vehicles had begun to replace the old fashioned horse-drawn carriages. Smooth macadamized roads were taking the place of bumpy cobbles and rutted dirt tracks befouled by the passing horses they served.

But nothing as yet rivaled the complexity of even such pointless creations as her uncle's latest, an unpunctual bunny. How much better would the world be if her uncle shared his remarkable talents beyond the idle amusements he built for Alice and her sisters?

It was not as though the world was entirely ignorant of his engineering abilities. Twice a week, sometimes twice a day, a suited industrialist complete with top hat and cane, or an engineer with the goggles and geared brooches of his guild, would beat a path to her uncle's door, carrying contracts or schematics and asking for his advice and help.

The professor would turn them all away.

Their schemes did not interest him, nor their inducements.

He was already quite comfortably well off, living on the generous stipend that Christ Church College paid in return for his occasional lectures and tutorials and for the respect that his purely academic papers, published in incomprehensible mathematics journals and read only by other equally dusty professors of mathematics, brought.

Only Alice had unfettered access to her uncle's library and, better even than that, to the wild designs that emerged from his workshop.

She learnt fast, dismantling her uncle's mechanical toys to see how they worked, trying to put them back together again, trying to improve them.

This despite her parents' steadfast refusal to take her passions seriously, confiscating the utility belt she'd fashioned for herself, and now, as late summer lingered over the wilting Oxfordshire countryside, forcing her outside to "play."

Unbeknown to them and even to her uncle, she had already established a discrete legal entity in the fictitious name of "Lewis and Carroll, Engineering Ltd" for the sole purpose of patenting her modest variations of his more novel inventions. As soon as she was of age, she would leverage these to build her very own workshop. She'd dedicate her life to solving mankind's many problems, to making things that were neither frivolous nor mere amusements, but were definitely, undeniably useful.

Sometimes she wondered if it wouldn't have been easier if she had been born a boy. Though this was an attitude she was increasingly determined she would change just as soon as she could. In these enlightened times, it was ridiculous that only men could vote or join one of London's many Guilds.

She came across the rabbit slumped at the foot of a large tree, a pile of cogs and gears spread about its feet and spilling from beneath its tartan waistcoat as though it had been rudely gutted. She turned away, upset by the image, before steeling herself to examine the steam rabbit more closely.

The fire within was fading fast, the eyes no longer glowing pink as they had before, and only the hands on the pocket watch still moved. Though, curiously, not the second hand.

That appeared to be stuck pointing at the base of the tree, which, now that she came to look at it, did appear quite unnaturally symmetrical.

She pried the watch from the rabbit's frozen grasp and allowed the wavering needle of the second hand to guide her to a spot half hidden beneath the tree's spreading limbs, where she discovered the entrance to a sizeable tunnel. She looked down at her pastel colored dress and her pretty little shoes and shrugged. Her preferred leather boots had that very morning been deemed "unladylike," and their impractical replacements were bound to be ruined. But perhaps that would serve as a lesson to her mother, who might in the future allow Alice to stay in the library, poring over the latest scientific journals rather than cruelly forcing her outside into

the sunshine with only a single smuggled textbook for company.

Alice peered down the dark hole, a warm gust of wind tugging at her hair. It wasn't clear how far down it went; she certainly couldn't see the bottom. But surely it couldn't go too far, not with the river so close by, not unless her uncle had branched out into hydraulic engineering. How long had he been digging it for? Or rather, knowing her uncle, what over-engineered device had he employed? A mechanical steam mole, perhaps?

She knew he'd been expanding his workshop; he always seemed to be short on space. What people took to be a small shed lurking in the grounds of her father's extensive gardens was merely the tip of an increasingly large iceberg. And she'd always known he had an alternative way in or out; it was that or accept he'd developed a teleportation device. Which is what he claimed when questioned, though Alice was far too sensible a young girl to believe half of what her uncle claimed.

Much though she had searched, she had not before now known where this hypothesized back entrance might be and doubted she would have ever found it if she hadn't followed the rabbit and its compass-like pocket watch. The bore was mostly smooth, though odd roots stuck out into the center of the hole from every direction and as far down as the eye could see. It was as she was reaching for one of these that she felt the edge crumble beneath her, and she couldn't help but emit a sharp shriek as she fell…

…and fell…

…and fell.

Drawing a stuttering breath, she realized she was hardly moving at all. The strong updraft, presumably steam generated, had only made it feel like she was falling. That, plus a steady rhythmic mechanical pulsing of the things that lined the tunnel, had effectively arrested her motion a few feet below the hole's sunlit entrance. She peered at them curiously. What she'd taken for roots were obviously artificial arms of some kind.

If she was still descending at all, it was only slowly.

Much too slowly.

She guessed the whole tunnel was meant to function as a lift, but one without the need for a car or a pulley. Perhaps it was rated for her uncle's more considerable bulk and what was capable of delivering him safely to some underground level might suspend her indefinitely mid-tunnel, as indeed this one had done.

Or, perhaps she simply didn't know how this lift of her uncle's was supposed to operate.

There were no obvious signs of any buttons, no levers like the ones she was used to in the hydraulic pressure lifts she rode on her occasional visits with her parents to London. So how did you choose whether to descend or to ascend?

And obviously it must have that control, because in addition to the artificial roots, there were also a number of shelves set into the tunnel wall: extra storage, something the professor was always short of, cluttered with empty jam jars and other assorted bits and bobs.

None of which seemed useful to her in her current predicament.

Even if she were to try to collect them all, they wouldn't, she calculated, alter her weight by anything like enough to drag her downwards. But it showed that control was possible. How else were the jars so neatly stacked on the shelves?

She was nearly horizontal, her skirt rustling in the wind like a miniature parachute. Perhaps if she made another shape? If she changed her angle? The updraft should be proportional to her cross section, so if she was vertical instead...

She tried it.

Gathering the loose material of her dress close to her, she tilted until her feet pointed straight down the hole. And down she shot, far too fast for her liking. She slackened her hold and allowed her petticoats to billow up around her waist, slowing her descent. Being unable to see where she was going was surely better than being able to see but not being able to stop.

Her legs folded gently under her as she hit the bottom of the shaft. She stood tiptoe to tiptoe with a large fan driving hot air up the tunnel, metal blades whizzing inches away from her face. She took a sharp step back and found herself being lifted into the air. Exasperated, she wriggled free of the root-like arms and darted to the side where she took a moment to catch her breath.

Typical of her uncle; a normal lift would surely have sufficed, but no, he had to invent a whole new, dangerous, and ultimately disagreeable method of getting from top to bottom.

Brushing the dirt and leaves from her dress, she looked around the room she found herself in. Gas mantel lamps flickered on the walls, but there wasn't much for them to reveal, just a three-legged stool, and at the far end of the room, a tiny door set into one of the walls.

Well, she thought, *I'm not going back up that shaft in a hurry.* She tried the handle of the miniature door and was annoyed to find it firmly locked.

Alice approached the stool and peered at the ornate bottle that sat upon it. Golden, almost glowing liquid swirled within, and a label attached to the neck said *Drink Me*. She picked up the bottle, tilted it back and forth trying to guess its contents, and noticed that there was a key glinting at the bottom.

"*Drink me*," she muttered to herself. "Not without a full chemical analysis – this bottle could contain anything." She didn't think her uncle would try to poison her, not deliberately, but then she couldn't be sure the bottle was intended for her in the first place, and her uncle was notoriously absentminded.

Why, only last week he had carefully carried a box to where the three girls had been listlessly waiting for a rare summer storm to play itself out. Lorina had her nose buried in some romantic novel or other, Edith stared out of the rain-splattered windows, and Alice tried to get her head around the latest publication by a certain Mr. Charles Darwin.

Edith had spotted the professor first. "What's that, Uncle?" she called out excitedly, eager for some new toy.

"It's my cat," he said.

"Cheshire is in the box?" Lorina looked put out by the very thought of anything that might be considered animal cruelty.

Nobody could quite remember why her uncle's cat was called Cheshire, and as his explanation changed every time he told it, the girls suspected even he had forgotten.

"No, no," their uncle said, "a photograph of Cheshire is in the box."

"Why not take it out, then?" Edith suggested.

He scratched his head. "It's not that the photograph is *in* the box. The photograph *is* the box. I've invented a new photographic technique, which needs neither lens nor shutter. It captures all of the light, you see, which means that when you use it, you can look at whichever bit of the cat you wanted to view the most, perfectly in focus. Gather round, children."

The three girls clustered around the box as it was gently laid on a cushion. "Well, open it then," Lorina said, impatient.

Their uncle shook his head. "That would let the captured light out. What we're going to do is to make small holes in the cardboard that you can look through. Hmm. Alice, my dear, could you close the curtains and the door for a moment?"

Alice quickly did so and flopped back to the floor in the semi-dark. Her uncle handed each of them a thumbtack. "Now, as soon as you have made your hole, put your eye to it quickly, and tell me what you can see."

Edith squealed with delight. "I've got his tail!"

Lorina gave her youngest sister a scowl. "Stop shaking the box," and then, "I think...I think I have Cheshire's front paws, but it's getting darker."

Alice didn't say anything, as she gazed on Cheshire's head, the torn ears and bright eyes fading slowly, until all she could see was the cat's whiskers and the slightly agape mouth, looking like a little grin.

Of course Cheshire always looked like he was grinning, and drooling for that matter. He wasn't a young cat, not anymore. And now that she thought about it, those bright eyes had looked somewhat alarmed.

"Uncle?" she said.

"Yes, Alice?"

"Where is Cheshire?"

And her uncle suddenly stood, spilling the now empty box to the floor, and exclaimed "Oh my!" before rushing from the room.

So yes, if a bottle had been left lying around by a man who could forget he had his own cat held tightly in a cage so that it didn't move while he was taking its photograph, then there was no trusting the contents. She pocketed the little bottle for later analysis and removed a hairpin, with which she made short work of the simple three-tumbler lock. The miniature door clicked open, and she lowered her head to peer through.

It looked an awfully tight fit. She thought about searching for an uncle-sized entrance instead, which there must surely be, because even if she could squeeze through, it

was a certainty that her uncle could not. But some sense told her time was of the essence.

She wormed her way into the space beyond, wriggling her shoulders when they threatened to get stuck, all the while being careful to make sure the bottle in her pocket wasn't crushed beneath her.

Panting again and looking even more disheveled than she had after her ride in her uncle's elevator, she found herself behind a heavy curtain. Edging it a little to the side, she looked out onto the main space of her uncle's workshop. Benches cluttered with gears and pistons and pipes, a small furnace in one corner for welding work, books and papers scattered around – the usual mess.

No, it was even messier than usual; there were delicate precision instruments spilled to the floor and ancient books with their spines cruelly bent and split. Now, that was unusual.

She was about to brush past the drapes, when she was suddenly aware that someone, or something, was watching her. She drew a breath and carefully looked around again. There! Her uncle's eyes were staring wide in her direction, and beneath them, a thin mask – no, not a mask, a gag – over his mouth. He was bound to a chair with heavy ropes and wire, his eyes frantically jerking toward the far end of the workshop. Alice nodded her head in silent acknowledgement of the warning. She let the curtain slide back, leaving just a gap, as she heard a frustrated rattling. A tall man dressed in a sharp black jacket and with goggles pushed up over his equally dark hair strode briskly forward.

He stood before the bound figure of her uncle, his engineer's gear brooch whirring as if mimicking his anger. "Professor Dodgson," the man snapped, "I'm growing impatient. Where is it?"

Her uncle raised his chin and stared defiantly at his interlocutor, who reached out and savagely yanked the gag down.

"That's…better," her uncle croaked. "No reason for unpleasantness. Perhaps, young sir, you could explain once again what it is you are looking for?"

"This!" the trespasser thundered, waving a sheaf of papers. "But a working version. You must have one, otherwise you would not have bothered to patent your device."

Her uncle licked his lips. "I'm afraid you're mistaken, Mister Jefferson. I'm not in the habit of patenting any of my designs; the fun is in the making of them, not in tired reproductions or in dreary commercial applications."

"The patent is yours."

"It is not," Charles calmly replied.

"It is!" the engineer insisted. "Oh, it might be via a proxy, a clumsy subterfuge to mask the true applicant, but the registered address leads back here."

For a moment her uncle's eyes flicked in Alice's direction, and she raised her hand to cover her mouth. It was not, of course, her uncle's patent that this Mr. Jefferson was so determined to find.

It was hers.

"So, one last time. Where is it, Professor?"

Her uncle emitted a short laugh, which turned into a cough before sputtering into an uncomfortable silence. "Now, really," he said, testily, "I'm still not at all sure what you mean. And even if I did, I can't help you tied up like this. You've seen how much of a muddle my workshop is in. A tad more perhaps, since your uninvited arrival, but even I struggle to find what I'm looking for sometimes."

"Hah. Do you think me such a fool? I'm fully aware of your little booby traps, your pitiful defenses, like that oh-so-obvious *Drink Me* bottle. What was that by the way? Cyanide? No, no, not your style, old man. You lack the necessary resolve to take such drastic actions. A potent sleeping draught, perhaps?"

"Ginger ale," mumbled the professor, lowering his head for an embarrassed moment.

Jefferson's scowl darkened further. "And still you try to play me for an idiot. You will rue your obstinacy. You could have joined me a year ago when first I came to you. I would never have thought to kill the goose that laid such golden eggs. But as it is, I'll gladly settle for this one device, as soon as you have told me how it really works."

"Perhaps...if you showed me the schematics again? My memory is not what it once was," Charles said. "What was it you said the patent was for?"

"You try my patience, old man. You think I would not resort to extreme measures to get what I want? Very well." He yanked the gag back into place. "I shall now search your office. Perhaps, if I do not find it there, you will have come to your senses by the time I return. I do hope so, for your sake."

The tall man strode from the room, swiping at a set of gear wheels as he went, spilling them noisily to the floor.

Alice waited until she could hear him in the other room before darting forward to her trussed uncle. She freed the gag first, but when she reached to tackle the ropes that bound him to the chair he quickly whispered, "No, Alice."

"But Uncle, I must untie you – "

Professor Charles Dodgson shook his head. "You may not have enough time. This fellow has a gun and might, I think, even stoop so low as to use you against me. I cannot risk you falling into his hands. You must seek help, tell your parents, contact the police. Now, quick my dear, replace the gag and go."

Alice did as she was told, but only retreated as far as her hiding place behind the curtains. She crouched there, trembling. She was terribly afraid. Of this man who threatened her uncle so casually, and for her two sisters innocently playing croquet on the lawns above. This tall engineer was more than a match for her father, the dean of Christ Church College. By the time she could contact the local constabulary, all manner of terrible things might already have occurred.

Most of all, of course, she was afraid it was all her fault.

She looked around the disorderly workshop, at the drawers of fine cogs, springs, and levers, desperate for inspiration. Hookah pipes and looking glasses and all manner of tools, both small and large, cluttered the walls. Nearby one whole desk was given over to what, in the dim light and with

a robust imagination, looked vaguely like a tea party, complete with the frayed frames of a number of automatons.

At one end of the table sat a frankly scary Hatter. By his side, a March Hare, who looked like an early prototype for the white rabbit. And a cutaway of a teapot contained a clockwork dormouse. At the other end of the table were the oversized magnets her uncle had used to levitate a cake that sang happy birthday and lit its own candles. They weren't normal magnets though, were they? They were powerful electromagnets, controllable with a switch, and that table wasn't a normal table either; it was a massive bank of batteries full of lead and mercury.

Surely there was something that could be used as a weapon.

But what sort of a weapon could a twelve-year-old girl use? And against a fully-grown and very determined man?

Nor did she have anything on her, except the *Drink Me* bottle, which only contained ginger ale and a key.

Still, it was a key, and this fellow was looking for a secret.

And every secret needs a clue. So why not give him one?

Alice darted out and placed the bottle on top of the large metal dish that formed the lower plate of the magnet and then darted back to safety, just as the engineer re-entered, his features contorted into black and ominous fury.

As he approached her bound uncle, Alice let out a soft sob.

And then, when that went unheeded, a rather louder one.

The engineer spun round, a clunky-looking revolver

instantly in his hand. But metal, obviously metal, Alice noted. A lot of it.

"Who's there?" he demanded.

And ignoring her uncle's frantic gestures with his eyes and his wild bushy eyebrows, Alice stepped out from behind the curtain, looking miserable and lost and awfully young.

"Please, sir…" she said. "Please don't hurt my uncle, sir. I know where he keeps the key to his safe."

Jefferson grinned an evil grin. "Well, at least one member of the Dodgson family has some sense. Tell me quickly, girl, where is this key?"

She pointed a trembling finger at the *Drink Me* bottle on the other end of the desk. "In…in there."

For a moment, the engineer looked at her with suspicion. Alice did not have to pretend the terror she felt. The bottle had been outside before, and now here it was, on a plate on a workbench. Would he smell a rat? But then, what harm could a little girl pose?

He took a quick pace forward and seized the bottle.

And Alice turned and kicked at the switch hidden by the drape over the mad tea party table.

She really hadn't expected such a dramatic effect. Though, if she'd thought about it, she'd have remembered the device had been designed to levitate a cake that had been baked by her two sisters. No wonder the magnets were strong.

The engineer gulped with surprise as he was gently lifted into the air and then accelerated upwards. She looked up to the ceiling where he lay spread-eagle against the upper

magnet, one hand bloodied by the smashed *Drink Me* bottle, the other trapped and mangled by the heavy metal gun, the rest of him held firmly in place by his engineer's brooch, the buckle on his belt, and by his sensible, steel-capped boots.

Alice cut her uncle's ropes, freeing him as two constables burst into the room. The older of the two shook his head in sad acknowledgement of the wickedness of the world. "Ah…Professor Dodgson, Alice, glad to see you're both safe. We had reports of an intruder. We tried to tell young Lorina that she was probably just imagining things, but she was awfully insistent. Wouldn't let us leave until we'd checked everywhere." The constable pursed his lips. "Seems she was right." He nodded at the engineer stuck to the ceiling. "Is that your doing, Professor?"

The professor gently squeezed his niece's shoulder. "Yes, I'm afraid it is. Shall I release him?"

"Probably best if you do. Harry, stand by just in case there's any fight left in him."

But there wasn't, not while he was pinned to the ceiling, and certainly not after he'd fallen the eight feet back onto the solid floor of her uncle's workshop. The policemen led him away, tipping their hats at the presumed hero of the day.

"Sorry about that, my dear," her uncle said, once they were alone, "but sometimes it's best not to appear too amazing. And you certainly are, and were, that. Now, please, could you hand me that patent the disreputable Mr. Jefferson was so interested in?"

Alice gathered the scattered pages, her heart still pounding as her uncle sat wearily back onto his chair, brushing the cut ropes aside.

He held the patent in his still-trembling hands and sighed. "Oh, Alice, my dear clever little girl. I think, alas, I may have to give up inventing altogether." He shook his head sadly from side to side. "With each new creation I make, each innovation, I see how it could be used not *for* man, but *against* him. It is fortunate indeed that your ingenious design, as specified, has a rather obvious flaw. A flaw, which for the sake of all of us, I'd be most relieved if you weren't to try to correct."

Alice bristled at that. "Flawed? No, I'm sure I didn't…" She caught her uncle's indulgent expression and frowned. "And it's not as if your mechanical devices are without their faults, Uncle."

"No, of course not," he agreed. "But I'm guessing you mean the rabbit. I pushed it past its original programming, made it do things other than what it was designed to do. It is hardly surprising if it malfunctioned. Indeed it is a small and thankful miracle that it succeeded in at least alerting you to my plight."

Alice sat there for a second, remembering the pitiful sight of the steam rabbit surrounded by its own workings. "Uncle, what was it programmed to do?"

"Exactly what it appears to do, my dear. A reminder of my appointments, an annoying interruption to prevent me from being, as I am so deplorably often, late." He smiled and shrugged. "It's my alarm clock."

Liam Hogan was abandoned in a library at the tender age of three, to emerge blinking into the sunlight many years later with a head full of words and an aversion to loud noises. He lives in London, hosts the monthly literary event Liars' League, and dreams in Dewey Decimals.

We hope you enjoyed *Beware the Little White Rabbit*! If you did, we'd be grateful if you left a review on your favorite vendor's site.

For details on upcoming releases sign up for our newsletter at leapbks.net/newsletter/

Also by Jackie Horsfall:
For the Love of Strangers

Also by Laura Lascarso:
Racing Hearts

www.leapbks.net

CPSIA information can be obtained
at www.ICGtesting.com
Printed in the USA
LVOW04s0419100116
469918LV00020B/609/P